Dying Echo

Books by Judy Clemens

The Stella Crown Series
Till the Cows Come Home
Three Can Keep a Secret
To Thine Own Self Be True
The Day Will Come
Different Paths

The Grim Reaper Series
Embrace the Grim Reaper
The Grim Reaper's Dance
Flowers for Her Grave
Dying Echo

Dying Echo

A Grim Reaper Mystery

Judy Clemens

Poisoned Pen Press

First Edition 2012

10 9 8 7 6 5 4 3 2 1

Library of Congress Catalog Card Number: 2012936465

ISBN: 9781464200212   Hardcover
       9781464200236   Trade Paperback

Poisoned Pen Press
6962 E. First Ave., Ste. 103
Scottsdale, AZ 85251
www.poisonedpenpress.com
info@poisonedpenpress.com

Printed in the United States of America

For Steve, my one and only

Acknowledgments

Thanks to all the wonderful folks who had a part in this book, including:

Jenny Baumgartner, who checked over the fight scenes and Casey's view of life from a hapkido perspective.

Nancy Clemens, who proofread the ARC, and always cheers me on.

Lee Diller, who lets me write when business is slow.

Those awesome readers who wrote to me, asking for more Grim Reaper adventures.

The great team at Poisoned Pen Press. I so love working with you all.

And always, Steve, Tristan, and Sophia, who support me all the way.

I've got so many lovely people in my life. I am forever thankful.

Chapter One

One week earlier

Alicia McManus made seventeen dollars and thirty-three cents in tips on the day she died. Ten hours on her feet, four of them because Bailey, the other waitress, had called in sick, even though everybody knew she was just hung over. Alicia normally wouldn't have minded, but lunch and dinner were both slower than a glacier, maybe because it was Thursday, maybe just because the food at the restaurant wasn't anything to get excited about. She shoved the money into her purse, not bothering to put it in her wallet. She'd have time for that when she was home with her feet up and the TV on. Maybe *Downton Abbey*. Maybe that cooking show with the chef that yelled at everybody, except that was a little too close to what she'd been around all day. Or maybe she'd just find the local PBS station, with the reruns of that guy from the seventies who painted with watercolors and spoke in that quiet, soothing manner. Nothing gritty. Nothing dark. Just elevator music for the eyes.

Maybe Ricky would come over. He'd rub her feet and let her sit there with her eyes closed while he talked about his day. He would tell her stories, and she'd listen quietly until he said something so silly she had to laugh and he'd stop rubbing and scoot onto the sofa with her, and maybe they'd make out for a while until they had to decide whether or not he was staying. Most often he wouldn't. He usually wanted to, but she was too tired from her job, from the day, from everything. But tonight… maybe she'd let him stay tonight.

She swung her bag over her shoulder, waved to the dishwasher and the cook—he wasn't good enough to call a chef—and let herself out the back door. She stopped outside, breathing in the crisp night air, and looked up at the ski slopes, lit brightly in the heavy darkness. They were a dream from where she stood, hazy and dim, like stars behind thin clouds. Even at that time of year, without the snow, the ski resorts were a popular tourist attraction. People would pay big money to ride the lifts up the mountains and view all those changing leaves. Not something Alicia would use her pitiful paycheck to experience. Not when she and Ricky could simply walk up on the rare occasion they had the same day off.

At the base of those expensive slopes sat the real restaurants. The ones with actual customers who paid decent tips and wouldn't slap her ass when she walked past. But those restaurants were pickier about who they hired. They'd want ID and a real Social Security Number and tax information. A few propositions and less than stellar cuisine were sacrifices she was willing to make for anonymity. It wasn't hell to work at The Slope. Just a dull sort of limbo.

She tore her eyes from the mountains and headed toward her apartment. It was a poor excuse for a home, but it had the necessities. Room for a bed, a bathroom, and a tiny kitchen more suited to a kindergarten playroom than a grown woman's place. The apartment had come furnished, which was the best situation for her, the only situation really, unless she was prepared to sleep on the floor and eat cold ravioli out of a can. Except then she'd have to buy a can opener. Her landlord was okay. He'd fixed the shower that one time, and replaced the outside light bulb when it had burned out. He never made her feel creepy, never spoke to her in any way other than like a dad, or a…well, a landlord. So she was content. But that would have to stop soon, her contentment. She'd been in town longer than she'd been anywhere else in the past almost twenty years. It wasn't safe. Not for her, not for anybody. Especially now that she'd messed up. She'd tried to be good. She really had.

So much for good intentions, and all that.

She liked being there. It was a pretty town. Her apartment was decent, and her job was okay. The name Alicia—genteel but not unusual—was one of her favorites. Lots of nicknames so people didn't get too used to any one thing, which was great. She'd always liked nicknames. They made her feel loved in a weird sort of way. Ali. Lisa. Leesh. She got called all of them. When customers and the manager weren't calling her honey. Or sweetie. Or hey you, girl with the menus.

And then there was Ricky. When she left town she'd be leaving him, too. He was the type of thing she needed to avoid. Always had in the past. But other guys in other towns at other times had been different. Fun and empty. She hadn't counted on Ricky being so…whatever he was. He didn't care she was older than he was. He didn't care she wasn't chatty and bouncy. He seemed to actually like her for who she was. Well, who she was as he knew her. But she supposed he'd get over it when she left. She supposed they always did.

Although she might not. Not this time. This could be even worse for her than losing Wayne, way back in that other lifetime. It would be far, far easier to leave now, though, before Ricky had a taste of what she could really offer, easier than to wait until her presence tore his world irreparably apart.

A sound, like a footfall on gravel, came from behind her, and she stopped, glancing over her shoulder. A plastic bag blew across the pavement, scuttling like a frightened animal. It wrapped around a light post, then wriggled away, scraping against the brick of a building before wafting into the air and down the block. She shook her head at her nervousness and continued walking.

A car came toward her, then passed, its lights flashing across her path and the storefronts, which were all closed this time of night. Tourists hardly ever found their dank little section of streets, not even during the day. There was really no point staying open past eight. Waste of money and electricity. Much better to be home, or better yet, in the nicer part of town. Alicia hardly ever went up there, though. Maybe with Ricky, when he felt like getting out. She preferred the quieter, darker, shadow life in the non-tourist streets. Fewer people, fewer chances to mess up.

She rounded the corner and looked up the street toward her apartment. It was a house, really, with the basement made into a separate living space. She didn't mind being underground. In fact, she sort of liked it. It was like a cocoon. Or a cave. Perfect for her.

The neighborhood was quiet that night. Nobody was out. Televisions flickered behind curtains, or could be seen right through the front windows. Crickets chirped in the cool night, probably one of their last hurrahs of the season, and a breeze ruffled the trees. Alicia stopped outside her door and breathed in again. This Colorado air was the best. Better than the humidity of northern Florida, or the frozen tundra of Alaska. This was fresh and cool, sort of like those days she'd spent in New England several years ago. Not like the weather of her childhood. That was different from all of the others.

She let herself into her apartment and flipped on the light in the tiny entryway. The mail lay scattered on the floor where the landlord had dropped it through the slot, and she picked it up. Nothing personal, of course. Coupons for the pizza place. An envelope saying that "Yes! She could own her own home!" And a promise that the local water company would give her the purity she deserved. Wouldn't that be something.

She dropped her purse onto the floor and stretched. It was good to be home. She walked past the kitchen door into the living-slash-bedroom and turned on the light. She turned a slow circle, happy in her little nest, and made her decision. A decision that would affect many people in the coming hours, days, and much, much longer. She decided that, "Yes. It was a good night for company." She pulled out her phone and dialed Ricky. "Want to come over?"

A smile colored his voice. "I'll be there in ten minutes."

He was knocking on the door when she emerged from the shower. She let him in, locked the door behind him, and dropped the towel.

He raised his eyebrows. "And hello to you, too."

She laughed, and he scooped her up, carrying her to the bed. She held him there for a moment, her hands on either side of his face, and studied him. "You're so good to me."

His eyes went serious, and he tucked a strand of wet hair behind her ear. "Just returning the favor." And then he kissed her.

Two hours later she jerked awake. Ricky was getting dressed.

"Where are you going?"

He glanced over, then bent to kiss her. "Would you believe an early morning delivery? As in *early* early. Four am. Do these people *really* need to host a breakfast before the break of dawn?"

She frowned. "I was hoping you would stay."

His face softened, and he sat on the edge of the bed. "I would like to. Believe me. It's not every day I get the offer. Can I take a raincheck? For tomorrow, maybe? If you can take two nights in a row."

She laughed. "I think I could manage it."

He tugged on his shoes and kissed her again. "You're beautiful when you've just been ravished."

She gave him a weak punch. "You got me all sweaty, you know. Now I have to take *another* shower."

He laughed and stood up, pulling on his jacket. "Go back to sleep. There's plenty of time for a shower in the morning."

"I guess."

"Goodnight, love."

She sighed, snuggling under the covers. "'Night. Love."

He ran his fingers gently over her face, then let himself out, with the soft *snick* of the lock moving into place.

She tried to go back to sleep, but couldn't. She had to pee. Why did sex do that? Why couldn't she just fall asleep in the warm aftereffects like they did in the movies? Well, she *had* fallen asleep, actually, when Ricky was still with her. So it was his fault, for getting out of bed and waking her up. She'd make him pay the next time.

Smiling at the thought of what exactly his consequences would be, she slipped out from under the covers and padded across to the bathroom. She took the time to wash up, rebrush her teeth, and run a comb through her hair. When she was done, she went back out to the living room.

A man she recognized was sitting on her bed.

He smiled. "Hello, Lizzie. It's been too long. Way, way too long."

She spun around, but the hallway was blocked by another man. She knew him, too. He was another one of the Three. Which meant….She whipped her head right and left, but saw only the man on the bed. He smiled again, and tilted his head sideways. "You looking for him?"

She followed his gaze to the corner, where the third man crouched on the floor. Just seeing him made her skin crawl. Those blank eyes. The pasty skin. She shuddered. All of her personal belongings—measly as they were—had been spread out on the floor in front of him. A couple of books, some money, the picture of her father. The third man picked up the photo and dangled it between his thumb and forefinger. He held a flaming cigarette lighter under the corner.

"Say good-bye to Daddy," the first man said.

Alicia closed her eyes. But she didn't say good-bye to Daddy. She'd done that many years before.

Chapter Two

"Ricky's in trouble. You have to come home."

Her lawyer's words had chilled her, and Casey had had no choice. Two days ago she'd left Florida, where she wasn't exactly welcome anymore, anyway, and made her journey west. The last trucker to give her a ride had dropped her off outside of town, and she'd walked the rest of the distance. She grabbed some cheap fast food on her way in, but her lack of appetite kept her from eating much of it. How could she eat when her little brother was in who knew what kind of trouble?

She made her way through back streets to Don's building, hoping he would somehow know she'd gotten to town. But of course he didn't, and his office was dark, completely locked up. She shouldn't have expected otherwise, as she hadn't called ahead, but she'd been hoping to avoid phone calls or late night visits to his house. She was too recognizable in this part of town, close to where she'd lived Before. There were still some tourists around, even though it wasn't yet the ski season, but they made her more of a stand-out, with her slept-in clothes and unwashed hair. So she skulked in the shadows by Don's building, afraid to let her face be seen. She wouldn't even attempt to visit Don's residential neighborhood, where Crime Stoppers had some of its staunchest—or should she just say, most fanatical—supporters.

"You want to use my phone?" Death held out what looked like the latest version of an iPhone.

"I can't use that. It will evaporate."

"Sorry. Forgot. Guess I should call it a *My*Phone."

Casey rolled her eyes.

"So now what?" Death said. "Go to your house and get some sleep?"

"I'm not going to my house."

"Right. You think there are *ghosts* there." Now it was Death's turn for eyerolling.

"I don't think there are ghosts. I just…don't want to go."

"Uh-huh. So are we going to spend the night here on Don's doorstep?"

"No. I'm going to call him."

"With what technology? A cup and string? Or are you going to send up a prayer and hope he catches it?"

Casey had ditched the last phone she'd owned when she'd left Florida. "I'm going to find a pay phone."

Death laughed. "Speaking of ghosts."

"There has to be one around here somewhere."

There was, but it took her almost an hour to find it, out in front of some dive of a restaurant in the nontourist part of town. Apparently pay phones were too tacky to be seen by out-of-state visitors, who were there to spend big bucks on apparel and clothes and tickets up the mountain.

Casey dug change out of her pocket and dialed Don's home number.

"This is Don Winter speaking."

Death snickered. "Chipper, isn't he? You'd think it was eleven in the morning instead of at night."

"Don," Casey said. "I'm here."

"Where?"

"Your office."

"*Now?*"

"Well, I'm at a pay phone a mile and a half away. I can be back there in twenty minutes."

"I'll be there in fifteen."

She hung up and turned away from the restaurant. She wasn't sure exactly what she was smelling—steak or cabbage or just a bunch of deep fried stuff—but it wasn't too appealing, especially since the place was obviously closed, and the smells were hanging around in the air, along with a sickly sweet odor like damp vegetation. Or something dead.

She jogged back to Don's office, grabbed her bag from where she'd stashed it behind a bush, and waited there in the shadows. In a few minutes, longer than he had anticipated, his headlights cut across the parking lot, washed over her hiding place, and turned off, leaving the small square of pavement in the dim glow of the street lights.

Don got out of his car and swept his eyes over the back of the building. "Casey?"

"I'm here." She stepped out of the darkness and waited for him to spot her.

When he did, he held still for a few moments. "It's good to see you."

"Don—"

He moved toward the door. "Come on."

She followed him inside, waiting while he reset the alarm and locks behind them. Then he turned to her, his eyes traveling from her hair to her feet. "You okay?"

"I'm fine. What's happened to Ricky?"

"I can make coffee. And we have some cake in the break room."

"I don't want *cake!*"

He inhaled, filling his cheeks with air, then gestured her toward the interior of the office, which was lit only by the security lamp on the ceiling. She walked behind him, thinking how very *same* the office was toward when she was last there. She'd spent a lot of time in those rooms, dealing with the law, with Pegasus—the car manufacturer who had basically killed her family—and with her own personal hell.

The place was pretty much like any independent lawyer's office. Neutral colors in the waiting room, a reception desk, a small conference room, Don's office space. The only difference from a normal visit, of which she'd had too many, was that they were there at night this time. His secretary was long gone, and the computers had been shut down. There was no comforting hum of the copier, no phones ringing, no fingers tapping on keyboards.

Don settled behind his desk and opened a fat file, with some photos face down.

Casey eyed the folder, her skin crawling. Face-down pictures weren't a good sign. "What are those?"

"As you probably realize from my phone call, Ricky got involved in something bad, Casey. A murder. It happened last Thursday night. I know I talked to you Friday, but Ricky hadn't gotten involved yet, and by the time I knew, I didn't know where to find you. "

"Tell me now. Or show me."

"It's not pretty. I don't think you should look at the pictures."

Casey held out her hand. "I'm not a little girl."

"I never said you were. I just…she didn't go easily." Don turned the top photo right-side up and held it just out of her reach.

Death sucked in a breath, peering over Don's shoulder. "I can vouch for that. Her killers didn't hold back. And don't yell at me for not telling you before. I didn't know who we were dealing with until I saw the picture just now."

"Who is she?"

"Her name was Alicia McManus," Don said. "Don't know her middle name. Cops got what we know from the landlord."

Death leaned further over Don's shoulder, and Don shuddered.

"That's not right," Death said. "Her name wasn't Alicia. It was Elizabeth. Elizabeth Paige Mann."

Casey swiveled the file toward her. Don gave only token resistance before letting her have it. She scanned the top paper. "You sure about her name?"

"Dead sure," Death said.

"It's the name everyone gave the police. Her landlord, her coworkers." Don cleared his throat and played with his pencil. "Ricky."

Casey turned over one of the photos, since Don was still holding on to his. It showed a woman lying on a carpet. Her face was beaten, so much so that Casey couldn't tell tell if she was young or old, pretty or plain, dark or light. Her body lay on its side, her neck at an impossible angle, her clothes barely covering her.

"She was dead when the police arrived," Don said. "It was lucky they even found her when they did. She could have lain there for days."

Casey glanced at Death, who shrugged. In and out at the death scene to take the woman's soul, and that was all the information Death had gotten from the earthly authorities. Everything else had to come from a woman newly dead, who wasn't exactly at peace with how she'd gone.

"Any clue who did this to her?"

Don shifted in his seat.

"*Other* than Ricky."

Death squinted onto the dark street between the blind and the window trim. "Don't know any names. But she called them the Three."

"There were *three* of them?"

Don blinked. "Three of who?"

Casey sat there, mouth open, unsure what to say. So she flipped over another photo, this one showing some burn marks on the woman's stomach, probably from a cigarette, or maybe a lighter, or a match, if the shape of the wound meant anything. Nasty. "So how did they find her?"

Don leaned his elbows on his desk and rubbed his forehead. "She didn't go in to work on Friday morning, and her manager called her. When he didn't get an answer, he got in touch with her landlord."

"Why? Did her landlord keep tabs on her?"

"No, not really. It was just…she didn't have many friends. Sort of kept to herself. They didn't know who else to call."

"No emergency contact in her employee file?"

Don looked out at her under his brows. "Let's say her employer doesn't keep the best records."

Not all that unusual. "So the landlord went looking for her?"

"He said he was worried. That maybe she was sick. It was unlike her to miss work, and I guess he felt sort of fatherly toward her."

Casey snorted. "Which means she was pretty?"

"No. I mean, sure, I guess she was, from what people say, and from seeing photos from before, but that's not what his deal is. He seems like a decent guy."

"Don't they all?"

"I do have *some* sense of people, Casey."

"I know, I know." She waved. "Go on."

"So he went looking. Her door was locked and there was no response to his knock, so he let himself in and…found her."

"I assume he did the normal thing and called the cops?"

"After running to the bathroom to throw up."

She nodded, understanding. "Anything unusual about the scene?"

"Other than a woman who'd been beaten and tortured to death?"

She looked up from the third photo, which showed a close up of ligature marks on the woman's neck. "Was this what actually killed her? She was strangled?"

"I believe so," Death said.

Don nodded. "Medical Examiner says it was the fatal injury, but, as you can see, it was only one of many things that was done to her."

"Other torture?"

"You can't even see her back in those photos. Or her feet."

"Raped?"

Don's lips pinched together, which she took as a yes.

"So could they find DNA from her killer?"

He shook his head. "No. they just found residue from con-doms—the same kind as on the ones in her trash."

Casey digested this bad news as she turned over several more grotesque crime scene shots until all that remained was a photo of two people, smiling, sitting behind a table, their heads close together. They were at a restaurant, where a waitress or someone at a close table had been called over to take the picture. The remains of a meal could be seen on the mostly empty plates in front of them.

"That's her, I take it?" She tilted the photo toward Don.

"It is."

She looked pleasant enough. And pretty. She was smiling, but Casey recognized something in her eyes—a haunted shadow, telling a deeper story of the woman's life. Casey was surprised to see that Alicia looked older than Ricky by several years. But again, maybe that was her experience showing through. Some past hurt or brokenness that colored her, even when she thought she could be happy.

The other person in the photo needed no explanation, except for what he was doing there. He looked happy. Relaxed. Familiar. And yet a stranger.

Casey sat back. "So. Tell me what my little brother has got to do with all this."

Chapter Three

Don took the photograph from Casey's hand and looked at it for a long moment before setting it on top of the pile. He scooted all of the pictures together and rapped them gently on the desktop to even them out. Finally, he pulled the folder across the desk, laid the photos on top of the papers, and closed it. "She was his girlfriend. They'd been dating a few months."

"That hardly makes her his girlfriend."

Death laughed. "So what does it make her? A friend with benefits?"

"Casey." Don's voice was gentle. "They were an item. He really liked her."

She closed her eyes and let the idea sink in. "Okay. So they were going out. The cops can't possibly think he did this to her."

Don stayed quiet for so long Casey had to open her eyes to see what was happening. He looked gray in the office light, and the bags under his eyes seemed to have darkened in the past minute.

"No," Casey said. "No *way* would Ricky do this."

"I know that. And you know that. But the cops have leads, and evidence, and…" He shrugged. "They think they have their man. They're not checking out anyone else."

Casey looked at Death, who now hovered behind Don, eyes on Don's cell phone, which lay alongside his briefcase on the edge of the desk. "What exactly did she say?"

"She didn't say anything, Casey," Don said. "She was dead."

The phone in Death's hand changed to imitate Don's. Death poked at it uncertainly. "She said nothing about Ricky. Except to tell him good-bye. Everything else was about the Three."

"The Three…"

Don's brow furrowed. "What is this with the number three? Are you talking about the evidence? The three main things they're banking on? But how did you even know about those?"

"I didn't. I…What's the evidence?"

"First, the final number called from her phone. According to the phone company, who had to check her records since her phone is missing, the last number dialed was Ricky's, at about nine o'clock. The call lasted almost thirty seconds. Enough time for a brief conversation."

"That doesn't mean anything. Anybody could have dialed that number using her phone. And if she was his *girlfriend* it shouldn't have been unusual for them to talk on the phone."

"Second, there were…" He cleared his throat. "Used condoms in the trash. They're guessing Ricky's DNA. They'll know for sure soon."

"Again, meaningless. You said she was his girlfriend, right?"

"Third." His eyes met hers. "Ricky was seen leaving her apartment Thursday night around eleven. The landlord was going to bed. He noticed movement on the street and saw Ricky's car. Ricky got in it and drove away."

"And the landlord felt the need to call the cops?"

"Only after he found Alicia's body the next day. In fact, he didn't remember about seeing Ricky at all until several hours later, long after he found her. He was in shock, I think, from seeing her that way."

"So he offered up my brother as a sacrifice?"

"He was doing his duty, Casey."

She shook her head, knowing he was right, but still angry. "He didn't see anyone else after Ricky that night? Nobody else came to her apartment?"

"Like I said, the guy was going to bed. Ricky being at Alicia's apartment wasn't exactly unusual. The landlord didn't think anything of it. He turned out the lights and went to sleep."

And let the *real* bad guys arrive unseen. "Great." Her mind spun. "Okay, those three pieces of evidence are all circumstantial. Phone calls, DNA they haven't matched, visiting his girlfriend's place. I suppose they raided Ricky's house, too?"

"They searched it, yes, the next night. With a warrant."

"And found…?"

He lifted his hands. "Nothing I've heard about. Well, except normal boyfriend kinds of things. This picture—" he tapped the folder, indicating the photo of the two of them at the restaurant "—notes in Alicia's handwriting, a take-out menu from the restaurant where she worked. Clothes, make-up, that sort of thing, you know, that she probably left at his place over the past few months."

"Everything that would show she actually was his girlfriend."

"And nothing to show he didn't kill her."

"But nothing to show he *did*." She stood up and paced in the small area in front of the desk. "Did they actually interview him after they found her, or only after the landlord called?"

"They didn't know *to* talk to him. Like I said, Alicia's phone was missing, and she had nothing else of his in her apartment. Not an address book with his information, or any kind of computer, or anything. The only reason the cops knew *her* name was because of the landlord."

"Didn't Ricky show up at her place, wondering where she was when he couldn't reach her by phone?"

"Yes, actually. That's the first the police talked to him. He went to her apartment on Friday, the night after she died. The landlord had remembered seeing him the night before, and the cops were getting ready to pay him a visit. They questioned him quite extensively right there at her place."

"Were you there?"

"Not that time. He wasn't a suspect yet—at least not officially."

"And he told them stuff?"

"Of course he did. After all, they hit him with the news, right there where she died, and he was devastated. He wanted to help."

"And incriminated himself."

Don held up his hands, and dropped them. "He didn't put up an argument about the night before. He confirmed he'd been there, and that he'd left her—*alive*—close to eleven. They arrested him the next morning, once they'd gotten her phone number so they could retrieve a list of calls."

"So what can I do? I have to help him."

"You can't help yet."

"Of course I can. It's why I came. Why you *told* me to come."

"Casey, the cops have other priorities where you're concerned. You know you're wanted for questioning about what happened in Ohio three weeks ago. If they see you, that's all they're going to care about, and you and Ricky will be headlined as homicidal siblings."

Casey didn't want to think about Ohio, about how she'd killed a man. About how she was on the run. Especially now that Ricky needed her.

"But you said Eric vouched for me. He told them it was self-defense." This would be Eric VanDiepenbos, a sweet, good-hearted, handsome young man who had befriended Casey three weeks earlier and then watched in horror as she'd killed the Louisville thug. She hadn't meant for him to see it. She hadn't meant for it to *happen*. "Besides, the cops know the guy was a mobster."

"*You* know it was self-defense," Don said. "And *Eric* knows that. But until the cops hear it directly from you, they're obligated to hunt you down. You can't just waltz into the police station—or the jail to visit Ricky—until your own issues are cleared up."

"Then let's go. Right now."

"We can't. The people we need are all asleep. And you're not going to get on their good side by pulling them out of bed on a Sunday night for something that could just as easily be done in the morning."

She glanced at Death, who was typing frantically on the smart phone. Death nodded, and said without looking up, "He's right. Everything's closed, and folks are finishing up the weekend. It's best to put it on the back burner till morning."

"Okay," Casey said, throwing up her hands. "Fine. You win."

"It's not a competition." Don put Alicia's folder in his briefcase and stood up. "You have somewhere to spend the night?"

"Ricky's is off-limits, I guess?"

"Still sealed off. How about your house? Or maybe," he added quickly, "your mother's?"

"She doesn't even know I'm in town."

"Right." He heaved a heavy sigh. "So I guess that means you'll be coming home with me."

"I can't. The cops will look there."

"They don't know you're in town, either."

"But don't they suspect I'll be coming around, with Ricky in trouble?"

"I don't know what they suspect. They're cops. They suspect everything."

"So here's what we'll do. I'll find a place to sleep—"

"Come home with me."

"—and I'll meet you here in the morning, at…what time does your office open?"

"Eight."

"Seven-thirty. And then we'll do it."

"Do what?"

"We'll go to the police station, and I'll turn myself in."

Chapter Four

Casey found a cheap motel on the edge of town, far from her old haunts, far from anything familiar, and in the morning she showed up at Don's office, showered and wearing her last set of clean clothes, which, unfortunately, was a pale blue warm-up suit with white tennis shoes. Not exactly what one would choose to wear to confront the cops, but at least it was comfy, and she could move freely, should she need to.

Don was already at his office, and the front door was unlocked. He met her in the reception area, briefcase in hand, wearing a dark suit. At least one of them would look professional.

Death sat in Don's waiting room, nose in a book, or, more accurately, in one of those new electronic tablets you can use to download things to read. Instead of a suit fit for court, Death wore footie pajamas with dancing bears on them.

"You ready?" Don said.

Casey stared at Death. "Seriously?"

Death blinked up at her. "What?"

"Um, yes," Don said. "Look, I understand you're nervous. But I believe it will be all right. Really." He opened the door. "Shall we go?"

Only after they were in Don's car with the doors shut did Death appear in the backseat, wearing a slightly more appropriate tan leisure suit and waggling the little computer beside Casey's head. "This is *amazing*. Have you *seen* these things? It's like a whole book in this skinny little pad."

Casey looked out her window.

"Or, actually, it's like *hundreds* of books. I'm never sure how to choose which one to read. This morning it's that one about the girl, what's her name, Scout? Her dad's a lawyer, and there's this guy they all think is guilty, and a weird neighbor who never comes outside and—"

"*To Kill a Mockingbird*," Casey said.

"What?" Don flicked his eyes toward her.

"That's it!" Death said. "It's a pretty good story."

"Why are you talking about that?" Don said. "Because you think they've arrested an innocent man?"

Casey glared at Death, who settled back into the seat. "They *have* arrested an innocent man. Anyway, why else would I be talking about it?"

Death gave a little cough, and Casey felt herself go hot. She knew she was grumpy. Knew it wasn't Don's fault.

"Sorry," she said. "I'm not exactly the world's best company today."

"To be expected." Don smiled grimly. "It's not every day you have to turn yourself in to the cops."

She watched the houses go past. "You really think this will work?"

"I do. It was self-defense. You have a witness. The victim was a criminal."

Casey closed her eyes and practiced some deep breathing she'd learned from her hapkido master. Speaking of whom, she wondered if *he* knew she was in town. He probably *felt* it somehow. He was like that.

"It *was* self-defense?" Don sounded casual, but Casey opened her eyes and could see how he was gripping the steering wheel.

"I swear. It was going to be me or him. And I didn't mean to do it. It was his knife. Not mine."

Don nodded once, sharply. "What I thought."

The police station was gray and built onto the side of a hill. The perfect back wall for a building with a lock-up on the first floor. No way would anyone be getting out *that* way. Not unless they were half groundhog. Don pulled into the parking lot and killed the engine. "Try to relax. Tell the truth, and it should be over soon."

"Don, who are you trying to convince? I think you're more worried than I am."

"Could easily be." He straightened his shoulders and gathered up his things. "Ready?"

They made their way to the building, Death walking right through the front doors, since the book—or reading device—was so fascinating. Casey, however, hesitated just outside, trying to picture Ricky's face. That was all she needed to convince herself she was doing the right thing. Her little brother did not deserve to be in prison with a murder rap hanging over him. He'd never hurt anyone, let alone a woman he loved, either for self-defense or intentionally. All violent tendencies seemed to have manifested in his older sister.

The police receptionist looked up, and immediately punched a number on her phone. Casey stiffened. Was she about to be arrested? She looked at the posters on the walls, expecting to see a "wanted" sign with her face on it.

A buzzer sounded, and a heavy door to the left swung open. Casey spun around, instinctively balancing on her back leg, arms loose, ready for a pack of officers to charge through with drawn guns, or maybe they'd just go for a full-fledged SWAT team. Instead, a middle-aged man in a dark blue suit jacket and gray pants strode casually through the door, while a young, uniformed officer held it open. The suit jacket on the older guy didn't look as good as Don's; it was just a little bit shiny, and had gold buttons on the cuffs. It was wide, too, like the man had lost weight but hadn't had the chance or the money to update his wardrobe. The pants were baggy, strengthening that theory, and his black shoes were scuffed. But he was clean and shaven and wore a tie—even though it was a little too fat and yellow.

The other cop was your typical young policeman. Dark blue uniform over a fit twenty-something body, shiny nameplate and shoes, wary eyes that couldn't hide his curiosity. The sort of look that could make Casey want to either pinch his cheeks or just appreciate the view, if he hadn't been waiting to arrest her.

"Don." The man in the cheap suit held out his hand, and Don shook it.

"Thanks for seeing us, Lloyd."

The man's eyes sparkled, and his mouth twitched. "You're welcome, I'm sure. Glad we could make the appointment." He turned toward Casey, and the half-smile stayed on his lips. "Hello, Casey. Mrs. Maldonado. It's good to see you again."

Casey frowned, still thinking an armed take-down team must be hiding in the background. "Do I know you?"

"We met just after your accident. Detective Watts. I helped with the investigation, but wasn't lead on it, since it took place outside the city limits."

"I don't remember."

"There's no reason you should. You had plenty of other things on your mind those days. I'm very sorry you had to go through that."

Casey held still, not sure how to respond. He didn't exactly sound like an arresting officer, or like he was even thinking of her as a potentially violent criminal. He sounded like he was giving her real condolences from a real person. Imagine that.

"Um, 'thank you' would probably be the appropriate response," Death said, glancing over, a finger on the e-reader to keep a spot.

Casey swallowed, but didn't get her voice to work before the detective was moving again.

"Shall we go through?" He held a hand toward the open door, where the uniformed cop made no secret of staring at Casey, like she was some specimen in the Crazy Wanted Killer Zoo. He apparently wasn't sure if he should be ready to defend himself, or to chase her if she ran. Obviously not in the same camp as the detective. Casey felt like saying, "Boo!" but instead leveled her eyes at him, and he ducked his head, looking at the floor. Casey preceded the others through the door, then waited on the other side, her arms wrapped around her stomach as she stared at the scuffed gray walls.

"Punk," Death said, pausing to look the young cop up and down. "Bet he doesn't read at all, except for maybe *Men's Health*."

Casey thought that was probably true, but wasn't ready to give the cop even that much credit.

"Right down here." Watts led them to an interview room where there was a table bolted to the floor, four plastic chairs, and fluorescent lighting. Very flattering, Casey was sure. Her pale blue warm-up suit, along with the light, would be leaching any color from her face that might have found its way there overnight. But then, she wasn't there to look good.

"Coffee?" Watts asked after Casey and Don had taken seats.

Don accepted, but Casey shook her head. Hot caffeine wouldn't do anything for her rumbling stomach. Watts sent out the cop, who hurried back with two coffees, creamer, and sugar packs, along with water for Casey. Casey nodded her thanks, and the cop nodded back. Maybe he wasn't so bad, after all. Just young, and inexperienced with dangerous criminals.

Watts took a sip of his coffee and made a face. "Terrible. Sorry about that, Don."

"It's fine."

Watts grunted a laugh. "Whatever you say." He pulled some of the creamer and sugar toward him, and took his time picking out a few packets.

"Ricky didn't kill that girl," Casey said.

The young cop jerked his head around, and Don widened his eyes, like he was trying to tell her to shut up. Watts picked up a sugar envelope and snapped it a couple of times to move the sugar to one end.

"He wouldn't do that," Casey said.

Watts stirred the sugar and several packs of cream into his coffee, and looked at Casey from under his brows. "Seems to me you've gotten your own self into some trouble these past few weeks."

Right. Her stuff before Ricky's. "It was self-defense."

Watts nodded, still stirring. "That's what I hear." He jerked his chin toward the officer, who laid a piece of paper on the table. Watts pushed at it with the tip of his pen. "We used your friend Eric's statement and came up with this one for you. Take a look and see what you think."

Casey glanced at the paper, and then at the detective. "You've just had this sitting around, waiting for me?"

Watts sucked on his teeth. "You want to tell her, Don?"

Don cleared his throat. "I kind of called him last night."

"Kind of? Him?" Casey frowned. "I thought we were worried about the cops hunting me down?"

"No. *You* were worried about that. I decided it would be better to be prepared. And there was no way they could find you last night, if you decided to stay hidden."

Casey looked at Watts, and at the officer, who'd gone back to staring at her like she was an exotic animal.

Watts took another sip of coffee, pursed his lips, and shrugged. "Still terrible. But why don't you take a look? See if the statement is something you can sign off on?"

"And if I can?"

Watts smiled. "Then I don't have to arrest you. Which I really don't want to do, anyway. You wouldn't believe the paperwork."

Casey hesitated.

"They're offering you an out, darlin'," Death said. "At least look at it. I'm scanning it right now on my reader, and it's looking pretty good."

Casey read the paper without touching it. Eric's recounting of the event was clear and concise. Casey came off as the victim of an attack, who was just trying to save herself. It was close enough.

"It's good," she said.

Watts nodded. "Nothing you want to change?"

"Not about the statement."

Watts studied her for a few moments, then handed her his pen. Casey signed. Watts handed the paper to the young cop. "You know what to do with that."

The officer nodded, took one last look at Casey, and left.

Casey watched him go. "What exactly is he doing?"

"Setting you free, my dear." Watts looked at her over the rim of his mug. "You do realize we're not the only police department interested in your whereabouts."

"Clymer?" Where she'd killed the guy.

"Among others. But this should satisfy them. Nobody—and I really mean nobody—wants anyone looking into this any further. The guy you killed wasn't exactly a boon to society, and the other side, well, let's just say they're happy to have us spending our time elsewhere."

She looked at Don, and back at Watts. "You mean that's it? We're done?"

"With that," Watts said. "Sure."

"But not with my brother."

He set down his mug. "Look, Mrs. Maldonado—"

"Casey."

"Casey. It's not good."

"He didn't do it."

"Yes, you said that before."

"Obviously, he got involved with this woman—"

"Alicia McManus."

"Alicia. Okay. But this has to be because of her, not him. He had nothing to do with it."

"And your reasoning for that is?"

Because the woman was using a fake name? Because Casey knew there were three murderers who came to get her in the dead of night? No way could she say either of those things, when her source was the King of the Dead.

"Because he's a sweet guy who stays out of trouble. Always has. What do we even know about the girl?"

Watts sat back. "Alicia McManus. Early thirties. Lived in the apartment where she was found. Came to town three months ago."

"That's it?"

"We have her rental agreement and job application at the restaurant. The information is...patchy."

"How?"

"The Social Security Number and birthdate were fake, so we don't know her exact age, and there was no phone number at which she could be reached. We didn't find out about her cell phone until later. Your brother gave the number to us, actually. She included no references on the apps, no next of kin, no former landlords or employers, and there was nothing about education, place of birth, or insurance. Or even a middle name. We can't find her anywhere in the federal databases."

"I see. So this Alicia, if that really is her name—" she glanced at Death, who pointed a finger at her like a gun "—was full of secrets, and her life here was basically a lie."

"You want to tell your brother that? Or do you think he found out on his own?"

"He did not do this! Look at the life this girl was leading. She probably dragged her past to town with her, and *that's* what killed her. Her own lies. Not my brother."

Watts smiled, but it wasn't friendly. "So you're saying this woman—who your brother happened to be in a romantic relationship with, by the way—brought this on herself?"

"Well, it can't have been Ricky's fault. Who would he have in his life who could do something like that? He doesn't know those kinds of people."

Don and Watts stared at her silently. Death let out a laugh, for a moment forgetting *Mockingbird*.

Casey went hot, and ran her fingers through her hair. "Look. I don't mean she got herself killed on purpose. Of course not. I feel terrible for her. I mean, the poor girl was tortured. And raped. No one deserves that. But you have to believe me. Ricky would not do that. To *anybody*."

Watts looked into the bottom of his mug. "Can I show you something?"

"Nothing will convince me he's guilty."

"Please. Just take a look."

"I won't—"

"For heaven's sake," Death said. "Don't make the man beg."

Casey held up her hands. "Fine. Show me."

Watts took his empty mug. "You stay put."

"Well," Don said when Watts was gone. "That went well."

"You mean the part about me basically saying the poor woman was asking for it? I can't believe I said that."

Death snorted. "Like you're usually a ray of sunshine."

"You've been under a lot of stress," Don said. "It's understandable."

"No," Casey said. "It's not."

Watts was back soon. Casey expected him to be carrying folders with the same things Don had showed her in the office—grisly crime scene photos and notes explaining why her brother was the guilty one. But he had only one clear plastic bag. He set it on the table in front of her. "Any idea what this is?"

She did. It was one of Ricky's old T-shirts, with Colorado U's name printed across the front. She knew it was his because the collar had a blood stain on it from when she'd accidentally busted him in the face when he'd volunteered as her sparring partner. He hadn't done that again. And he hadn't thrown away the stupid shirt.

Watts held it a little closer. "Recognize it?"

"It's my brother's."

"Yes. Guess where we found it?"

"The victim's house, probably, since it's in an evidence bag. But that doesn't mean anything, assuming she really was his girlfriend. There's bound to be lots of his stuff there."

"I'm sure there might have been. But do you think all of his 'stuff' has this?"

He flipped the bag over. The bottom half of the shirt was spattered with blood. New blood. Not from when Casey had busted his nose.

Casey stared at it. "*This* is your evidence? A shirt from her apartment that anybody could have put on? Or maybe they used it to mop up the blood when they were done. Don't tell me you haven't considered that someone else wore it, then left it there to make Ricky look like the attacker."

"Of course I would have considered that."

"Would have?"

He set the shirt on the table. "We didn't find it at the crime scene. We found it in your brother's house."

Chapter Five

"I don't understand it," Casey said.

"Doesn't seem too confusing to me," Death said from the driver's seat. They were waiting for Don to finish up the last of the paperwork which would make Casey a completely free woman. "They found her blood on Ricky's shirt. In his house. Perhaps he's not the golden boy, after all."

"There has to be an explanation."

"Of course there is. Maybe he was *there*."

Casey spun sideways. "Maybe if you were better at your job, you could find out these things right at the beginning."

"You mean at the end. For them. But I told you. She didn't say the names of the men. And the way things were during her last few minutes, Ricky could have been there and she wouldn't have known. She wouldn't have been all too coherent just then."

Casey collapsed back against the seat. "It's all just…too awful."

Don got in the car, barely missing Death, who oozed to the back, and sat for a moment with his eyes shut. "Your part went remarkably well."

"You *called* them."

"It worked out, didn't it?"

"But what if it hadn't?"

He started the car. "No use worrying about it."

He was right, of course.

"What *didn't* go well was that I hadn't known about the shirt before."

Casey could tell from the set of his jaw that he was angry. "What was their excuse?"

"That we aren't at trial yet, and they still had time before disclosing it."

"Is that true?"

"Even if it is, it's unfair. Watts should have told me. He should be giving me every chance to prove your brother's innocence."

Death made a choking noise. "So a bloody shirt found in Ricky's house means he *didn't* do it?"

"He *is* innocent," Casey said. "We *will* prove it."

Don was silent.

"So, can you get me in?"

Don didn't pretend not to understand. "I asked the detective to put our names on the prison's visitation list. We're set up for a lawyer appointment during open hours this afternoon."

"And until then?"

"I've got work to do. You can hang out in my waiting room. Unless, of course, you have other places to go."

Casey heard the suggestion in his voice, along with what was probably criticism.

"How can I possibly visit my mother without seeing Ricky first?"

"Easy," Death said. "You go to her place."

Don shook his head. "I don't know, Casey. But this has been a hard time for her."

Casey rested her forehead on the side window, letting the coolness soothe her.

"I know," Don said. "It's been a hard time for you, too. But think about it…"

"Scout doesn't even *have* a mother," Death said. "I'm sure she would have been overjoyed to spend time with one if she had been lucky enough—"

"Will you shut up about that book?"

"What book?" Don's forehead wrinkled. "You have been having the strangest outbursts today."

"Oh, *God*. I know. I'm sorry. It's…the stress. And I haven't been sleeping well."

"Sure." Although he didn't *look* too sure. "You want to take a nap at my house? I'm sure Mel would be fine with that."

"I don't want to bother her. I'll just…I have some places to go."

"All right." He put the car in gear. "So where should I drop you?"

"Actually, nowhere." She got out and leaned back in the open door. "I'll walk."

"Casey—"

She shut the door and held up three fingers. Three o'clock. That's when she'd be back at his office to go visit her little brother in jail. She could see Don wanted to say more, that he would argue with her about being on her own that far across town, so she waved, and walked away.

Chapter Six

"You okay? You look a little pale." Death leaned toward Casey. "I'm really not so sure this was a good idea."

Casey ignored the nagging and breathed in the surroundings. It had taken her almost an hour and a half to walk there from the police station. As Watts had said, the accident site was outside the city limits. Not super far, but enough for a good hike. Casey gazed up at the mountains. They remained the same as they always had been. Permanent. Unfeeling. Beautiful. The sky was blue, with puffy white clouds. The trees glowed with autumn.

Their car had been going a decent speed when it went out of control. Not over the limit. Not reckless. Just a normal straight-road kind of speed. One moment they were moving along, singing a nursery rhyme, and the next they were sliding into the guardrail with a clash of metal and glass, hood buckling, tires screaming, leaving their blackened tire trails on the pavement. Once the movement stilled, Casey had glanced quickly toward her husband, confirmed that he was shaken but intact, then yanked off her seatbelt and stumbled out of the car, shoving the door open with her shoulder, calling all the while to her crying son in the back seat that *Everything is okay, baby, I'm right here.*

But then she wasn't.

The force of the blast had catapulted her backward, the car's door a steel wall between her and the shrapnel and flame. When she awoke, the faces she saw were not Reuben's or Omar's, but the detached, professional expressions of two paramedics.

"My family," she'd croaked.

The man holding her wrist looked away. The other one slumped his shoulders only a fraction. But it was enough.

"Reuben!" Casey struggled to break free. The men held her down with hands and even knees, but she wasn't trained to accept submission. A head butt to the first guy's nose sent him flying backward into the second, who lost his grip on her legs. The second guy scrambled to grab her again, but a swift kick to his solar plexus stopped him as he buckled in half, gasping for air.

Casey stumbled forward, where firefighters in bright yellow uniforms surrounded the blackened hull of what had been her car. They didn't see her coming, or they would have stopped her from barging through, from seeing the melted upholstery, the steel frames of the seats, and her husband, still clasping the steering wheel, even though he could no longer see where the car was headed. His hands, charred and exposed, were the last part of him she'd ever see.

The firefighters had wrestled her away, kicking, screaming, and biting, before she could see into the back seat, where her baby had died. The coroner all but refused to let her see him once he was in the morgue, and in her shock and despair she didn't realize most of what was happening during the next week until it was too late. Her son was buried without her being able to say a last good-bye. She would be thankful after it all that her final image of Omar hadn't been of his broken, blackened body.

The guardrail must have been repaired some time later. Now it shone silver in the sun, brighter than the sections to the right and left. The burned grass had replenished itself, and the gravel along the shoulder looked the same as all the rest. There were no crosses or plaques or any other outward sign to show that this was where Casey's life had changed forever. Where she had lost everything.

Except she hadn't lost her brother. *He* was something. A big something. And he needed her.

"Okay. I'm ready to go." Casey turned, expecting Death to be waiting.

But Death was nowhere to be seen.

Chapter Seven

The house looked the same as it always had as Casey was growing up. A pleasant enough white two-story on a small, winding street, with an attached garage, brass numbers on the door, and a cast iron lamppost at the end of the sidewalk. The mountains stood magnificently in the background, and the neighborhood gave off the feeling of comfort and stability.

What was different about the house was the state of repair. It wasn't horrible. It didn't look empty. But the bushes had become overgrown, and the flowerbeds lay dormant and brown. The lawn was a mixture of too-long grass and leaves, and weeds grew up in cracks in the driveway.

A stab of worry sent Casey a little faster up the walk. Her mother had always been meticulous about the yard. Flowers in every season but winter—and then the poinsettias bloomed inside—mown grass, cleared driveway. One of the shutters hung crookedly, and several shingles were missing from the roof. Had this really all happened in the last week since Ricky had been in prison?

It wasn't possible.

Casey felt a flood of shame. Ricky had been so busy keeping track of *her* place during the past couple of years, making sure it was up for realtor walk-throughs and prospective buyers, that he hadn't been able to help their mother. Had her mom really gone downhill so much since Casey had seen her that she couldn't even maintain her place on her own?

Casey stood at the door, her hand raised, as if to knock.

"You don't just walk into your mother's house?" Death waited beside her, twisting over the railing to see in the window.

"I used to."

"And now is different because…"

"I'm a bad daughter."

"I see. Only good daughters get to go in unannounced? Then I will go out on a limb and say there are a lot of women who shouldn't have keys to their parents' homes."

"You mean there are *more* people who have abandoned their mothers, and left their little brothers to rot in prison?"

"He's been in for a week, Casey. That's hardly rotten. A little ripe, maybe, but that's about it."

Casey took a deep breath through her nose. It wasn't worth getting angry with Death. Death had a mouth that flapped a lot, but she couldn't exactly slap it.

"So?" Death gestured to the door.

Casey slowly turned the doorknob. It didn't budge.

"You could kick it down," Death suggested.

Casey didn't bother replying. Instead, she rang the doorbell. And then she knocked. There was no answer.

"Back door?" Death hopped over the rail, already on the way around the corner. Casey followed, trying to look past the drawn curtains to the interior, but all she could see was fabric. When she got to the back, Death was coming out the door. Actually, coming *through* it.

"What's going on?" Casey said.

"Your mom's just sitting there. Staring into space."

"You were not invited in."

"Tell me about it. I'm never invited. But it's not like I'm a vampire in those books kids read these days. I don't *have* to be invited. You know, I'm wondering where that myth came from, anyway." Death pulled the ebook reader out and began tapping the screen.

Casey put her hand over it. "You don't have to be polite, either? You can just walk into non-dying people's houses?"

"For heaven's sake." Death brushed her hand away, and she drew back, shivering. "Like you're Miss Manners."

Casey blew on her fingers, then tried the door. It was locked, just like the front. The window in the door was clear of obstruction, the curtains drawn to the side, so Casey cupped her hands around her eyes to peer in. "The kitchen looks exactly the same as when I was a kid. Except dark."

"How about knocking?"

Casey tried. Again, no response.

"I'd say she doesn't want company," Death said. "What are you doing?"

Casey was crouched beside a flowerpot that held a dead plant. "There's a key under here. Or at least there used to be. Here we go." She stood up, dusting her hand off on her jeans and holding up a silver key. She took another deep breath and slid the key into the lock. The door opened, like it always had when she would come home from school.

"Mom?" Casey poked her head through the doorway, then walked all the way in. The smell of her childhood tickled her nose. Lysol and gardenia mixed together, but only faintly, as if they were merely distant memories, rather than anything present day. "Mom?"

Death swirled around her to materialize in the doorway to the dining room. "This way, Casey."

Casey followed, shivering in the air Death left behind.

Her mother sat by the front window, but she wasn't looking out of it. Instead, she sat stiff-backed, staring at the far wall, her hands clasped together on her lap. She wore a light blue sweatshirt with cardinals on it, and a loose, elastic-waisted pair of jeans. Her hair looked like it hadn't been washed—or even combed—for a very long time. Perhaps since Ricky had been arrested the week before. She had become, in the two years since Casey had left, an old woman.

Casey followed her mother's gaze to the wall and went weak-kneed. The little shelf that had always held Casey and Ricky's school pictures was still full. Only now the shelf held photos of

Omar. His first baby picture, his three-month, the six-month taken only days before his death. In each photo—well, except for the newborn one—he was grinning that gummy smile, his dark eyes bright, his shock of black hair sticking up, even after they'd worked so hard to plaster it down.

"You okay?" Death stood between Casey and the photos, almost solid enough to block the view.

"I'm fine." Casey wrenched her eyes from the pictures and knelt by her mother's chair. "Mom?"

"I don't know," Death said. "She's not looking so good. Kinda like you right now, all white and everything, except older. She has definitely lost weight since we last saw her. I mean, look at those skinny arms." Death pulled out an iPad and held it up. "See? Photo from before the accident. It's like she's not even the same person."

Casey waved the iPad out of her face and touched her mother's arm. "Mom. It's me, Casey."

"Of course it's you." Her mom's head snapped toward her, and her eyes flashed. "I think I still know my own daughter. Even if you have forgotten us."

Casey sat frozen, shocked into silence.

Death, however, had no such issues. "Woo-wee! You are your mother's daughter, aren't you? Good thing she doesn't know kung fu."

"You take off, leave me, leave Ricky. Let that woman come into our lives. *His* life. And now look what's happened. Your little brother is in jail. Locked away with criminals. How do you think he'll be treated in there?"

Not something Casey wanted to consider. "I'm sorry, Mom. I'm back now. I'm here to help."

"Like that will work, with the cops all hunting you."

"Not anymore."

Her mother's eyes filled. "They caught you, too?"

"No, Mom. I'm free. It's taken care of. I'm here now. The cops aren't after me."

Her mother grabbed Casey's arm with spidery fingers. "You're home? For good?"

Casey glanced at Death, who waited with undisguised interest for her answer. "I don't know, Mom. I came home to help Ricky."

Her mother's clutch loosened, but she didn't let go. "Well, that's something. Isn't it?"

"It's something."

Her mom picked at Casey's sleeve. "Have you been to see your brother?"

"Going this afternoon. Do you want to come along? I can have Don put you on the list."

Her mother shook her head, slowly at first, and then vehemently. "No. I can't see him there. I can't. It was bad enough losing him to…to that woman. Now I've lost him for good."

"Not for good. We'll get him out."

Her mother's eyes bored into hers. "I don't see how you'll do that. She fixed him up good. That little…witch."

"The plot thickens," Death said. "Or at least gets interesting."

"Mom, from what I hear, Ricky loved her."

Her mother grumbled. "He was *obsessed* with her. There's a difference. Your brother is a sweetheart, we all know that. Would do anything for anybody. Has done everything for *you*." She shook her head. "I thought he was smarter than other men. I guess I was wrong. A pretty face comes along and he's as dumb as they come."

Death whistled. "I am so feeling the love."

"Mom, what made her so bad?"

"Besides getting herself killed and accusing him?"

"She didn't…why didn't you like her *before*?"

Her mother let go of Casey's sleeve and again clasped her hands in her lap. "She took him over. His whole life. It was all *Alicia this* and *Alicia that*. I couldn't…" She closed her eyes again, and her knuckles went white from the strain of her grip.

"She couldn't compete," Death said.

It sounded that way.

Death rushed on. "And she apparently had no idea Alicia wasn't the girl's real name. You realize Ricky probably didn't know, either. He gave the police this fake one. Makes you wonder just how well he knew her, after all."

It made Casey wonder a lot of things. "When did Ricky meet her, Mom?"

Her mother's eyes didn't open, and she talked in a low voice. "A few months ago. July? June? I can't remember. I don't know. It was probably going on long before I knew about it."

Certainly before Casey had known about it. She'd talked with him a few weeks ago, before all this had happened, and he hadn't said a word. She'd even teased him about women, and had warned him to stay away from another one he'd dated who Casey hadn't liked. He hadn't said anything about Alicia. Probably afraid Casey wouldn't like this one, either. Ironically, having her mother hate the girl so much made Casey feel less angry with Alicia, and even sorrier that she'd ended up the way she had.

"What do you know about her, Mom? Where was she from? How long has she been here in town?"

Her mother shrugged her bony shoulders. "Ricky never told me much. She worked at some awful diner on North Jackson. Terrible food. Your brother convinced me to go there one time. The mashed potatoes were fake, and the gravy came from a can. The pie was cold and doughy." She shivered. "I wonder when the health department last checked up on the kitchen."

"Alicia was a waitress?"

"I suppose. Ricky met her when he made a food run for that catering company he works for. Not that the girl's restaurant had the good sense to buy their food. This was for some huge banquet or other. The girl had been hired on as extra wait staff for the event. Ricky took one look and…" Her jaw came forward. "That's all."

"She never visited here? You didn't get to know her?"

Her lips twitched. "Ricky never brought her. My opinion apparently didn't matter."

"Ah," Death said. "Now we're getting to it."

"Or," Casey said, "he was forming his own opinion before getting yours, Mom. That's only natural."

"Hmpf."

Casey glance at Death. Her mother had never been this snarky before. The whole affair had obviously been more than she could handle.

"Plus, you haven't exactly been here for her," Death said. "Who knows how long she's been this way?"

Great.

"Anything else I should know, Mom? Anything that might help Ricky?"

"I've already said. It was the girl. You find out about her, you'll find out who really killed her."

"You've told me *all* you know?"

Her mother leveled her eyes at her. "I told you—I don't know much. Your brother—and that girl—made sure of it. Why would that be if she didn't have something to hide?"

Casey stood up, knees cracking. "Okay, Mom. I'll look into it. I'll find out why she was such a mystery."

Her mother grabbed her hand. "Casey. I am glad you're home. I've missed you."

Casey put her arms around her mother's shoulders, which were so much frailer that she remembered.

"I've missed you, too, Mom."

Her mother stiffened, and Casey backed away.

"Come back and see me," her mother said.

"Of course I will."

"Don't let me hear that you've left town again."

"I'll be back, Mom. I promise."

Her mother turned away, returning to her posture of staring at the far wall, her hands knotted together on her lap.

"Bye, Mom. Just for now."

Her mother's only response was a tightening of her lips.

Casey avoided looking at the photos on the shelf, even though they pulled at her like living things. Omar. Her sweet baby. Dead and gone.

Once outside, she took a deep breath and made her way toward the front yard. Out on the sidewalk she paused and glanced toward the front window, where she could imagine her mother hiding behind the curtain. "Why would Ricky and Alicia stay away from Mom? Why keep everything so secret?"

"Because they were afraid," Death said.

"Of the Three? You think Alicia told Ricky about them?"

Death pulled out an iPod and stuck in the earbuds. "No, I'm sure she never mentioned them to him. It would have freaked him out, and most likely she was trying to forget them herself."

"Then what were she and Ricky afraid of?"

Death looked back toward the house and laughed.

"What?" Casey said. "You think they were afraid of *Mom*?"

Death turned up the volume and spoke loudly, like people do when they have music in their ears. "For the life of me, I can't imagine why they *wouldn't* have been.

Chapter Eight

The restaurant where Alicia had worked was called The Slope, and it seemed to be walking a slippery one. Casey took a booth at the back, where she could sit against the far wall and see both the front door and the doors to the kitchen and unisex bathroom. It resembled the restaurant from the day before, where Casey had found the pay phone amidst the competing smells of stale fry oil and dead rats. She could hardly imagine her mother there, trying not to touch anything, and only picking at the food she was served for fear of contracting some deadly—or just gross—disease.

"You know," Death said. "I think I'm going to leave you to it. I'm feeling all…greasy." And Death evaporated in a cloud of french-fried mist.

After a few minutes of examining the cover of the not-quite-clean-enough menu, Casey studied the waitress who sauntered over to her table. Her name tag had been made with an old-fashioned Labelmaker; dark green tape with raised white letters, which read simply, "Bailey." The girl's brown uniform shirt strained at the seams around her ample breasts, and her jeans were so tight they couldn't possibly have been easy to move in, let alone allow circulation. Dark circles surrounded her washed out blue eyes, as if she hadn't had enough sleep in the last year, and her skin would charitably be called pale and pasty. But that could have been the poor lighting.

"Get you something?" Bailey held her order pad and pen at the ready.

Casey pushed the menu away. It wasn't likely she'd be eating anything out of *that*. "You know Alicia? The woman who got killed?"

Bailey fumbled with her pen, almost dropping it. She snatched it up and scribbled something on her pad, avoiding Casey's eyes. "Of course I knew her. We worked together."

"Here at The Slope?"

Bailey gave a jerky nod. "Where else? She started back a few months ago, in the summer. I've been here for, like, ever."

"What can you tell me about her?"

Bailey's eyes narrowed. "You a reporter?"

"Do I *look* like a reporter?"

Bailey checked out the pale blue warm-ups. "Hardly. You look like a soccer mom."

Casey kept her face neutral. "I'm not that, either. So what was she like?"

"Why do you care?"

Casey refrained from jabbing the girl's pen in her eye. "Because I want to know what happened to her."

"Why?"

What was this girl? A four-year old? "I think they have the wrong guy in prison."

Bailey sucked in a breath, and her eyes went wide. "You *do*?"

Casey almost laughed. "Why is that such a surprise?"

Bailey looked over her shoulder, then scooted in the opposite bench, leaning forward on the table. "Because nobody else seems to think so. Everybody just wants to think he's the guy and forget about it."

"Why?" Now Casey was asking.

"Dunno. Scared, I guess. I mean, if it wasn't Ricky, who was it?"

Casey felt like she'd been punched in the gut. Hearing this girl use her brother's name so casually, naming him a scapegoat, was too much. "But you feel differently?"

Bailey's eyes shot first one way, then the other, before settling on Casey's. "Look, Leesh and I didn't get along, okay? I wanted to be friends, but she was all 'I'm too good for you.' I didn't hold it against her, though. We did fine here, but it's not like we were close." She messed with the salt shaker. "Ricky was out of her league. I told him so, too, whenever he stopped by and she wasn't here. Or even if she was, but, like, in the back. He should have found somebody better."

"Like you?"

Her chin jutted out. "What? You don't think *I'm* good enough for him? Not like *her*?"

"Didn't say that."

"Oh, I get it. You want him for yourself. Well, I was the one who was here first, not you, so you can just—"

"He's my brother."

She paused, her mouth hanging open. "What? Your *brother*? Oh, gosh, Sorry. That's kind of gross, isn't it? Me thinking you wanted to hook up with him. Anyway, unlike some people, like *Alicia*, at least I tell the truth. I don't lie about—" She stopped.

"Don't lie about what?"

She shook her head again, like it was an automatic reflex. "Look. This restaurant, they don't ask a lot of questions, okay? People like me, I do all right. I have a real driver's license, and folks in town actually know me. Other guys, like our dishwasher, or even the janitors, they don't always have the right stuff. The Slope helps them out. But then Alicia comes along…" She picked at a dried glob of ketchup on the table.

"And?"

"I don't know. Her story, it's all wrong. She's just this white woman from 'out of town,' she says. Looking for a job while she 'gets her head together.'" She rolled her eyes. "Whatever that's supposed to mean. Says she's trying to stay under the radar just for a while. So Karl, he's the manager, he says it's no problem, she can just fill out what she wants on the application. See, we had another waitress quit—ran off with some ski instructor from up the hill—and Karl was freaking out. Girls don't want to come work here. They'd rather work across town with all the rich folks." She went back to picking at the ketchup.

"You don't want to work up there?"

"Nah. Rich folks can be a real pain in the ass. Anyway, she comes in here all quiet and hot, and Karl signs her up. Just like that. No questions asked."

"And you think she lied about herself?"

"I'm sure of it. The first time I called her Alicia I had to say it like five times before she answered me. And another time..." She lowered her voice and leaned forward again. "She was dealing with this old lady who comes in here, who couldn't hear a bomb go off in her underwear, and it was taking her, like, forever just to take the woman's order. I went into her locker and looked through her purse. And guess what?"

Casey sighed. "What?"

"No license. No credit cards. Nothing with her name on it. Just cash and chap stick and some lame picture."

"Picture of what?"

"I don't know. Some old guy. I didn't look real close because I heard her coming."

She looked at Casey all knowingly, like Casey should be able to read her mind.

"What?" Casey said.

"Didn't you hear me? She had *zero* papers with her ID. If Alicia McManus was her real name, where was her stuff? Driver's license? Bank card? Heck, even a note or a frequent customer card or something. She wasn't only flying under the radar, she'd completely dropped off the map."

Which Casey happened to understand.

"Bailey!" A man was calling. Karl the Manager, Casey assumed. He leaned over the cook counter that separated the kitchen from the rest of the room and was pointing to a couple who had come into the restaurant and stood uncertainly at the front door.

Bailey pushed herself out of the bench seat, her lack of excitement oozing from every pore.

"Bailey…"

Casey sat so Bailey blocked the view of her manager. She lowered her voice.

"You want to help me get Ricky out of jail, right?"

"Sure. Don't know what I can do, though."

"Think you can get me a copy of Alicia's employee file? The fake application and whatever else?"

Bailey's eyes did the swivel thing, and she gave a little smile. "I'm sure I can. Not right now, though."

"That's fine. I'll come back. It'll have to be later, though. I'm going to see Ricky this afternoon."

"Try tomorrow, or later tonight. I get off at eight. Karl will have to leave at some point to go to the store or bank or some other place. I'll try then. And give Ricky a hug for me, okay?" She went off to put the other customers at a table, leaving Casey in view of the manager. He made no secret of watching her.

Casey decided to go somewhere else to wash her hands, although she really would have preferred a complete shower and a dry cleaner. She stood, and tried very carefully not to touch anything else until she was out in the fresh air.

Chapter Nine

"Did you get some lunch?" Don was eating in his conference room, with papers spread out on the table all around him.

"Wasn't hungry," Casey said. "Although now I see *that*..."

Don waved at the second half of a gigantic turkey sandwich. "Please. Take some. Mel has been killing me with healthy food. What she tends to forget is that healthy food becomes *un*healthy when it's doubled in size."

Casey took a seat, moving a few papers out of harm's way, and devoured the sandwich, an apple, and a slice of the cake Don had mentioned the night before.

"Better?" Don looked at her over his glasses.

"Much. Are we ready to go?"

He glanced at his watch. "Fifteen minutes. We'll give ourselves plenty of time for getting through security, and for the inevitable wait."

"Not looking forward to all that."

"No one ever does."

Forty-five minutes later they were in the parking lot of the jail. It was a huge block of a building about twenty miles out of town, and just looking at it gave Casey a greater understanding of her mother's state. To think her little brother was behind those walls was enough to make her want to curl up into a ball and cry. But that wouldn't help Ricky. And it wouldn't make her feel better for long.

"This," Death said, "is totally cool." Red and green images cavorted on the screen of an iPad. "I hacked into the security system. This is showing all the heat signatures behind the walls."

"Doesn't look very full," Casey said.

"Don't know how you can tell that," Don said. "But you're wrong, anyway. Place is packed to the gills. They've been paroling people faster than ever, just to make room for the new criminals."

"Like Ricky," Death said. "Anyway, this thing just reads through the first layer of these walls. Too much iron and concrete and God knows what else."

Casey shuddered. "How far in have you gotten in person?"

"All the way," Death said. "Folks die in there all the time. Some naturally, some…not."

"I've been in pretty deep," Don said. "Literally and figuratively. Gives me the creeps, getting closed up in there, but I don't always choose who my clients are, you know. Some of them are buried about as far in as they go."

"And where's Ricky?"

"I've been assured he's safe. Although what exactly they mean by that, I'm not sure. The two times I've been able to get in to see him, he insisted he'd been treated all right. He's got a clean record up till now, and the blowback, should he be innocent and something happened to him in there, would be terrible for the facility."

"Glad to hear they're so concerned about him as a person."

"You've got to take what you can get, and as long as he's safe, I don't care why they're doing it. *We* know what he's like. We'll just have to be content with that for now. There's no way the system can know people like their families do."

"He's got a point," Death said. "You can't expect law enforcement to actually *care* about the prisoners. It's not like they're regular people. Drug dealers, child molesters, murderers…oh. Sorry."

"I'm not a *murderer*."

Don stopped halfway out of the car. "Look, Casey, I understand how you must feel coming here. But you've got to put the past few weeks behind you. No one is looking at you for the death of that man anymore. It's over. Completely forgotten."

Casey got out of the car.

The process to see Ricky was as involved and time-consuming as she'd feared. Every moment, from when they first stepped into the building until they were left alone in a room, she expected someone to realize who she was, and to have old paperwork saying she was a wanted criminal. But they got through without incident, and within the hour she and Don were waiting for her little brother in a cold, off-white box of a room, with a bolted-down table and three chairs, much like the room where she'd met with Detective Watts that morning. Only this one smelled a lot worse.

Death had taken off during the screening process—"Waaay too boring, and the technology is *so* yesterday"—but was now back, holding up the iPad and checking out heat signatures again. "Someone's coming."

When the door opened, Casey jumped up. Don grabbed her wrist. "Stay behind the table until the guards tell you it's okay."

She shook him off, but stayed where she was, even when Ricky appeared.

The first sight of him took her breath away. Pale, blotchy skin, sunken, dull eyes, and a buzz cut. His prison-issued clothes hung loosely on him, and the slump of his shoulders turned him into an old man. But what really got her were the handcuffs. They held his arms stiffly behind him, in a posture Casey had never seen, or even imagined, on her little brother.

Two guards followed him in, one staying by the door, the other with a hand on Ricky's elbow. "Okay," the one touching Ricky said. "Hold still."

Ricky waited, his eyes averted from Casey's, as the guard unlocked the cuffs. When he was free he shrugged, then pulled his arms forward to rub his wrists.

"Call if you need anything," the guard said, "or bang on the door. We'll be waiting outside." The guard gave a little salute and let himself out.

Casey walked around the table. "Ricky—"

He ducked, hands up, as if expecting to get hit.

Casey froze. "Ricky, it's me. Casey. Your sister." She felt almost like she had at her mother's, except her mother hadn't acted *afraid* of her. Casey walked slowly toward him, hands out, as if she were approaching a nervous dog. "I'm sorry I haven't been here for you. But I'm here now. I'll get you out of here, I promise."

He lowered his hands and peered up at her with wide eyes.

She couldn't manage a smile, but she tried to look confident and loving. "It will be okay."

His eyes filled. "It will never be okay."

"Look, whatever has happened to you in here, we'll deal with it together. I'll get you any help you need. I'll stay with you."

His eyes flashed. "I don't care about what's happened to *me*. *I'm* fine. It's what they did to *her*. What they did. They..." He closed his eyes and swayed on his feet.

Casey grabbed him, and Don hopped up from behind the table. Together they lowered Ricky onto a chair. When they were sure he wasn't going to fall over, Don went back to his seat.

"He means it, you know," Death said. "What they did to her is far worse in his mind than what's been done to him in here."

Casey knelt beside her brother. "I know what they did to her. I'm sorry about that, too. It was terrible."

"Terrible?" He gave a manic laugh. "It was...more than that."

Casey dragged another chair around the table so she could sit next to him. "I want to help find out who did this, Ricky. You don't deserve to be in here. And she deserves the truth."

He looked away. "She doesn't care about the truth anymore."

"No, but you do, don't you?"

"The truth won't bring her back."

Casey had way more experience with going after "truth" than she ever wanted. Courtrooms, test drives, payoffs. All of them were designed to "bring closure," but in reality brought nothing other than wasted time and money. She was more alone after all the legal crap than she'd ever been. Which was why she'd given up on the "truth" of her family's accident long ago. But this situation was different. No innocent person had ever been charged with killing her family, not like Ricky was being blamed now. Not even Pegasus, the guilty car company, had paid very many consequences for the accident. No matter what sort of "closure" there was supposed to have been, Casey—and her husband and son—had paid all there was to pay.

"Listen, Ricky, I didn't know this girl—"

"Alicia."

Casey hesitated.

"He thinks it's her real name," Death said. "You going to tell him, or should I?"

Casey let it go. "I didn't know Alicia, but it sounds like you knew her pretty well. What can you tell me about her?"

His eyes went soft. "She was sweet. And quiet. And kind of…mysterious."

"Secretive?"

"No! Just…" He sat for a few moments. "She wasn't the kind to go blabbing about herself everywhere. She was…private."

"But she talked to you?"

"Of course. We talked all the time."

"About what?"

"What do you think? Normal stuff. Work. Food. I don't know."

"Where was she from?"

"All over, I guess. She moved around a lot. Oregon. California. Lots of places. But I told her this should be her final stop. I'd convinced her, I'm sure of it. She liked it here better than anywhere else." A little color stole into his cheeks, indicating his hope that he was the reason for her contentment.

"What about her past?"

"What about it?"

"Did she talk about it, other than just where she'd lived? Houses, friends, jobs? You know. Actual details?"

His eyes slid away.

"Ricky? What is it?"

He shook his head. "Nothing."

"But—"

"Forget it, all right, Casey? Please?"

Casey watched as his face went through a change from sad and depressed to stubborn, his mouth a thin line.

"Okay," she said. "Fine. What about her childhood?"

"Her *childhood?*"

"Sure. You'd been going out for a few months. It would be normal for you to talk about your childhoods. You would see things around here that you remember, so you'd tell her, and that would trigger her memories. You know. You share stuff when you're dating."

"She didn't talk about her *childhood.*"

"Not even—"

"At *all.*"

"Casey," Don said, "perhaps we should just let him tell us what he *wants* to tell us."

Casey looked at her brother, who suddenly resembled a sullen teenager. Too bad he was actually ten years past that.

Ricky closed his eyes. When he opened them, the despair was back. "Look, I'm sorry. I'm just…" This time the tears overflowed onto his cheeks, and he swiped at them with his sleeves.

Casey leaned forward. "It's okay. Just remember I want to help you. The more I know about her, the better chance I have of figuring out who did this to her."

"It wasn't me."

"Of course it wasn't. I never thought so for an instant."

Death swooshed around, then hovered up by the ceiling, checking out the jail's video camera. "This isn't on. Just wanted to make sure."

Casey ignored the interruption. "Did Alicia have any other friends?"

Ricky frowned. "Not really. There was one other waitress at the restaurant who was about her age, but she kind of drove Alicia crazy. Ali said she never shut up."

"Would this be Bailey?"

"You *know* her?"

"I stopped by The Slope before coming here. She was working. And very eager to talk."

"You can't believe anything she says."

"Then I guess you *are* guilty."

"What?"

"She's one of the few people in this whole town, apparently, who thinks you're innocent. She's going to help me. So I wouldn't go bad-mouthing her right now if I were you."

"She's going to *help* you? But she always hated—" He stopped.

"Hated Alicia?"

"Look, I don't think she killed her, okay? She just never thought...She always said..."

"That you should be with her instead of Alicia? I know. She told me the same thing. It's not exactly a secret."

"So if she wants to help it's not because she wants to help Alicia."

"Does it matter?"

"Of course it matters! She doesn't care that Ali got killed. She just wants to use this to prove she was right. Or something."

"It doesn't matter *why* she wants to help. We'll take whatever help we can get."

"I don't want her making Alicia look bad."

"Ricky." Casey grabbed his hand. "You said it before. Alicia doesn't care anymore. She's gone. But I care. And you should. You don't want to be in here the rest of your life for a murder you didn't commit. Accused of killing the woman you loved. I mean, you did, right?"

"Did what?"

"Love her."

"Of course I did."

"And you didn't kill her?"

He yanked his hand away and stumbled from his chair, hanging onto the back. "I already told you—"

"Then we'll take Bailey's help. Won't we?"

He thrust out his chin, but then his shoulders drooped again, and he sank back into the chair. "You'll be careful what you believe?"

"About Alicia? Or about you?"

"About any of it."

She studied him. "So, what *should* I believe?"

"The only thing that really matters is that she was a good person. She really was."

A good person who had lied to him about such a basic thing as her name, and hadn't shared the slightest detail about her past except a list of multiple, gigantic states. Never a good sign.

"So tell me why someone would kill her."

"It wasn't her. I mean, it wasn't *because* it was her. It was a random break-in. It had to be."

Don cleared his throat. "I really don't think it was random, not from the way they—"

Casey glared at him, and Don stopped talking before he said anything too upsetting.

Ricky didn't seem to have heard, anyway. "She didn't have anything worth stealing. There was no secret stash of money—"

"And you know this how?"

"Because she wasn't the kind of person to hoard cash, or even care about it. She wore hand-me-down clothes. She never ate out on her own, even at The Slope. She didn't even have a computer, for God's sake."

"Why would God want her to have a computer?" Death said.

"She never bought things," Ricky continued. "If I did take her out to eat, she might pay her part—because she'd insist, not because I didn't want to—but she didn't go shopping, or skiing, or anything. There was nothing in her apartment people would plan to take. It had to be totally by chance."

"Okay." Casey drummed her fingers on the table. "So let's say it was random. How did they find her? She lived in a basement apartment, underneath a nosey landlord, in a residential neighborhood that wasn't exactly fancy, but wasn't a slum. You said yourself there was nothing obvious worth stealing. So why her?"

"I don't know. They followed her, maybe. She always walked home from work, and she was always alone. It would have been close to dark if it was after work. They could have been waiting for someone like her. Someone they could overpower and—"

"Stop." Casey held up her hand. "You're saying 'they.' What makes you think it was more than one person?"

Ricky went even paler, and his mouth dropped open. "What?"

"You know *what*. There's something you're not telling me."

His mouth clamped shut, and he shook his head. "There's not."

She looked over at Don, and he raised his eyebrows. He saw it, too.

"Look, Ricky, this is just like the Bailey thing. If you want me to help, you've got to tell me what you know."

He closed his eyes and breathed out through his nose, obviously struggling with something. Casey waited him out.

"She didn't tell me."

"Tell you what?"

"I mean, she didn't tell me on purpose. She was asleep."

"So you feel like you're betraying her if you tell us."

He shrugged, obviously embarrassed. "I guess. Kind of."

"I understand, Ricky. Really, I do. But the way I see it, you're betraying her if you *don't* tell. If it's something that could help us find her killers. And you know there was more than one."

He took a shuddering breath. "Have you seen the pictures?"

"Of Alicia? Yes. You have, too?"

His jaw trembled. "I wish I hadn't. What they did to her…"

"*Tell me*, Ricky."

He glanced at Don, and lowered his voice, as if he didn't want Don to hear. Don pulled a paper out of his briefcase and pretended to be reading it. Casey could tell he was faking, because his eyes weren't moving.

"We were sleeping," Ricky said. "One of the few nights she let me stay." He flushed. "Not because she didn't want me to, but because we were both so tired, and we had to get up early. You know how my shifts are, and if she had to work breakfast she'd be there at five. Usually I'd be at her place for a while in the evening, and then go home. It worked well for us. Or okay, anyway. Sometimes I'd ask if I could stay when it was late after we—" He stopped, and his flush grew deeper.

"It's all right, Ricky. You don't have to explain that part. I do remember what men and women do when they're in love."

He gave a brief smile, which looked more like a cringe. "Anyway, we were sleeping, and she started thrashing around. I woke up when she yanked the covers off of me. I tried to wake her up, too, because she was mumbling weird stuff, but she grabbed me. Both arms, like she was trying to get me to listen to her. Her eyes were wide open, and she was scared, really scared..."

Casey held his hand. "It's okay, Ricky."

"She kept saying, 'They found me. Oh, my God, they found me.' I asked her who, but she just said 'they.' It was freaky. She finally went back to sleep when I...I held her tight enough. When she woke up in the morning she didn't say anything about it, so I didn't, either. I figured if she wanted to tell me, she would." His face crumpled and he dropped it into his hands. "I should have asked her about it. If I had, she might still be alive. This wouldn't have happened."

"Ricky, you don't know—"

"I could have *protected* her! She wouldn't have been alone! She wouldn't have been walking *alone*." He fell onto Casey's shoulder and sobbed. She rubbed his back and looked up at Death, who was filming the whole exchange.

"I know," Death said. "I'm exploiting your brother's emotions. But you have to admit, his sense of grief is so raw it makes even me feel like weeping. It's so astounding I needed to record it."

She didn't stop glaring.

Don caught her expression. "Um, Casey? You okay?"

She shook her head and closed her eyes, leaning against Ricky's hair.

"The other question," Death said, coming in for a close-up, "is this. Does he really think he could have prevented what happened? Or is he simply angry that she didn't let him help? Does he know there were big things she wasn't telling him?"

Good questions, Casey thought. But ones that really didn't need to be answered. Either way, her brother was screwed up for life.

"Ricky," she said. "One more thing."

He sat up, his face red from crying.

"You know your Colorado U T-shirt, the one with the stain from where I busted your lip?"

"Yeah. Haven't thought about that shirt for ages."

"Do you know where it is?"

"Not for sure. It's probably in my dresser somewhere, buried under all the other shirts. Why?"

"The police found it in your house. It had Alicia's blood on it."

He stared at her, as if he couldn't comprehend what she was saying. "But…how? I never wore that around her. I never—" He looked at Don. "They think I was wearing it when she died. They think I wore it when I *killed* her."

Don nodded. "I didn't know about it until this morning. They hadn't told me."

"I don't know how it got blood on it, I don't know how—"

"Of course you don't." Casey patted his knee. "But don't you worry, Ricky. I'm going to find out."

How she was going to find out was a mystery.

But she didn't say that part out loud.

Chapter Ten

Getting out of the prison was a lot quicker than getting in. Death still chose to go elsewhere as they waited, saying the inmates were much more interesting than security checks could ever be. Casey believed that.

It was wrenching leaving Ricky in that awful place. The smells, the sounds, the angry people. Not anywhere she ever imagined her little brother would end up. But she assured him—and herself, in the process—that she would get him out quickly. She wasn't sure she actually believed herself, but she talked a good talk.

"So," Don said once they were back on the road. "I'm not sure we got anything good from him."

"Of course we did."

"Really? Enlighten me, please."

"Alicia obviously didn't share about her past. And when she spoke in her sleep she was worried about somebody finding her. The woman was in hiding. That proves it."

"You think?"

"Have they found out anything more about her, or are we still going with the lies she told on her job application and rental agreement?"

"I haven't heard anything new."

"We don't even know that Alicia McManus was her real name."

"Nice," Death said, giving a thumbs up. "Way to sneak that information into the conversation."

"Right," Don said. "You mentioned that back at the police station when Watts was telling you everything we don't know about her. It would make sense if it wasn't her name, since they can't find a record of her anywhere. But how would we go about finding her real one? Ricky obviously doesn't know it."

"Hmm," Death said. "This could be tricky."

Casey had no idea how to get Don to discover Alicia's real name of 'Elizabeth Mann' without actually saying it.

Death jumped in. "What if you suggest something close to Alicia?"

"Could it be a name sort of *like* Alicia?" she said to Don. "That might have the same nickname?"

"Could be. I've heard that people will do that, or use the same initials. So that could be Alice, I suppose, although there aren't a whole lot of women her age named that these days. Or Allison, maybe? Or some other form of Alicia, even. Lisa. Or just Ali."

Casey felt like thudding her head with her hand.

"And that doesn't help with the last name," Don said. "There are thousands of surnames that start with M."

"Could we go with the same idea as the first name? That it would be something close?"

"McMillan? McCarthy? McArthur? I'll suggest the idea to Watts. Maybe he can get someone on it. I'll tell them to start with the initials being the same."

Casey groaned. This was impossible.

"So where to?" Don said. "I don't suppose you'll come to my house for supper?"

"I'd like to, but I kind of promised Mom I'd come back after seeing Ricky."

"Of course. I'll drop you off there."

Death's tongue clicked. "Did you just *lie* to your lawyer?"

Ignoring Death, Casey convinced Don to drive to his office, where she grabbed her duffel bag, which she had left there that morning, told him she'd be in touch the next day, and walked toward her mother's. Once out of sight, she stopped at the next intersection. Death kept going across the street, listening to an iPod, walking in rhythm, until realizing that Casey was gone.

Death yanked out the earbuds and walked back to her, being run through twice by passing cars whose drivers suddenly reached for their heater controls. "What?"

"I have to."

"Have to what? Oh. That's the way to your house, isn't it? Think your mother will mind?"

"I didn't actually say I'd be back *today*, as you know. Just that I'd see her again before I left town."

"Then let's go."

Casey hesitated.

"Do we have to go over this again, Casey? No ghosts. No demons. No lingering spirits. It's just an empty house."

"But that's the thing. It's not. It's full of all kinds of things."

"I know. Furniture. Mementos. *Stuff*. But Casey, those material things don't really mean anything, do they? The important things are up here." Death touched her temple, and the coolness actually felt good, for once. "Your memories don't need tangible symbols. All they need is for your brain to function, and once that stops working, well, you'll be with Reuben and Omar in person. Or, not in *person*, exactly." Death swooped toward her and peered deep into her eyes. "Right?"

Casey averted her face and looked down the street, imagining she could see her rooftop through the trees and the other houses. Wood, metal, concrete, fabric. That's all a house was made of. Perhaps it would even be comforting to be within its walls. "All right. Let's go."

She soon began to see houses that looked familiar. Some of them had memories attached, as well. The house where she learned her first swear word—definitely not from her mother; the yard where she avenged a slight to Ricky by tying the offending boy to a post and telling him she was sending the neighborhood's stray dog over—which of course she didn't, and even if she had it wouldn't have mattered because the dog was a big, slobbery sweetie; the playground where she'd gone with Omar, and had swung him in the baby swing, surrounded by other moms and their babies. Babies who would now be toddlers, walking around, talking in broken sentences and giving their parents hugs throughout the day.

"Oh." She'd forgotten that Ricky's house sat on that road, only blocks from her own place, making a sort of triangle from their childhood home. He had bought it a few weeks before Casey's accident, so she never got used to visiting. Its existence had slipped her mind entirely. She stood on the sidewalk, looking it over. No one had been there for quite some time, it seemed. The week he'd been in jail had shown its colors.

She swung up the front walk and checked the door. Don had been wrong. It wasn't being held as a crime scene anymore. But it was locked. The police would have bolted it behind them when they were done investigating. She walked into the garage and checked for the kind of place she and Ricky had always hidden their key when they were kids. She found it in the third possibility, under a tub of ice cream in the deep freeze.

"I don't know why you humans even bother to lock your doors," Death muttered.

Casey used the key and stepped into the front foyer. There was no doubt the police had been there. Black fingerprint dust coated the surfaces, drawers had been emptied and not refilled, and the coat closet door was open, with empty hangers cluttering the rail.

She walked through to the kitchen. There again was the search disaster, with the fingerprint dust, all sorts of little household items piled on the counters and table, and photographs stuck back onto the refrigerator in a jumbled mess. Pots and pans lay scattered on the floor, and there was a conspicuous spot on the wall where Ricky had obviously hung a calendar. The nail was still there, along with a few sticky notes of dates and times, and a mug of pens sat close by on the counter.

Casey opened what looked like a pantry and found the cleaning supplies. Ricky had taken care of her place for almost two years while she'd been on the road. It was her turn, now.

"Music while you work?" Death said, and propped an iPad on an iHome with the playlist on shuffle.

Casey listened to the very eclectic mix of blues, hip-hop, rock, and opera while sweeping, scrubbing, refilling drawers, and organizing photos. She spent almost an hour in the kitchen before moving on to the rest of the first floor, and finally upstairs. Those rooms were just as bad, except for what looked like the guest room. There had only been minimal tossing and dusting there. Probably because there wasn't much furniture in the first place. She had finished that bedroom and moved on to Ricky's and the master bath when she sat heavily on the stripped bed. Even the mattress pad was gone.

"Tired?" Death said.

"Exhausted."

"Why don't you take a nap? You could put sheets on the guest room bed."

"I want to finish cleaning. *Then* I'll take a nap."

Death eyed the bedside stand and the dresser in the corner. "Think the cops took *everything*?"

"You mean, Ricky might have hidden something they didn't find?"

"What if he *did* have questions about Alicia? What if he wasn't telling you—or her—the complete truth? You saw how he hesitated when you asked him about her past."

Casey looked around the room. Where might Ricky have hidden something? She looked under the mattress, but that was a clichéd hiding place, and the police had certainly checked there. She looked for false drawers in the bedside table, extra walls in the closet, and behind the toilet in the master bath. She went through what shoe boxes were left in the closet—which actually held shoes—and each one of his dresser drawers. She found nothing but clothing, toilet articles, and condoms, which made her squirm. She threw them back in the bedside table.

"Casey," Death said. "I'm disappointed in you."

"Because seeing my brother's birth control makes me queasy?"

"No."

"Because I couldn't find something trained law enforcement missed?"

"No. Because you're not using your noggin."

"My noggin."

Death knocked her head with a cold knuckle that didn't knock so much as hiss.

"What? Am I missing something?"

"I think so. You remember how you knew exactly where to look for the house key when we got here?"

"Yeah, because it's the same place we hid it when we were— Oh. Duh."

"So where did Ricky hide his private things when he was a kid?"

"You mean stuff he didn't want me to find?"

Death smiled. "That's what private means. Don't tell me you never found his stash."

"Of course I did. But he doesn't know that, so don't tell him."

Death made a zipping motion. "My lips are sealed."

Casey took off downstairs.

"Not in his room?" Death slid past her, down the bannister.

"First place I would have looked. He knew better."

"But you found it."

"Eventually. It took me a while, and then I had to be careful when and how often I'd check it, or he'd know."

She walked into the office, where Ricky had a desk—empty now of a computer or anything else useful—a reading chair, and—*ta da*—shelves lined with books.

"He hid stuff in the *library?*" Death said, then giggled. "He did it in the library with the reading lamp."

Casey scanned the books, and found it on the second shelf. *The Chronicles of Narnia*. The boxed set that was released when she and Ricky were kids. She pulled the whole set down and sat in the chair.

"I love those books," Death said, and held out the ereader, which displayed the cover of *Prince Caspian*. "Which one was your favorite?"

Casey didn't answer. She was too busy sliding the books out of the box.

"How could he fit anything in there?"

"Doesn't have to be much."

Casey set the books gently to the side and picked at the back with her fingernail. The cardboard stuck for a moment before coming free. When it did, a paper fluttered out.

Death swooped in. "What does it mean?"

"I have no idea."

It was a scrap of paper, obviously torn from a larger one. Two lines were written on it, each in a different color pen, like they'd been put there two separate times.

Fine as cream gravy.

Sharp as mashed potatoes.

Death's forehead furrowed. "He's keeping track of clichés?"

Casey didn't answer, but dug in the back of the book box to peel one more thing from the hiding place. Another copy of that photo. The one of Ricky and Alicia at the restaurant.

"Must be the only shot they had," Death said. "Seems everybody's got a copy."

Casey slid the photo into her pocket and left the dismantled book series to go to the kitchen. Death followed.

Casey opened the pantry where the cleaning supplies were kept and dug around until she found a box for dustrags. "I can't believe I didn't think of this when I was in here earlier."

"You're going to dust *now*?"

She opened the box and dumped out the rags to discover a Ziploc bag underneath. There were two things inside. One was a wrapped candy bar called a Chick-o-Sticks. The description under the name said it was a "Crunchy Peanut Butter and Toasted Coconut Candy."

"Ricky is a secret candy stasher?" Death said. "Was this a favorite or something?"

Casey shook her head. "Never heard of it."

The second item was even more curious. It was a biography of Carol Burnett.

Casey squatted and slumped against the wall. "I don't get it."

"You will."

"You do already? Tell me!"

"I have no idea. But I have faith in your power of deduction."

Casey was ready to give a smart reply when the doorbell rang.

Chapter Eleven

"Uh-oh," Death said.

Casey held her breath. Perhaps if she pretended she wasn't there, the person would go away. But less than ten seconds later the doorbell rang again, followed by loud knocking. Death disappeared for a moment, then returned, trying not to laugh.

"She knows you're in here."

"Who?"

"Ricky's neighbor, from across the street. And she is a picture, let me tell you."

"Have I met her?"

"Can't tell you that, sweetheart. But if you did, it was before you and I started hanging out together. Here." Death pulled out a digital camera and showed Casey a photo of a very colorful woman on Ricky's front step. As she watched, the photo moved, presenting an image of the woman leaning over the side rail of the front steps to try to see in the front windows, as Death had at Casey's mom's.

Casey sighed. "I guess I'd better go see what she wants before she falls on her *noggin*."

She stashed the candy and biography back in the dustrag box and stopped in the office to put the Narnia series back together. She left the photo and the slip of paper with clichés in her pocket. The doorbell kept chiming all the while, alternated with vigorous knocking. Casey opened the door during one of the lulls to receive a view of the woman's rather large backside as she again bent over the rail to see in the window. The woman almost toppled over when she heard the door, but righted herself and turned to Casey with her hands outstretched. Casey recoiled. The woman's fake eyelashes were so huge and thick it looked like she had spiders on her face. Her hair had been dyed a brilliant orange, and her lipstick was the color of a ripe tomato. Her caftan-like blouse-dress thing was a mixture of the brightest colors imaginable, and her feet were bare, with several rings on brightly painted toes. It was like a circus has landed on the doorstep.

"Are you the cleaning lady?" she asked Casey.

Death laughed.

"No," Casey said.

"Oh, I thought…" the woman gestured at Casey's pale blue warm-ups and the dustrag she'd stuck in her pocket during her search. Casey had to admit she saw her point.

"Police?" the woman tried again.

"No, I'm—"

"Another *girlfriend*?"

"I'm Ricky's sister."

The woman stopped short. "His sister? He has a *sister*?"

"I haven't been around much lately. I don't live here."

"And where *do* you live?"

Casey frowned. "Who are you?"

The woman clapped a hand to her mouth and laughed uproariously. "You must think I'm terrible. I am. I'm awful. I'm also Geraldine, and I live over there. I moved in last year, came from Vegas, can you imagine?" She pointed a long, crimson fingernail toward the house across the street, where pink flamingoes and oversized whirligigs filled the small lawn. The house would have been normal otherwise, except for the bright orange shutters and the life-sized buffalo statue in between the house and garage. "I've just been devastated about what's happened, and wanted to know if there's anything I can do to help. That's why I came over. There hasn't been anybody here since the police—those *horrible* people!—left yesterday. They took things out, you know. Ricky's computer and his phone and sheets and who knows what else. Like they really think he could have done anything to that sweet girl."

"You knew her?"

Geraldine opened her mouth to say something else, but then stopped and peered over Casey's shoulder into the house.

"You know what she wants," Death said. "Might as well go with it, if you're thinking of getting any information out of her. If she has some, she'll share it if the circumstances are right. Which basically means she needs to feel a part of things."

Casey wanted to shut the door on the woman's face, but instead she said, "Would you like to come in?" with what she hoped was a welcoming voice.

"I hate to impose," Geraldine said as she shouldered past. She lumbered right through the foyer into the kitchen and around the side to the living room where she plopped herself down on the sofa. She situated herself where she had a view of the side and front yards, then crossed her ankles and placed her hands in her lap, like a genteel southern belle. "I only met the girl once, you see, and it wasn't here. The two of them were at the grocery store, picking out fruit, and I went right up and introduced myself. She was a pretty little thing, wasn't she, and Ricky looked so happy!"

"Did she tell you her name?"

"Of course, which is more than you've done." She looked at Casey knowingly.

"Casey."

"Well, *Casey*, Ricky introduced her as Alicia and said they were getting snacks for watching a movie that night. Now, isn't that romantic?"

Sounded pretty normal to Casey, but what did she know?

"I never saw her here," Geraldine continued. "I'm not sure why. I pretty much know everything that happens on this block, and why Ricky never brought her home is a mystery to me. They were holding hands and looking at each other all lovey-dovey when I ran into them at the store. It's not like she was hideous or deformed or anything. She looked like a nice, normal girl."

"Most girls do."

"Well, that's true. But the things I've seen!" She fanned herself with her hand. "Delivery men staying longer than they should, girls out running with hardly a stitch on, people, you know, *doing it*, in their yards at night. It's enough to make a grown woman blush."

The thought of this woman adding one more color to her palette made Casey shudder.

"But Ricky and his girl—woman, I suppose I should say, you know, to be what they call *politically correct*—they acted in love, not in *lust*, if you know what I mean. Very sweet, actually. It made me remember my young days, when I first met my Arthur."

Casey groaned inwardly. Was this woman really going to go on about her past? But no…

"I saw Ricky come home that night, you know. The night the girl was *murdered*. Late, of course. But he looked completely normal. At least, what I could see through his car window, and when he got out of the car before the garage door closed. I really think I would have noticed blood or torn clothing or even if he looked upset."

"What did he look like?"

Geraldine smiled, her expression going all dreamy. "Happy."

It was like a punch to Casey's solar plexus. Her poor brother. He might have been happy then, but the next morning it was like his world had exploded. But that's how life worked. One moment you were content, feeling like nothing could touch you, and the next…

"Relaxed," Geraldine said again. "Like those nights when Arthur and I had been, you know, *intimate*—"

"Aah!" Death screamed.

"Is there something I can do for you, Geraldine?" Casey said, hoping she didn't sound as desperate as she felt.

"Oh, you don't need to do anything for me," Geraldine said, not even fazed by the interruption. "But I think there's something *I* can do for *you*."

"And what's that?"

She smiled mysteriously. "I can tell you about the man who showed up here at your brother's house the day after she died."

Casey gripped her chair's arms. "What man? And do the police know about him?"

"Of course they do. I told them right away. He was a bad man, I could tell. He had that look in his eye."

"You saw him up close?"

"Of course I did. He was over at Ricky's house after Ricky went to work. This was before we knew anything had happened to his girlfriend, you know. The man was wearing a uniform, like from a home repair place or something like that. *Hometown Interiors*, the patch said. I wasn't able to find them anywhere in the phone book, but you know how things are these days, with cell phones. If you don't have a landline you have to move heaven and earth to get your name in the yellow pages."

"What did the man say?"

"Well, I watched him go right around the back of the house, and when I didn't see him for a while I went over. He was just coming out, and I asked him what he was doing. He was very polite, I must say, but like I said, his eyes were all wrong. He said he was fixing something in Ricky's bathroom, that Ricky had left the back door open for him, which I suppose could be right because we live in a very safe neighborhood, and people do that sort of thing."

"What did the police say?"

"They checked on him, said it was a legitimate business, and there was paperwork and on-line correspondence to corroborate what he said."

Ricky hadn't said anything about a repairman. But then, when Casey had seen him that afternoon he wasn't exactly in the state of mind to be talking about his bathroom. And she hadn't known to ask.

"I called again the next day to ask the police about the man," Geraldine said, "but they brushed me off, said they'd already gone down that avenue. I told them—"

Casey got up and walked to the bathroom on the first floor. Geraldine skittered along behind, watching over Casey's shoulder. There was no sign of any recent work. No stickers on the window, no unmatched wood or fresh paint. And when she had cleaned the room there hadn't been any sawdust or dirty footprints. Nothing but regular bathroom grime and fingerprint dust.

They trooped upstairs, but there were no signs of new repair or construction in that bathroom, either.

"That man wasn't working on anything," Geraldine gushed. "But he spent quite some time in here. What do you suppose he was doing?"

There was no way to be sure, but Casey figured she had a good idea. He was planting things. Things like bloody shirts and paper trails.

Chapter Twelve

"Time to hound the cops?"

Geraldine had gone back home—after Casey gave several varied and right-out blunt hints that she really should—and Death held out a phone that now looked like a Droid.

Exhausted, Casey lay on the couch in Ricky's living room, feeling grimy and dusty. "It doesn't sound like speaking to law enforcement would do any good. Geraldine's already told them everything I could."

"Not about Ricky's stash."

"Like they'd care about a few scribbled sayings, stale candy, and a biography of a comedienne. What I need is hard evidence, not stuff that has no meaning to anyone but Ricky."

"So you need to ask Ricky what it means."

"Don't you think I realize that? It's not like I can just call him up and ask."

Death stepped away, hands up. "Just trying to be helpful."

"What time is it?"

"Almost seven-thirty. Why? Hungry?"

"Well, yes, but it's also about time for Bailey to get off work. She said I could check with her about Alicia's faked job application."

"Perfect. You can grab supper while you're there."

"Not. I'd rather go hungry. You coming?"

Ricky's car had been taken away by the cops, so Casey strapped her bag onto her back, jumped on Ricky's bicycle, and headed to the other side of town, Death keeping pace on an airborne Segway. Casey made it to the Slope just before closing and waited outside. When Bailey appeared, it took Casey a moment to recognize her. She'd changed into a different tight shirt, this one with open buttons revealing cleavage, and a clean pair of skinny jeans. She'd obviously made a stop in the bathroom to put on fresh make-up, and her hair was loose, falling around her face.

She headed for her car, confident in high heeled boots, and slid into the driver's seat. Casey got into the passenger side just as Bailey inserted her key in the ignition.

Bailey yelped and laid her hand on her chest. "Geez, you scared me."

"Sorry. Didn't think you'd want your manager to see you talking to me."

"Yeah, he was awfully crabby this afternoon. I think it's all getting to him."

"Did you find it?"

Bailey looked blank for a moment before understanding lit her eyes and she dug in her purse. "It's been a long day. I forgot for a second what it was you wanted. But here it is."

Just one side of one sheet of paper. Alicia's job application. "You need it back?"

"Nah. I made a copy while Karl was out."

Casey scanned the form. It was everything she feared. All lies, nothing that would help. At least not at first sight.

"So did you get in to see him?" Bailey's hand waved in front of Casey's face, like she'd been trying to get her attention, but had failed.

"Who? Your boss?"

"No, Ricky. You said you were going to the prison."

"Yeah, I saw him."

"How was he?"

"How do you think?"

Bailey frowned. "I do care about him, you know. Just because Alicia was his actual *girlfriend* doesn't mean I didn't like him. I told you I don't think he did it, and I *will* help you find the real killer. Ricky deserves a second chance."

Poor girl. She had it bad. And Casey had spent so much breath trying to convince Ricky to give her a second chance, Casey should probably follow her own advice. "He wasn't good. Pretty much a mess. I have to get him out."

"*We* have to." Bailey's eyes were hard. Determined. "What else can I do?"

Casey considered the offer. "Do you think the other people you work with know anything?"

"About who killed her?"

"Or just about her. Would she have told them anything?"

"I really doubt it. She pretty much kept to herself, and they're not exactly her type. Not my type, either," she added quickly.

"Who's type are they?"

She made a face. "Can't imagine."

"What about customers? Any of them she was especially friendly with?"

"Some of the dinner folks, I guess. I get along better with the breakfast and lunch crowds. The working men, you know. Alicia wasn't real friendly with them. Got them their food and whatever, but they thought she was stuck up. They seem to like me."

Casey eyed the girl's clothes. "I wonder why."

Bailey had the grace to blush. "So do you want me to talk to them? The dinner people or the dishwasher and cook? Some of the older couples who come in for late breakfasts might be good, too."

"Are you working tomorrow?"

"Got to. There's no one else, not till Karl hires another waitress." She brightened. "You interested?"

"No. But I'm going to come by. We can question the other employees together. What's a good time?"

"Depends. If you want the cook and dishwasher, you'd better wait till after the breakfast rush. You want the dinner folks, you'll have to come later on."

"Karl won't mind?"

"He won't care. Not if you're applying for the waitress job."

"I told you—"

Bailey grinned slyly. "Or you can try to find the guys wherever they went tonight after work."

"They don't tell you?"

"I never ask. Don't really want to know."

"What about you? Are you headed to the other side of town?"

"I'm meeting some friends there."

"I thought you didn't like rich people."

"Not when they're treating me like a servant. When I meet them on their terms they're not so bad."

"And they don't see through it?"

Bailey's eyes were bleak, and she hesitated just a little too long. "Not all of them."

"All right." Casey opened her door. "I'll see you tomorrow morning. About nine?"

"That's fine."

Casey got out of the car and watched the girl drive away before heading down the sidewalk. She stopped under a dim parking lot light to study the job application, but had to squint. Death held the Droid over the paper to add illumination.

"I don't get it," Casey said. "The manager didn't ask for any ID? He let it all go, no questions asked? How does he get away with that?"

"Come on, Casey; you can't be completely surprised."

She folded up the paper and began pedaling. Death rode on the back axles, like a nine-year old, but didn't need to hang onto Casey to stay put. "So, where are we headed?"

Casey wobbled, but kept the bike upright. "I guess…home."

"Home. Doesn't that sound strange?"

But Casey couldn't let herself think about their destination as she rode. She wasn't even sure she could think about it when they got there. "Alicia made up a name, supplied only a brand new address, and didn't even put the number of the phone she was using. Who knows how many places she lived before coming here? And Ricky believed her about wanting to stay."

"Maybe she really was going to this time."

"No. People like that, who move around with new names, and fill out fake applications, they don't stay. They just drop everything and leave people, and jobs, and landlords behind. They can't be trusted. Not with important things."

Death laughed. "Do you *hear* yourself?"

"I know."

"You're so self-righteous about her changing her name and hiding her past. But it's like she's another you. A Mini Me, like in that movie. Except for, well, it's You. And she's not a midget."

Casey kept riding, turning onto the road where her house sat. It felt like she was riding uphill, even though that stretch of road was flat. "What Alicia did hurt Ricky. I never got in a relationship. Never hurt anybody."

"I guess it depends on how you define 'relationship.' And 'hurt.'"

"I never made any promises to anyone in the past two years. Especially a man."

"You sure about that?"

"Yes, I'm sure!"

"Then why is Eric VanDiepenbos, that sweet young man from Clymer who just saved your ass, sitting in front of your house?"

Chapter Thirteen

Casey skidded the bike to a stop, and Eric looked up from his perch on the front steps. She breathed in deeply through her mouth and out her nose, unsure how to proceed. She hardly knew the kid, right? She'd only met him a few weeks ago. He was young—younger than she was, anyway. He was also idealistic, damaged from the murder of his lover, and the son of a criminal. His presence here in her home town couldn't possibly be good.

"Casey?"

The sound of his voice brought back other memories, as well. The murder of the Louisville mobster, a killer's head exploding in front of them, and a passionate near-sex experience in the back of a darkened theater. Casey went hot, then cold. This man, with whom she'd experienced so much in such a short amount of time, stood in front of the house where she'd shared a complete life with Reuben. Complete in the sense that she'd given her total self. Incomplete in that it had lasted only a few years.

The house still looked the same. Better, actually. Ricky had taken good care of it. The lawn must have been mown just before Ricky went to prison, because it still looked fairly neat. A few leaves had scattered over it, but nothing that couldn't be explained away by a light breeze. The paint was fresh, the flowerbeds weed-free, and the stump that had been a beautiful oak tree held a pot of rust-colored mums. It was like she'd just come home from the *dojang*, and Reuben and Omar would be waiting inside. The house would smell like tamales, and flour dustings would decorate Reuben's shirt. Omar would be strapped to Reuben's back, watching as Reuben steamed the filled corn husks. The moment felt so real Casey almost believed it.

But Eric VanDiepenbos, not at all a part of that life, waited by the steps as she walked the bike across the street and laid it in her yard, along with her bag. She stood at the end of the walk.

"Thank you," she said.

"You're welcome."

He took a step forward.

She took one back. "Why are you still here?"

"I'm actually not *still* here. I went home. And then I came back. So the question should actually be, why did I come back?"

She waited. "And the answer?"

"I heard about your brother. I want to help."

"What could you do?"

"I don't know. Something." He shifted on his feet. "Plus, I wanted to see you."

"Why?"

He gave a little laugh. "Why? Casey, do you not remember *anything* that happened three weeks ago?"

She looked around, wondering where Death was when she needed a hand. Or a distraction.

"That's over," she said.

"Not for me."

"Right. What with your dad going to prison and everything…"

He shoved his hands in his pockets and kicked at something on the walk. "At least your brother is innocent."

"You believe that?"

"I don't need to. You do."

Casey looked at Eric, his hair flopping over his forehead, kicking at pebbles like a twelve-year-old. What on earth was she going to do with him?

"You really want to help?"

His head jerked up, like a puppy expecting a treat. "Yes."

"Fine. Come back tomorrow morning."

His face fell. "Tomorrow—"

"I haven't even been back to this house yet. This is the first I'm seeing it. And I can't do that with anybody else." She gave him what she hoped was a gentle smile. "Not even you."

"I'll stay out of your way. I promise. I'll…be here for you."

"Eric, you have no idea—"

"I know what happened to you two years ago. I know about the accident, and about your baby. I know about…Reuben."

Of course he did. She had called him her dead husband's name while they were ripping each other's clothes off in the back of that theater three weeks earlier. That, obviously, had been the end of that little affair.

"Eric, look. I like you, you know I do. I'll be eternally grateful for how you kept me out of jail. And I appreciate that you want to help with my brother—I'll take whatever help you can give me with that. But this…" She looked up at the house. "This I have to do by myself. It has nothing to do with you. It has everything to do with the life I lost. Please try to understand."

"Can I just wait out here? In case you need someone to talk to after you go in?"

She shook her head. "Where are you staying tonight?"

"Well, I was hoping to stay here."

Wasn't going to happen. "Okay, here's what we'll do. You have a phone?"

"Of course."

Of course. Like everybody had one. Well, she supposed, every *normal* person did. Actually…"I think the landline is still on in the house. Ricky kept everything going in case I came back. So I can call you if I need to, right?"

"But—"

"And you can go stay in my brother's house."

He wrinkled his nose.

"Or you can find a hotel. But Eric, you can't stay here. Not tonight." Maybe not ever.

He sighed. "Fine. But you have to promise to call if you need me."

"I promise. All right? Now here's the key to his house." She gave him directions, as well as her phone number, which was burned into her brain from Before.

He plugged the number into his iPhone, which looked exactly like Death's replica, and scribbled his on the back of a gas receipt. "Casey Maldonado? Or Kaufmann? Or should we simply go with Smith?"

A joke. Sort of. That was how she'd first introduced herself to him way back three weeks ago—it felt like three years. And he'd told her his name was Eric Jones. Cute. A far cry from VanDiepenbos.

She glanced at the mailbox, which had the house number, but no last name. "Maldonado. My last name is Maldonado. My husband's name."

Eric became very busy inputting the information. "How about I use all three? That way I'm sure to know I'll get one of you." He shifted on his feet, looking even more like a child waiting for recognition. But at the same time like a man, with strong arms and kind eyes and warm skin…

"Goodnight, Eric."

He looked around at the street and the house, but not at her. "All right. I'll see you in the morning. Unless you call me."

"Do you have a car?"

He gestured to a generic gold Taurus. Rental.

"How about you come get me at eight-forty-five?"

"I can come earlier."

"No, that will be fine. I—we—have an appointment at nine."

"Okay. Should I eat breakfast first? Or will we be eating there?"

The poor boy. He had no idea what he was asking. "Eat first. You won't want even one bite at the place we're going."

He nodded, looking at his car, his keys, the sidewalk. "You sure I can't—"

"*Goodnight*, Eric."

He stopped speaking and studied the car key like it held the answers to the universe. "Goodnight, Casey." He got in the car and pulled slowly away. From the shape of his silhouette as he drove, Casey could tell he was watching her in his rear view mirror.

And then he turned the corner and was out of sight.

Chapter Fourteen

The house didn't smell like tamales.

It smelled like cleaning solution. Not the same combination as at her mother's house. More like how she'd left Ricky's. Clean and fresh, and sterile. No actual life. Not even a fern.

Casey had dreaded that first step into the kitchen, the room she entered from the back door. She'd used the key from the garage, the one hidden under the tee ball stand Omar had never had the chance to break. The key slid in easily, and the doorknob turned like it had been used daily over the past two years.

The kitchen felt strange. Not strange as if something were wrong. Just…alien. No familiar odors. No well-worn articles of clothing strewn across the backs of chairs. No food crumbs or dishes on the counter. It was a show home, which was what she'd wanted Ricky to make it into. Something that could be bought and sold, as if it meant nothing more than a piece of paper declaring it real estate.

She wandered into the living room. Again, nothing personal. No pictures of her family. No *Taste of Home* or *Hapkido Times* magazines on the coffee table. No shoes left in the middle of the room. There was an afghan on the back of the couch, one her grandmother had made. But that held only memories of her childhood. None from the years with her own family. Omar had been too tiny for the heavy blanket, which had been crocheted for Casey's father, a large man who favored black and hunter green. A memory did float up of a child-made fort, made with Ricky, the afghan serving as the roof. It had been too heavy to stay up, and she and Ricky had fought about how best to use it in their construction. For some reason she'd inherited it when her dad died. Nobody had ever really used it since.

She went through the front hallway and stared up the hardwood steps. The upstairs. That was where the real test would be. The answer to whether or not ghosts did exist. She took a deep breath and started up, running her hand along the smooth railing. As she climbed, her heart raced—a sure sign of anxiety, as it would take hundreds of stairs to make her body react to mere physical activity. She paused halfway up, taking in the smooth white wall, where there used to be family photos displayed. Now it was a testament to Ricky's hard work and care for her home.

She continued up until she hit the landing. Straight ahead was the bathroom, where she'd given Omar countless baths. More than once she'd gotten as wet as he had, when he had splashed and played. He'd always loved those times in the warm water, with Casey or Reuben blowing bubbles to entertain him. The little bath cushion was gone now, and the baby shampoo and wash had been replaced with Bath and Body Works bottles. The mirror was free of spots, and the only thing on the counter was a ceramic liquid soap dispenser. The towel even looked unused, as if it were there just for looks. Which it was.

Casey stood in the hallway. Which should be first? The bedroom she had shared with Reuben, where they'd spent countless hours talking, sleeping beside each other, and, of course, those other things Geraldine had been going on about with her Arthur? Or Omar's bedroom, where she'd spent those late nights and early mornings when he'd woken up hungry or over-tired or teething? Come to think of it, why should she go in either?

Because if she was going to spend the night, she would be sleeping in one of those rooms, unless she wanted to spend the night on the couch.

She'd slept worse places.

She went back downstairs and sat on the sofa. Her stomach rumbled. She went to the kitchen and looked through the cupboards. Completely empty, like she was Old Mother Hubbard. The refrigerator was unplugged, so of course it was empty. There was nothing—not even a can of beans—to eat. She went back to the living room.

She could order out for pizza. Or Chinese. Or walk down to the 24/7 convenience store and get one of those crappy burritos and an Icee.

Or she could just tough it out till morning.

She drank some water from the spigot, lay on her back, and pulled her father's afghan over her. She should be tired. It had been a late night, and an emotional day. She was in her own home after being on the road for two years. That in itself should be exhausting. She closed her eyes and concentrated on her breathing. In and out, even, deep, slow. Counting sheep. Counting stars. Going through the alphabet, naming different kinds of food for each letter.

She opened her eyes.

The refrigerator was clean. Just warm. She plugged it in. And then she put her shoes back on, grabbed her wallet, and walked out the front door.

"Midnight snack?" Death sat on the front step, holding an electronic tablet and watching an episode of *Everybody Loves Raymond*. "This family drives me crazy. If I were a part of it I'd shoot myself."

"Go right ahead."

Death pushed a button and the show disappeared. "Wow. You're not any nicer in the middle of the night than you are during the day."

"It's not like you shooting yourself would do any harm."

"True." Death stood and stretched. "So where are we going?"

"*I* am going to the convenience store."

"Burrito?"

"I was thinking frozen pizza. Or maybe some rotisserie chicken, if they have some this time of night."

Death made a face. "Sounds wonderful. I think I'll stay here where I won't die of food poisoning." Death turned the tablet back on, resuming the *Raymond* episode where it had left off. "Maybe you'll find someone of your type there."

"What type would that be?"

"Honestly?"

"No."

Casey left Death and walked toward the store, which sat at the end of the street several blocks down. The night was quiet, and hardly any lights glowed behind curtains of the neighboring houses. She and Reuben really had picked the family part of town. No late-night partiers or guys hanging out on the street with their hot rods and beers. The few lights she saw were probably for parents up with babies. She turned her mind away from that thought and broke into a jog. She hadn't gotten a run for a couple of days and she was feeling it.

When she reached the store she kept going. It was the middle of the night, but she was still wearing the blue warm-up suit, after all. If she couldn't sleep, she might as well exercise. She headed down the hill toward the lower side of town. Alicia's side. She remembered Alicia's address from the information on the job application—assuming *that* at least wasn't a lie—and glanced at the street names. Alicia lived on a president street. The same names that popped up in every town across the country—Washington, Lincoln, Jackson, *Jefferson*. There it was. Casey found the number on the nearest house and used that to make her way toward Alicia's place. When she reached it she stood in the middle of the dark street and studied the place.

It looked like a regular house. There was no indication that there was an apartment in the basement. Nothing to say a woman lived there alone, or, as Ricky had stated, that there was anything in the vicinity worth stealing. It was a nice enough house, in a decent location, but not a place Casey would imagine thieves would frequent—it was neither a feast of riches nor a harbor for drug dealers and gangs. Just a dark, quiet neighborhood with lower-middle-class status. The mountains loomed like black sentinels over the roofs, close enough to be seen, and almost felt. Far enough away they weren't a direct moneymaker. The landlord wouldn't be able to charge top dollar to a renter, because getting anywhere touristy would mean using public transportation, or taking a long walk, like Alicia used to do every night after work.

A siren sounded in the night, but it was in the distance, and moving away. A car accident, maybe, or a break-in at a house that would be more profitable than these modest dwellings. Still, Casey moved out of the middle of the street, into the shadows. Her light-colored warm-up suit glowed like a beacon under the streetlights, and the last thing she needed was some nosy neighbor calling the cops.

There was no sign in the house that the landlord was awake. No movement. No lights. And no dogs paced the lawn inside the small fence. Casey walked around the house and found what she assumed was Alicia's door, at the base of a narrow cement staircase. The entryway was free of police tape, and through the small window in the door Casey could see that the interior was pitch black. The door was locked.

Casey ran her fingers over the top of the doorjamb, but there weren't any keys. She moved several rocks, the small planter on the steps, and one of those ceramic frogs meant for hiding things, and looked underneath. Nothing. She wasn't surprised—if Alicia was lying about her life and afraid of her past creeping up on her, she wasn't going to make it easy for anyone to get in. Even if she thought she couldn't be found, her innate sense of self-preservation would keep her from using any security shortcuts.

Casey turned to walk back up the steps.

A man stood at the top of the stairwell with a baseball bat.

Chapter Fifteen

"Who's there?" He raised the bat to shoulder level.

Casey put up her hands. In the darkness she couldn't see much about the man—young or old, strong or weak. But a baseball bat could do damage no matter who was wielding it, especially when she was trapped in a brick stairwell, with no room to maneuver.

"I'm unarmed," she said. If you didn't count her feet and hands. Or elbows.

The man held his ground. "What do you want? I called the cops."

"I'm Ricky's sister. Ricky Kaufmann. I came to look at Alicia's apartment."

The bat lowered a few inches. "You mean Ricky, Alicia's boyfriend?"

"Yes. The guy you turned in."

He slumped and the bat tip went all the way to the ground. He leaned on it, like it was a cane, and rubbed his forehead with his other hand. "I didn't turn him in. The cops wanted to know if I saw anything. I had to tell them. He was here."

"But you didn't tell them about the other men."

"I didn't *see* any other men. If there *were* any."

"You really think Ricky did this?"

He closed his eyes and took a deep breath. "I can't believe he would. That's why it took so long…I didn't even think about his visit until hours later. He came over to see her often. She introduced him to me, and he treated her really nice. He was a…a good kid."

"He still is. Can I come up?"

He stepped aside, still holding the bat, but not as a weapon. "I can't imagine who would…" He shook his head, apparently unable to speak.

"Do you have a copy of your rental agreement?"

"Alicia's? Sure. In the house."

"May I see it?"

He considered. "You have ID?"

She pulled out her wallet and showed him. He tilted it toward the light that came from the street. It still had her maiden name, since she hadn't had to renew her license during the few years she'd been with Reuben, so it matched with what she'd told the landlord.

He handed it back. "So, Casey Kaufmann, why do you want to see the papers?"

"Like you, I don't believe Ricky killed her. I'm trying to find out who did."

"You think she wrote it on the lease?" He obviously thought she was bonkers.

"I just want to figure out who she was. The cops can't find her anywhere, and I think her past caught up with her."

"You think someone from some other place killed her?"

"It makes more sense than my little brother doing it."

He spun the baseball bat in his hand and looked up at the mountains. "All right. I'll show you."

"What about the cops?"

"What? Oh, I didn't really call them. I've had enough police during the past week to last me a lifetime. They've been helpful, I suppose, and I haven't had any problems with them, but still…" He led her to the side of the house and opened the door.

"You're not afraid of me?"

"You look pretty harmless."

A sharp laugh startled Casey, and she jumped. Death, standing in the open doorway, pushed a button on a digital recording device and played back the landlord's words. *You look pretty harmless.* "Talk about words that shouldn't go together. 'You' and 'harmless.' I guess 'pretty' is all right, when you get cleaned up. Not now, necessarily. But once in a great while."

"So come on in, then," the landlord said.

Casey followed him into the dark foyer, and he snapped the light on, temporarily blinding her. She squinted, and he led her through to a cozy sitting room. "I'm Gerard Brooks, by the way. Figure since I know your name, you ought to know mine. Have a seat. I'll get the papers."

The clock on the wall said it was after midnight. Not a polite time to be calling on people, but she knew she hadn't woken him—she hadn't been loud enough. He must have been awake already. Another person too unsettled to sleep. Too rattled by dreams, or things he'd actually seen.

The room spoke of wear and maintenance. Everything was neat and clean, but also patched and faded, as if it had been there since the house was built. Curtains covered the windows, but they were made of heavy burlap-like material—no frilly, or even colorful, window dressings. The carpet was worn almost bare in some spots, and the sofa where she sat felt like she was sitting directly on the springs. This landlord most likely wasn't renting out rooms to get rich. He was renting them out so he could survive. Or at least keep his home.

"Not sure what you're going to learn here," Death said. "It's not like she confided in him."

"How do you know?"

"I guess I don't *know*. I would just be surprised. If she wasn't telling Ricky things, and she was *sleeping* with him, I don't see why she would be telling her landlord."

"Father figure? The whole thing about it being easier talking to strangers?"

"You would know. But wasn't everybody here in town basically a stranger? She'd only been here a few months."

"Here you go." Brooks came back, reading glasses perched on his nose. Casey could see him better now they were inside and her eyes had adjusted. He looked like a typical middle-aged, white, American male. Balding, a little paunchy, but nice, too. Like Casey assumed her dad would look, had he lived to be that age. His clothes were in the same condition as the house—clean but worn. Dark blue sweats, a white, long-sleeved T-shirt, and leather moccasin slippers. Nothing new or fashionable. Just practical. And comfortable, as if he had been in bed when she'd arrived, even if he wasn't sleeping.

Brooks dropped the papers onto the sofa. "These are actually copies. The police took the originals. I'm not sure how they can help you, but if it helps Alicia, I'm happy to let you have a look."

It couldn't help Alicia anymore, but Casey didn't bother to say it. It could help Ricky, though, and if she needed to appeal to the landlord's sense of protectiveness—or was that guilt?— she'd do it.

The short stack of papers included copies of a completed rental agreement, a signed security deposit form, a receipt for the first payment—first and last month, plus the security deposit— and what should have been a copy of Alicia's first paycheck. Instead of a paycheck, there was a signed letter from Karl, the manager, saying Alicia had a job at The Slope. Casey figured that when you were paying someone under the table there wouldn't be as many official forms at hand.

The rental agreement had mostly the same information as her job application from The Slope, except this had the reference from Karl, as well as the phone number of the cell phone she'd been using, which was apparently a throw-away. The security agreement was basically just Alicia saying she promised not to trash the place, or she would give up her deposit. And the letter from Karl was on obviously mocked-up letterhead, and had a date from June.

"You took this at face value? From a place called The Slope?"

The landlord sighed. "I know the restaurant. It's a terrible place, and someone would only want to work there if she were desperate."

"So you like to rent out to desperate people?"

"It's not the smartest business model, I realize that. But she was…she reminded me of my daughter."

The daughter, Casey assumed, whom she saw highlighted in framed photos on the walls, along with scads of children. How she stayed looking so young was a mystery. Having just one baby had done a number on Casey—she couldn't imagine having five. But then, perhaps when they lived past the first six months it was different.

"How did Alicia find you?"

"Advertisement in the paper. Usually I go by word of mouth, but this time there were no takers. Kids want to live right at the base of the mountains, you see. They don't want to have to walk farther than down the block to hook up with their friends and go skiing or dancing. And that's where all the modern clubs and things are. That's where the young people want to be. So this time I had to resort to advertising."

"Why did your last tenant leave?"

"Who knows? None of my business. But I'm assuming he had a better offer elsewhere. I wasn't sorry to see him go. My daughter never did approve of him, either."

"Did he give you trouble?"

"Nothing criminal. At least I don't think so. Just lazy. The place was a mess when he left. Beer bottles, fast food trash, and the *dirt*. You'd think he worked in the mines. Plus he brought all kinds of women home at all times of night. I finally had to say something." He shrugged. "Could be part of the reason he left."

Death was busy photoshopping Alicia into Brooks' family photo on the iPad, but paused to say, "Think that's a connection?"

Casey couldn't imagine how, but asked Brooks what he thought.

"No. He was here and gone long before Alicia showed up. I never heard from or saw him again after he left. It's a good thing I got his last month's rent when he moved in. I never trusted his face."

"Hmm," Death said. "Can you trust a face? Do faces have independent thinking?"

Ignoring the comment, Casey said, "What about Alicia? She showed up with your advertisement and you just took her in?"

"She must have had a trustworthy face," Death said.

"She'd been staying at the youth hostel," Brooks said. "That one on the edge of town. Only she wasn't exactly a youth anymore, and I could see it had taken its toll on her. The kids who go there generally don't care about curfews or, well, sleep. And they definitely don't care about *others'* sleep. The supervision isn't very strict, so the place is basically a party house. Alicia had been there for over a week while she job hunted and began her days at the restaurant, so she was looking rather…exhausted."

"She had the money to pay you?"

He shifted in his seat. "Not all of it."

"Told you," Death said. "The face thing."

Casey looked at the papers again. Now that she was looking for it, she could see that the receipt for the first month's rent and the deposit was in June, but the last month's rent was dated the middle of August. "You gave her a free month?"

"No. Not that I wouldn't have considered it, but she insisted on paying it all. Said she didn't want to owe anyone. She had enough to pay first month and the deposit, but not the entire last month. She didn't look like much of a risk—" he flicked a glance at Casey, probably to see if she would judge him for his assessment "—so I put half the payment off until she had it all."

"Plus the months of August and September?"

"She paid for each month in addition to the last month requirement. Actually, she overpaid, because she didn't use all her time before…" He swallowed and looked down at his hand, clenched into a fist on the table.

"What will you do now? With the apartment, I mean?"

"I suppose I should rent it out. That's what my daughter would tell me. There's no point in having a space like that just sitting there. That's what she would say."

"She has a point."

"I know, but I hate going down there. And the thought of someone else moving in, and maybe something happening to them…"

"Would you be willing to let me have a look?"

"You want to rent it?"

"No, I have my own place. I just want to see where Alicia was living."

"All that's left is my furniture. She rented the place as it was. Didn't bring much of her own. Only what fit into her bag."

"Now who in the world would live like that?" Death said.

Casey stood. "Could I just take a quick look? A few minutes, and I'll be out of your hair."

"It's no bother," Brooks said. "Although I'll stay in the doorway, if you don't mind. Ever since that day I can't…"

"I understand."

Casey followed him back outside and around to the basement door. The air that came out was already stale, and Casey's nostrils twitched. She moved past Brooks and into the apartment. There was a light switch on the wall, and she flipped it on, revealing the foyer. It looked like Ricky's place, with the black fingerprint dust. There weren't personal items strewn around, however. Apparently because the girl hadn't had any.

There was a little table and a rug in the hall, but nothing else, other than the dust. She walked to the first doorway, which led to the kitchen. No one there, of course. The counters were covered with black, and most of the cupboard doors hung open, revealing the meager kitchenware. A few plates, two glasses, a bowl.

The next doorway was for a little bathroom. Casey turned on the light to reveal a freestanding shower stall, a small sink, and the toilet. Not much room for moving around, but then, a bathroom wasn't usually a big social area. Again, black dust covered most surfaces, including the counter, the edge of the mirror on the medicine cabinet, and the toilet seat.

Finally, Casey came to the living area. It looked like any furnished apartment, except for the blood stains on the floor. Casey should know. Spindly desk, a woven rag rug, generic prints on the walls alongside empty shelves, a couch that had seen better days, and a small table with two wooden chairs, the only place to eat, since the kitchen was so small. The double bed had been stripped, just like Ricky's, and two flat pillows lay without cases, one on the mattress, one on the floor. The door to a tiny closet stood open, revealing a thin jacket and a clean, pressed uniform shirt for The Slope, each on a wire hanger, and a pair of sneakers sat neatly on the floor. A dresser had been wedged into the corner of the room, its drawers hanging open. Casey stepped around the dark stains and poked through the meager collection of underwear, socks, and bras before moving down one drawer to two neatly folded T-shirts and a pair of faded jeans.

The only thing on top of the dresser was a pair of earrings in a box. Turquoise tear drops on silver posts. The box bore the name of a local store. Ricky had probably given her those.

Casey heard a footfall and turned to see Brooks standing in the entrance to the room. He'd overcome his queasiness, apparently.

"She kept the place perfect." His jaw clenched. "The only mess she ever made was when she…when she died, and I can hardly blame her for that." He kept his gaze averted from the spot Alicia had lain.

Casey made a small circuit of the room, inspecting the walls, checking under the opposite half of the rug, opening the empty desk drawer. "Where are the rest of her things?"

"Cops took them, I guess."

"Everything?"

He looked around. "Like I said, there wasn't much. I came down to fix a light once, and her shower, and it didn't look any different then. Her purse was there on the table, I think. But she hadn't brought boxes or anything. She showed up for our rent interview with one bag, and she moved in immediately. I never saw her bring anything else. No furniture, no other luggage…"

"Didn't that make you suspicious?"

"No. Curious, maybe, but it was really none of my business. She seemed like a nice girl, and someone who needed a place. I was glad to give it to her. She never caused any…any trouble."

Casey gave him a moment to collect himself by going into the kitchen. The only things in the fridge were a carton of old milk, some yogurt, and a half-empty egg carton. In the cupboard beside it, the only one that was still closed, sat a box of cereal and a partial loaf of bread. Nothing in the freezer. No canned goods. The sink was empty, and there were no dirty cups.

"She must have been so lonely," Casey said.

"Kind of makes you glad you have me to keep you company, doesn't it?" Death leaned against the counter, holding a digital meat thermometer. "Amazing what they've come up with. This can read a roasted turkey's temperature in *seconds*. No more waiting for that silly button to pop out, or for the old kind of thermometer to drag itself up to one-eighty."

Casey shivered at the sudden chill in the room and hugged herself as she went back to the bathroom. There had to be *something* to help her get to know Ricky's girlfriend. But the bathroom was just as bare as the living room. The shampoo was the cheapest kind, and the bath soap was a freebie from some hotel. One well-worn towel hung on the drying bar, along with a mismatched washcloth. Nothing but another bar of freebie soap sat on the sink counter. Casey opened the medicine cabinet. Alicia's toothbrush was gone, but a well-squeezed tube of toothpaste lay on the bottom shelf beside a small bottle of Advil and a tube of mascara. Her hairbrush was probably in her purse, along with any other make-up.

What a life. What a solitary, lonely, very single life.

Casey shut the cabinet, pushing on it to snap it closed. She looked at herself in the mirror. And then she looked at the mirrored surface itself. The cops had only dusted the edges, where someone might touch when they opened or shut the door, so the center of the mirror was free of dust. But it wasn't free of smudges. Smudges that looked like they were in a pattern.

Casey leaned forward and breathed on the mirror.

Death sat on the toilet tank, legs crossed. "What are you *doing*?"

Casey kept breathing until the mirror was fogged up and she could see what the smears turned out to be. Tears stung her eyes, and she pressed her fingers against her mouth.

"Oh," Death said.

They stood together silently, staring at Alicia's last words, already fading in the fluorescent light.

I was here.

Chapter Sixteen

"You're awfully quiet." Death was back on the Segway, keeping up with Casey as she jogged toward her house.

"Hard to run and talk at the same time."

"Plus you're quiet when you're upset."

"I'm not upset."

The night had gotten cooler while Casey was in Alicia's apartment, which made Casey shiver even as she ran. She sped up, hoping to raise her body temperature and erase the jitters.

Death matched her speed. "Do you buy it that Brooks wanted to help out a desperate young woman? That there was no other agenda?"

"Yes."

"Really? Was it his *face*?"

Casey didn't bother replying. She continued pounding down the street. The lights for the convenience store—her original destination that night—came into view in the distance. But something made the hairs on the back of her neck rise.

"Uh-oh," Death said.

A man stepped out of the shadows about ten yards in front of her, from between two cars parked along the road. Casey slowed. He stood in the middle of the street, waiting for her. As she got closer, his eyes flicked to something behind her.

"Another one," Death said.

She glanced back to see the one behind her angling to her right. A third man appeared on her left.

"I'm not liking this," Death said.

Casey wasn't, either. It was too much like that other time, in Clymer. The dark of night, on a deserted street. Only that time she was faced with one attacker, not three. Three. These weren't *the* three, were they? The ones who had left Alicia broken and dead? Casey remained where she was under the glow of a streetlight and judged the distance between the men. No angle for running, not with the cars and the men in a triangle. She could scream, but as soon as she did the men would be upon her.

She couldn't see much detail about any of them. They all hovered at the edge of the light, wearing loose clothes that hid their builds, and hats which turned their faces into angles and plains. They moved loosely, unafraid. The light glinted off the teeth of the man in front of her. He was smiling.

The guy on her left stumbled and bumped into a car. He weaved away from it, giggling, waving his hands at the others. "I'm okay!" More giggling.

"Oh," Death said. "Maybe I'm liking this a little better."

So the one guy, at least, was drunk. Still no clear shot away, even past him, not with the cars lining the street. But if *he* was drunk…She took another look at the guy's partners. Their loose movements spoke more now of alcohol than of competence.

Death swooped away and was back in seconds. "Yup, all three. Drunk as skunks. Although that saying never made much sense to me. Are skunks notorious drinkers in the animal kingdom? They've always seemed so antisocial to me. But then, maybe they're solitary drunks, which of course makes them more dangerous."

"Shut up," Casey said.

"What did you say, darlin'?" It was the guy in front of her. He was closer now, and she could see more than shining teeth. He was young. Probably twenty. Not as drunk as his buddy on her left, but enough to make his posture loose-limbed. He wore a University of Colorado hoodie, which reminded her of Ricky's T-shirt. The one with the blood spatters on it.

The guy behind her, to her right, had stopped, and swayed on his feet.

"Not even a challenge," Death said. "I think I'll sit this one out."

"What do you want?" Casey said in a firm voice.

The guy on her left giggled again, and staggered back to rest against the hood of the car.

The hoodie guy stopped his forward movement but kept smiling. "Just looking for a little fun, baby, that's all."

"Too bad I can't warn them," Death said from a seat on the roof of a Jeep, where he was filming everything with a palm-sized digital recorder. "You're not a fun-seeker."

Casey sighed. She didn't want to fight these guys. "I wouldn't be any fun, guys. Honestly."

"Aw, I don't believe that." Hoodie guy took another step forward. "You look like fun to me. Out in the middle of the night. You must be looking for some action."

"Were you looking for action a week ago?"

"We're always looking for action, baby."

"With a woman who looked like this?" Casey pulled the photo of Ricky and Alicia from her pocket and held it up.

Hoodie guy squinted, most likely trying to focus. "Hey, she's hot. But no. No, I'd remember. And she's a little old."

Death laughed. "Talk about beer goggles. What does he think you are? A high school student?"

"So you don't know her? And you never did anything with her?"

"Never."

"What about your friends?"

"If I didn't have her, my friends didn't have her. I'd know. We share everything."

Lovely.

The guy behind Casey stopped swaying and began moving forward. Casey put the photo back in her pocket and stepped away, but that only took her closer to the guy on the car.

"Might as well accept it," Death said. "You're going to have to deal with this."

She feinted left, on an angle that would have been between Car guy and Hoodie. Hoodie swung that way, and she moved right. The guy from behind staggered forward to cut off that direction, so all that was left was backward. She turned to go back the way she came.

Hoodie guy lunged forward and grabbed her wrist. She held her breath and counted to three so she wouldn't break his arm.

"Seriously, guys, come on, you don't want to mess with me."

Hoodie laughed. "But we do, hottie. We *do*." He pulled her closer.

Casey yanked him forward, sticking out her foot and sliding her arm from his grasp as he tripped and fell onto his knees.

"Owww!" He pouted, then lurched upright. "Why did you *doooo* that?"

Death *tsked*. "Didn't his mother teach him not to whine?"

"I'm not interested," Casey said to the kid. "Not in having fun or beating you up. Can we just call it a night?"

"Not after *that*. That wasn't very nice."

"Assaulting women who are walking alone—"

"Gee, thanks," Death said.

"—isn't nice, either."

"We weren't assaulting. We were…flirting."

"Is that what you call it? I'm going home now. You guys should do that, too, before something bad happens."

Hoodie guy's eyes flicked over her shoulder, and Casey could hear the third one coming. She balanced herself on her left foot and kicked back with her right heel, connecting almost waist high with a sensitive part of the guy's anatomy. He grunted, then sank slowly to the ground.

Hoodie guy watched with his mouth open, then frowned heavily, like a kindergartner showing his disapproval. Casey saw in his eyes what was going to happen. She stepped to the left just as he grabbed for her, and he stumbled forward, catching his foot on his fallen friend and dropping face first onto the road. He stayed there, apparently unable—or perhaps just unwilling—to move.

Casey looked over toward the car guy. He was gone.

"That way," Death said, pointing without looking.

Car guy was hustling down the sidewalk, dimming as he left the circle of light from one street lamp, then brightening as he reached the next. Casey watched until he reached the next intersection. He stopped there and looked back. Casey waved. He jerked a wave of his own, then realized what he was doing and speedwalked around the corner and out of sight.

"Now what?" Death hovered over the unconscious boys.

"Is there a rule about what you do with idiots?"

"None that would be acceptable to you, I don't think."

A light on a house across the street turned on, and a face appeared in a front window.

"Great," Casey said. "A nosy neighbor. That's all we need. Wouldn't the cops love hearing how I beat up two guys the same day they dropped the murder charges? You know whoever's looking out the window has his finger on the 911 button."

"Most women would be glad if a neighbor took interest while they were being attacked. In fact, one might say something to the paper, like, 'If it hadn't been for Mr. Billingsly I wouldn't be here right now.' And she'd be all weepy, and fragile, and everybody would feel sorry for her, and she and the neighbor would bond, you know, at least for a month until they realized they have nothing in common, and they would get back to their regular lives. You know the cycle. That whole 'Save someone's life, be responsible forever' stuff is really just crap."

"You should know by now I'm not 'most women.' And that whole cycle sounds exhausting."

"Oh, it is. But it serves a purpose, not the least of which is saving the woman from a worse fate on the night in question. It's your own fault you don't need saving. At least not from these guys."

Casey took a few steps away from the house, where the light still shone, then stopped and looked back at the heap in the middle of the road. "Stupid kids. They're going to get run over."

"Serve them right."

"How 'bout I leave them over on the sidewalk and you call the cops?"

"Can I do that?"

"I don't know. You've got enough phones."

"Here." Death held out a Droid. "Say something."

"What?"

"About these two. To tell the police. I doubt they'd be able to hear my voice, even if I could get through."

"Maybe I can just call from the nosy neighbor's house. Unless he's already called."

"Come on, at least let me try."

"Fine." She gestured for Death to start recording. "Some drunk guys assaulted a woman on…"

"Pine," Death said.

"…on Pine. Between…"

"Third and Fourth."

She repeated the streets. "Two of the men are waiting on the sidewalk for you. You might want to bring a breathalizer. The third one got away. There, will that do?"

Death giggled. "We'll see!"

Casey dragged Hoodie and his friend to the sidewalk on the opposite side of the street from the neighbor, and jogged away, leaving the drunk guys and Death behind. It would be interesting to see if the cops could make any sense of the recorded message. She was sure Death would regale her with every detail as soon as it was all over.

The lights of the all-night convenience store reminded Casey why she'd come out in the middle of the night in the first place. She'd been hungry then. Now she was famished. Nothing like examining a murder scene and dealing with three frat boys to work up an appetite.

The convenience store was empty of people except for the clerk, who was sitting behind the counter on a high stool reading a romance novel. She looked up when the bell on the door jingled, and pushed a strand of limp blonde hair behind her ear. "Help you?"

Casey studied the food under the glass-fronted counter. "Any chicken?"

"Just fried drumsticks. They're dry as bones. Even ketchup doesn't help."

"What's that?" Casey pointed at something sitting in sauce.

"Supposed to be barbecued pork. I'd avoid it if I were you. It's been sitting there forever."

"Tater Tots?"

"Ick."

"Potato salad?"

"Disgusting."

"So what would you suggest?"

"Something from the freezer section. That is, if you want to avoid a painful and messy death."

Now there was a saleswoman for you.

Casey settled for a burrito and a bottle of Lifewater. She took both back to the house, ate them while sitting at the bare kitchen table, and lay down on the couch, pulling her dad's afghan over her legs for another try at sleeping.

It still didn't work.

"You know where you need to be." It was Death's voice, but Casey was still alone.

"I can't," she said out loud to the empty house.

But Death's response was as clear as if it had been spoken. She would never sleep if she didn't do what needed doing. Maybe she should call Eric. Nah. She didn't want to wake him up.

"You think he's *sleeping*?" Death's voice dripped with incredulity. "With you three blocks away?"

Even more reason not to call him.

The clock on the wall ticked. The heater kicked on. The wind made the drying leaves on the trees rustle. Something skittered across the roof. Or in the ceiling.

"Okay. *Okay*. I'll go."

Casey flung off the afghan and got up, before she could change her mind. She hesitated only briefly before heading up the stairs, and went directly to Omar's door. She stood there, listening, as she used to when she would check on him before going to bed. Of course there was no sound now. Nothing but the heater and the wind and her rodent visitor. She opened the door.

Omar's crib still sat against the wall, under the mobile. Ricky must have thought it would sell the house better that way, with the Noah's Ark wallpaper and the blonde wood changing table. Omar's dresser, drawers empty, sat beside it, a collection of Webkinz on the top, complementing the decorative border. Casey ran her hands along the top of the crib, and used a finger to start the mobile turning. The rocking chair sat in the corner along with memories of late nights, and Casey decided she'd had enough.

She shut the door behind her, her heart in her throat, wondering if she should just cut her losses and spend the night on the street.

Her feet propelled her across the landing until she stood outside her own bedroom door. Hers and Reuben's. She was tempted to listen there, as she had at Omar's, but the sounds she might hear from behind that door were too painful to contemplate. She turned the doorknob and flung the door open.

Her breath left her in a wild rush, and she grabbed at the doorjamb, her head spinning. How could the room still smell like him after all this time? That mixture of Reuben's natural musk and Sybaris, his Mexican cologne. He'd been gone *two years*. The house had seen many cleanings and walk-throughs and days. How was it possible? How could it still hurt that much?

"Go on then, sweetheart." Death stood beside her, for once empty-handed, so close she could feel the chill. "The first step is the hardest. I promise."

"Like you would know."

Death looked at her with such kindness she thought her heart would break.

"You think I don't know pain?" Death said. "Or sorrow? My dear, they're part of what I do. Part of who I am. Not a day goes by I don't feel it a hundred and fifty thousand times. So I do know, my love."

"You took him."

Death sighed the sigh of many losses. "It wasn't my decision. You know that. It's never my decision. I just follow the rules."

"The *rules*."

"They're what make the world go 'round. And no matter how creative we try to be, we can't break them. Your voice on my phone? Didn't work a bit. Good thing the nosy neighbor had a phone handy, because apparently you have to use human devices, since you're a human. And I have to do what I do. Because no matter how we feel about them, no matter how bent and crooked we think they are, we have to follow the rules."

Casey took a deep breath through her nose and let it out her mouth, centering herself. "The first step is really the hardest?"

"I promise."

So Casey let go of the doorjamb, clenched her jaw, and took that first step.

She didn't collapse.

She didn't break down into a sobbing mass.

She didn't pass out.

"He's not here," she said.

Death smiled sadly. "Of course he isn't."

Casey turned on the light and spun in a slow circle, taking in the details of the room. Most of the personal effects were gone. No *dobaks* were draped over the footboard. No dress shoes sat in a perfect line under Reuben's side of the bed. No messy pile of books and magazines lay on the nightstands next to the matching lamps. But the quilt was still the same, since it went with the walls and the curtains. The blown-up photo from their trip to the Grand Canyon still hung over the headboard. And the antique toy ferris wheel, the one that had belonged to Casey's grandmother, sat on top of the dresser, the clown on the axle smiling insanely.

Casey ran her hand over the bed, feeling the handmade stitches, so lovingly sewn there by her mother, before...well, before everything.

"Go on," Death said. "You're exhausted."

"But—"

"Sleep, child."

Casey pulled down the corner of the quilt on her side of the bed. And she crawled in. And she went to sleep.

Chapter Seventeen

Someone was pounding on the front door. Casey dragged herself from sleep and looked at the clock. Eight o'clock. Crap. Again, where was Death when she could actually use some help?

She stumbled down the stairs and flung open the door. Eric stared at her, apparently not sure whether to smile or run screaming.

Casey looked at him for several seconds before backing up and gesturing for him to come in. "Weren't you supposed to come later?"

"Couldn't sleep. Thought maybe you couldn't, either."

Should she tell him just how little sleep she'd gotten? No. "Fine," she said instead. "Give me a minute. Or ten."

He held up a bag and some coffee from one of the local coffee shops. "Got breakfast."

"Awesome. Make yourself at home in the kitchen. Not that there's much there."

She left him standing in the foyer and went upstairs to take a shower. Fifteen minutes later she was back down, unfortunately still wearing the same clothes as the day before. She threw the rest of her clothes in the washer and joined Eric in the kitchen.

He set some coffee in front of her, along with creamer and sugar packs. "So you got some sleep, then?"

"I guess. Some. You?"

"Few hours. Your brother's place is nice. I used the guest room. Found some sheets in one of the closets."

She sipped the coffee black and pointed at the bag. "What's in there?"

He pulled out a couple of scones, two hot egg and sausage biscuits, and some cherry Danishes. "Take your pick."

Casey picked one of each and ate them all. The burrito hadn't exactly been satisfying the night before.

"So tell me where we're going," Eric said.

"A crappy restaurant, where Alicia worked."

"She's the woman who was murdered?"

"Raped, tortured, and murdered. Yes. And she was my brother's girlfriend."

Eric had paled at her description, but asked, "What do we know so far?"

"That my brother didn't do it."

"Assume I'm not an idiot, okay?"

"Sorry. We don't know a lot. Alicia McManus wasn't her real name, and we don't know where she came from when she showed up this summer."

"How do we know about the name?"

Whoops. Back-pedaling time. "Law enforcement can't find her anywhere in the system, so it makes sense that she didn't exist under it." Not a lie. Just not the whole truth.

"Any ideas on that?"

"They're looking into it. Trying some new combinations."

He looked at her over his Danish. "There's something you're not telling me."

"There's a lot I'm not telling you. I haven't had time."

"Fair enough. So keep going."

She took him through the basics—that Alicia was running from a dangerous past, she carried almost nothing with her as she ran, and she supposedly loved Ricky. She told him about Ricky's neighbor Geraldine and what she'd seen, and about the stash of sayings, candy, and books that Ricky had hidden away.

"Carol Burnett?" Eric said. "Is he a fan?"

"Not that I ever knew of. Maybe Alicia was."

"Weird."

"Tell me about it. And other than those bizarre offerings, we've got nothing."

"What about this restaurant? What are we looking for there?"

"I want to talk to the other employees, in case Alicia told them anything. I doubt she did, since she barely even talked to Ricky, but she might have let something slip. What?"

"People can find things out, even if you don't tell them."

"You mean like how you figured out who I was?"

He shrugged.

"But you had my ID. I'd left it in my bag. It's not like it was hard."

"I knew before that."

"I don't believe you. How?"

"Remember? I told you. Your first name. Some Internet searches."

"But we don't know her real fir—" But she did. In fact, she knew Alicia's entire name. She just hadn't considered a computer, which was dumb, seeing how Death had been parading around with every technology known to humankind. "You have something we can use to look online?"

"Sure. I have an iPad in the car. I'll get it."

Soon he was back, and Casey had a dilemma. How was she supposed to look this up with Eric watching? She couldn't possibly explain to him how she knew Alicia's real name.

"So I think we've gotten to whatever it is you're not telling me." Eric's mouth twitched into a smile.

"I don't know *how* to tell you." Again, Death was nowhere to be found when she needed advice. Not that she ever really wanted the advice Death had to offer.

Eric sat quietly and waited.

"I know her real name."

"And you haven't told law enforcement because…"

"They would lock me up."

"What did you do to get it?"

"It's not what I've done. It's how I know. And they wouldn't lock me up for being a criminal. It would be because they'd think I'm nuts."

"Whereas you're telling me because I already know you are?"

"You have to wonder, don't you?"

"I've seen nuttier." A shadow crossed his face, and Casey knew he was thinking of three weeks earlier, when a woman crazy with greed and a man with grief ended up a bloody mess. He shook himself, and the shadow left his face. "So what's her name?"

"That's what you want to know? Not how I found out?"

"For now. You'll tell me more when you want to."

She hesitated.

"Come on." He nudged her knee with his own. "What is it?"

"It's just, I don't think you'll believe me."

"No, I mean, what's her name?"

"Elizabeth Mann. Two 'n's."

He typed the name into his iPad and seventeen thousand hits came up. The daughter of Thomas Mann, a research physicist, a holocaust survivor, a lawyer, and a flutist. Plus scores and scores of other people, none of them the late Alicia McManus. There were a few women who looked a little like her, but on close examination were far from the person they sought.

"Any other suggestions?" Eric said.

Casey leaned back in her chair and stretched out her feet, accidentally bumping Eric. She pulled away. "It's time to head to the restaurant. You up for driving?"

"Sure. You up for riding?" Three weeks ago Casey had been right on the edge about being in moving vehicles. She just hadn't done it much since the accident, preferring instead to walk or ride a bike, or even hop a train. But there came a time when there was nothing else to be done. Once over the first hurdle—kind of like that first step upstairs—she was able to ride in, and even drive, cars and trucks. She didn't love it, but she knew it was the way things had to be.

"I'll manage. Thanks for breakfast."

"You're welcome."

She looked across the table at his open, friendly, handsome face, and felt a sudden pang. What was she doing in her house—*Reuben's* house—alone with another man? She stood up, making the chair screech. "Let's go."

She followed Eric out to the car. Death leaned against the rear door, jabbing at something on a Kindle Fire. "Die, you stupid pig! *Die!*"

Casey peered at the screen, which was filled with colorful exploding birds and crashing wooden structures.

"Something wrong?" Eric asked.

"Nothing I can explain."

They drove to The Slope, Casey hyper-aware of Eric's hand on his knee. Really. What was wrong with her? She'd shared a passionate kiss with a different man in Florida only days before, simply because he reminded her of Reuben. Now, here she was, feeling all tingly over a guy who was nothing like him, who she happened to almost sleep with a few weeks earlier. She had to get her hormones under control.

Death groaned and threw the Kindle at the window, where it exploded in a cloud of mist before it could shatter the glass. "Those *pigs*. I *hate* them!"

They pulled into the parking lot of the restaurant and Eric wrinkled his nose. "Definitely glad we ate at your place."

They went in, Death following, still grumbling about the game. Casey caught Bailey's eye, where she was waiting on a table of two elderly couples. When she'd gotten the order she came over. "Well, who's this?" She eyed Eric up and down.

Casey stiffened. "A friend."

"Eric." He held out his hand.

Bailey took it, cocking her hips and shoving her chest a little more forward, as if that were possible. She leaned toward him, keeping a hold on his hand. "I'm Bailey. And I didn't know Casey had any friends. Especially ones I'd like."

Eric slid his hand from hers. "Nice to meet you."

Bailey giggled, and flung her hair over her shoulder, pulling her shirt collar farther open.

Death laughed. "Whew! She's something, isn't she?

"So, *Bailey*," Casey said, "can we talk to the guys?"

Bailey smirked, as if she knew exactly what she was doing to Casey *and* to Eric. "Let me make sure Karl's busy in his office. He'd say you couldn't be back there because of regulations. Yeah, I know. As if this place is big on that. Give me a minute. I'll be right back. *Eric*." She smiled and flung her hair again as she spun in a slow half-circle and meandered away, hips swinging.

"Well," Eric said when she was gone. "At least one woman around here likes me." He gave Casey a half-smile.

"That's your opening to say you like him, too," Death said.

"Well," Casey said, "I never would have expected Bailey to have good taste in men."

Eric's smile grew, but he ducked his head, like he was embarrassed.

Casey looked around at the tables in the dining room. Mostly they were empty, with dirty dishes and cups of melting ice, surrounded by greasy, ketchup-ridden plates. But there were still a few tables with customers—mostly older couples, not exactly the blue-collar crowd Alicia had avoided and Bailey depended on. Maybe they would be willing to talk about Alicia.

Casey stopped by the first table, but the couple there hadn't known any of the waitresses other than Bailey. The next group, the two couples Bailey had been serving when Casey and Eric had arrived, remembered Alicia, but didn't have anything to say other than that she was polite and efficient and always kept their coffee hot.

"Um, I think someone over there is trying to get your attention." Eric gestured to a group of five women, none under the age of eighty. They waved her over from across the room, eyes glistening, red lipstick smudged from breakfast.

"I don't know," Eric said. "It looks a bit dangerous."

"We're living on the edge."

They made their way to the women, who sat around three two-person tables that had been pushed together. Death had taken the sixth chair, and was trying to avoid the dirty plates and crumpled napkins piled in the empty spot.

"Honey." The woman in the nearest chair clutched Casey's wrist with a bony, bejeweled hand.

Casey's first instinct was to twist the woman's arm behind her back and shove her face onto the table, but she had enough control to realize that would have been over-reacting. And she probably would have snapped that frail old radius right in half. Instead, she swallowed her defensive response and forced a smile.

"What are you going around talking to everyone about?" Ring Lady said. "There's nothing boring old Pearl and Ethan over there know that we couldn't tell you ten times more about. It's a group effort here, you know, with centuries represented. Sort of like those groups of really smart people who all try to figure out how to make the world a better place, or stop it from ending, or whatever—what are they called?" She flapped her hand at the others.

"A brain trust!" one hollered.

"Mensa!"

"A consortium!"

A tiny woman with tortoise-shell glasses winked at Casey. "Librarians."

The first one let go and patted her arm. "So what was it you wanted to know about, sweetie-pie?"

Death poked a finger at some congealing eggs. "Other than why they're here eating in this dive when it's obvious they could afford higher class cuisine?"

"There was another waitress here before," Casey said. "Alicia McManus. Early thirties, brown hair, pretty."

Several tongues clicked, and there was general shuffling around the table.

"You mean that poor girl who got…killed?" Ring woman leaned in like it was a secret.

"Yes. Did you know her?"

"Of course we did, dear." This was a woman across the table. She wore a bright red hat, and the hair Casey could see was pure white. "She was our waitress whenever the other girl wasn't here, ever since early summer."

They looked at each other, their eyes shifting back and forth between their friends and the back counter.

"She was very different from the other girl, you know," Ring woman confided.

"Not so…how might I say it?" said Red Hat, tapping her mouth with her fingers. "*Forward*."

"Bailey is forward with you?"

The smallest, oldest woman cackled from her seat beside Death. "Hardly, honey. But with those working men…she doesn't leave much to the imagination, if you know what I mean. But then, she's got to use what she's got, doesn't she? I find her entertaining. I thought at first she was all hat and no cattle, but I was wrong. She's got *spunk*."

"I like this one," Death said with a hoot. "Bet she was just like Bailey in her day. I mean, *look* at that *hair*." The shellacked hairstyle was dyed black, as in midnight, darkest of dark. It made the woman's wrinkled face seem ghostly white—except for the red spots she'd rouged onto her cheeks—as white as the huge, pearl clip-ons hanging from her stretched out lobes.

Blackie wasn't finished. "I'm sure your young man here would agree. Bailey certainly has something that keeps the men interested."

They all swung to look at Eric, who went beet red.

"Well?" Blackie said.

He cleared his throat. "She's very…" He stopped and looked to Casey for help because he obviously didn't know what to say. He couldn't exactly say "busty" or "sex-riddled" to a group of female octogenarians.

"Anyway," Ring Woman said, saving him, "we liked Alicia. She was very sweet."

They chorused agreements, except for one woman who hadn't yet said anything. She huddled in the seat by the wall, her thin hair pulled back in a tight bun, causing her cheekbones to poke out in an almost skeletal manner. Despite the hair and skull-like appearance, she was probably the youngest of the clan, a mere eighty or so, and her teeth—or dentures—were bright white. Casey could see them, because the woman was wrinkling her nose so hard her upper lip left them exposed.

"Oh, don't mind her," the librarian said. "Eleanor never likes anyone. Even us."

Eleanor pinched her lips shut. "That is unfair, Rita. I have been a part of this group as long as the rest of you, haven't I? If I hated you all so much I certainly wouldn't have kept coming to breakfast."

Rita patted her hand. "Of course, dear."

Eleanor yanked her hand away. "Don't patronize me. We all know that woman was hiding something."

"You do?" Casey said.

"Well, of course. Why else would she change the subject every time we asked her a question other than the name of the daily special?"

"As if any of the food here could be special," Death muttered.

"Not like that Bailey girl," Eleanor continued. "I know more about her and her goings-on than I want to know about anybody. Why the rest of them encourage her, I'll never know."

There was collective eye-rolling around the table, but no one actually responded.

"So did you get any information from Alicia?" Casey asked. "Besides the food stuff?"

Ring woman sighed. "Not anything we could *use*."

"Use?"

"To make up our scenarios. Not with any detail, anyway."

Casey glanced at Eric, who shrugged.

"You see," Ring Woman continued, "we love to come up with stories. Like after you leave we'll talk all about you two and why it is you stand five feet away from each other, even though you're together, and why you, honey, are wearing clothes that obviously haven't been washed in some time, while he looks neat and clean. Even shaven. And you didn't eat breakfast here, which makes us think you probably ate it elsewhere, and probably together, but that doesn't add up with the awkward way you behave around each other. If you'd spent the night together, you would be much more comfortable."

Casey was feeling anything but comfortable under the scrutiny—and imagination—of such a crew. Eric had gone from his reddish blush to almost as white as Blackie.

"So what kind of scenario did you come up with for Alicia?" Casey asked, for multiple reasons.

Ring Woman shook her head. "She was like one of those formula romance novels. She came out of nowhere, no history, no friends, nothing she would share with us. She could have been an exiled Romanian princess, for all we knew."

"Except she had light hair," Red hat said. "Romanian princesses wouldn't have light hair."

"The only clue we ever got about her personal life," Ring woman continued, "was that sweet boy who apparently found out more than we ever did."

Ricky.

"And," Red Hat said, "*that* made for some good discussion because obviously the *other* girl—" she glanced toward the kitchen again "—felt like he should be with *her*. They certainly were opposites, the girls, I mean. Alicia the cold, silent type, and Bailey the…well, you know. *Warmer* type."

Casey sighed. "So you've got nothing for me. I guess Pearl and Ethan do know as much as you."

"Hold on now!" Ring Woman sat up, her expression almost panicked. "I'm sure we have something. Girls? Huddle."

They leaned in toward the center of the table and began talking all at once. It was hard to pick out anything specific—Casey could only hear snippets.

"What about that horrible haircut?"

"I still think those circles under her eyes meant something."

"Pinto beans and hot links, remember?"

"Working those double shifts for Bailey."

"Sweetest smile when she flashed it."

"Like a long-tailed cat in a room of rocking chairs."

"Hid those tips away like they were pure gold."

"What about that time she…?

They went silent, and Ring woman sat up, triumphant. "We know something."

"Will you share?"

She looked smugly over at Pearl and Ethan, who were tucking into their biscuits and gravy, seemingly oblivious to the battle that was being waged. Rings cleared her throat, but still the couple ignored her.

"Go ahead," the librarian said. "Tell her."

Rings leaned forward. "She called him *Wayne*."

"Who? Ricky?"

Rings blinked. "You know her young man's name?"

"Yes."

"Hmm. But anyway, it wasn't him. The one she called Wayne. That was the dishwasher." They all very obviously didn't look back toward the kitchen. Casey did, though, and she caught a glimpse of the kid through the window. He saw her, and went back to work, acting like he hadn't noticed her looking.

"That's not his name?"

"Hardly. This one's name is Samuel."

"Sammy," Red Hat corrected.

"He's worked here since he turned fourteen. He'll come bus our tables sometimes, when we want to stay for coffee and the girls are busy."

Blackie's eyes sparkled. "Alicia didn't even realize what she'd done until she asked why he was looking at her funny. He'd followed her out with a dish tub, you see."

"And what did she do when he told her?"

"Looked like she'd swallowed an orange. Went all white, and closed her eyes for a second. I thought she was going to faint."

"We all did." Rings was back in charge. "Samuel wasn't sure whether to put down the dish tub to catch her, or go running for someone bigger."

"He's kind of little," the librarian explained.

"Did Alicia tell you why she called him that?"

"Nope, although we did ask her."

Of course they did.

"So." Casey looked at Eric for affirmation. "I guess the name Wayne must have meant something to her."

He nodded. "Doesn't help us a whole lot, though, since we don't know his last name."

"Unless—"

"Nope," Rings said. "We have no idea. But it's a start, right? Better than Pearl and Ethan."

"A hundred percent." Since the old couple had given them nothing.

"Hey." Bailey was gesturing to them from the kitchen door. She glanced down the little hallway that led to the back and waved harder. "Karl's in the back. Come on, quick."

"Thanks a lot," Casey said to the ladies.

"Whoa, Nellie," Rings said, clutching Casey's wrist again. "You owe us."

Casey raised her eyebrows. "Excuse me?"

"We gave you information, now it's your turn."

"But I don't have anything."

"I think you do."

The other women were all nodding.

Eric nudged her and whispered, "Your relationship to Ricky."

"Oh." Casey pulled her wrist from Ring Woman's grip. "So you know how I knew the name of Alicia's boyfriend before you mentioned it?"

They nodded and leaned forward, as if one body. Eyes sparkling, mouths slightly open.

"I know his name because he's my brother, and he's been arrested for her murder. I'm going to prove he's innocent."

Ka-ching.

Her debt was paid.

Chapter Eighteen

Casey and Eric followed Bailey into a dark room with some hooks on the wall, and a few plastic bins. A tiny bathroom was tucked into the corner.

"This is where we change, if we need to." Bailey pointed at a small Rubbermaid tub. "We generally just hang stuff up, but I was looking for something in the pantry this morning and found this. It must have been Alicia's, because nobody else recognizes any of it. I guess I'm supposed to show it to the cops, but I thought you might want to see it first. Not that there's anything much in there."

Casey squatted beside the box and took off the lid. Bailey was right—there wasn't much. A brush, some tampons, a paperback novel…and a photo of a man. He was in his thirties or forties, probably, and was putting something into the back of an old station wagon. His face was turned toward the camera in a candid shot—like the picture was a surprise. His face was unshaven in a scraggly way, but his expression was pleasant, and he wore dirty work clothes, as if he'd just finished a day on the job, working construction or mowing the lawn.

"Anything?" Eric eased down beside her, not setting his knees on the dirty floor.

She showed him the photo, and said to Bailey, "Any idea who this is?"

"Nah. Never saw it before. Never saw him, either. Only guy Alicia was ever with was Ricky." She snapped her fingers. "Unless this was the dude she had a picture of in her purse. Guess it could be him."

"You have a copier?"

"In the office. I'll make a copy when you go. I can just tell Karl I want one before we give this stuff to the police. Now, let's get to the guys before Karl oozes out of his lair."

They followed her into the steamy kitchen. Casey tried not to gag at the mixing smells of bacon and burnt eggs, and purposely kept her eyes forward, not even glancing into the actual cooking area, where she could detect someone in her peripheral vision, moving around.

Death drifted in as the saloon-style door flapped shut, swishing through the cracks and materializing again in mid-air. "I am not touching anything in here. Who knows what I might contract? In fact…ugh. You have back-up. You two are on your own. But take notes—I want to hear every detail." And Death was gone, blowing through the doors, making them flap back and forth. Bailey jerked around, then put her hand on her chest when no one appeared. "I thought it was Karl. He'd have my head."

"You mean he'll fire you if he sees us?"

She gave one of those sarcastic head moves young women are so good at. "Hardly. You think he's going to leave himself with no waitresses? He can't find one to replace the one he already lost. So nah, he'd just make my life hell for a few days. As if working here could be any worse. Now, come on."

The dishwasher—Sammy or Samuel, depending on which of the old ladies you wanted to listen to—was along the far wall, spraying off a rack of plates to put through an industrial-sized, stainless steel machine. Water misted everywhere, making the floor a slippery, dangerous mess, despite the rubber mats. Sammy was small, as the group of women had implied, but he wasn't puny. Just…short. He was probably eighteen or nineteen, and very obviously still living through those days of acne and sparse facial hair. Casey supposed it hardly seemed worth the effort to shave when all you had were scraggly little patches at random spots. He wore a rubber apron, elbow-length yellow rubber gloves, and a burnt-orange bandanna over his hair. He looked like a human-sized rubber duckie.

"Sammy." He didn't hear Bailey calling him, so she spoke again, raising her voice over the sound of the sprayer. He jerked his head around, and she motioned for him to come over.

He shoved the rack into the washer, locked the sliding steel door, and squelched over in his soggy tennis shoes, the one part of him that wasn't encased in waterproof gear. "What?"

Bailey hooked a thumb toward Casey and Eric. "These folks want to know about Alicia."

His expression remained impassive. "What about her?"

"Anything you could tell us." Casey tried to ignore the steamy, smelly atmosphere and look pleasant. She doubted she was succeeding. "I'm Casey. This is Eric."

Eric and Sammy gave each other one of those nods that seem to come naturally to guys. Sammy gave Casey only a cursory glance, which wasn't surprising. Casey knew she wasn't the most charismatic person in the world, plus teenage boys generally didn't know how to talk to women and look at them at the same time.

"Casey is Ricky's sister," Alicia said. "You know, the guy who was Alicia's boyfriend."

"Sure, I remember him," the kid said. "Sounds like he wasn't such a good choice, after all."

Casey bristled. "He didn't do it."

"Whatever."

"Are you saying she had other choices? You? Are you even out of high school?"

He looked at the ground and poked his toe at something that wasn't there, making Casey think of a puppy who'd just been told he wouldn't be getting any more treats. She should have felt bad, she supposed, for embarrassing him, but if he was going to talk that way about Ricky, her heart wouldn't be bleeding for him. She waited for him to stop sulking.

"*Anyway*," Bailey said, "Casey wants to know if Alicia ever told you anything…personal."

"Personal?" Sammy looked up. "Like what? About...*him*?"

Casey refrained from kicking him in the knee. "I know about *him*. Did she tell you anything about *herself*? Where she was before she came here, why she showed up here in the first place, who might have wanted her dead?"

He shrugged that way teenagers do when they think adults are asking stupid questions. "Why should I tell you?"

"Look, kid—"

Eric swiveled so he stood in front of Casey, hiding the dishwasher from her view and looking down into her face.

She made a move to get around him, but he held up his hands. "Casey, you've got to cool it."

She gave a little laugh. "Excuse me?"

"Casey..." His earnest expression and kind eyes were enough to make her pause, and she allowed him to lead her back almost to the dining room door, where he spoke quietly just for her ears. "Look, I know you want answers, but this isn't the way to go about it. You've got the kid half scared and half pissed off. Not the way to encourage confidences."

She took a deep breath and looked straight ahead at his throat, where his Adam's Apple bobbed up and down once as he waited. The tendons stood out, like he was clenching his jaw, and there was a tiny patch of stubble he'd missed that morning when he'd shaved. She wondered if it would feel scratchy if she kissed it.

"Okay," she said. "You do it."

"I didn't mean you couldn't—"

"Please, Eric."

He swallowed again, and the tendons relaxed. "Okay." He stood there for a moment more before making his way back across the room. He crossed his arms and leaned against the counter. "So, Sam...may I call you Sam? We understand this must be hard for you, especially if Alicia was your friend. I know it's hard for Bailey, here—"

Casey must have made a sound, because Eric paused, and he and the other two looked at her. Casey cleared her throat. "Sorry. Must have been a frog."

Eric frowned, then turned back to Sam. "Sam, we all want to know who did this to Alicia. What happened to her was terrible, and devastating to everyone who knew her. Including Ricky. Casey doesn't believe her brother would have done such awful things, and Bailey agrees. Do you really think Ricky seems like the type to hurt her?"

Sam shifted on his feet, not looking Eric in the eye.

Bailey stomped her foot. "Sammy, come on—"

Eric shook his head at her, and she clamped her mouth into a thin line.

Sam mumbled something.

"Sorry?" Eric said.

"I guess he's not. I just…why would he even like her? I mean, she was kinda cool, sure. Not friendly or anything, just pretty, I guess, for her age, I mean, she was kind of old, and she seemed smart. But she worked *here*. How did he even meet her? She never went out in the evenings, and he worked for some fancy place."

Really? Casey was surprised at that. She'd never considered Ricky's catering job fancy, but then, she supposed it was when compared to The Slope.

"How do you know she didn't go out?" Eric asked. "Did she talk about what she did on her off hours?"

Sam went pink. "Well, I asked her if she wanted to catch a movie one time—this was before I knew about *him*—and she said she just wanted to go back to her place. By herself. Not with me. I mean, it wasn't an invitation. She wasn't like that. Not even with the customers. Not like some people." He glanced at Bailey, who didn't seem to catch what he was implying.

Eric nodded. "So she kept to herself. Did she ever say anything that seemed strange or out of character? Or anything that could have meant she was scared?"

"She never seemed scared. She always walked home by herself, even when it was dark out. I offered her rides different times, but she always said she was fine on her own. I wish…" He shook his head and looked at something above Eric's head. Maybe one of the cobwebs in the corner.

"And you don't know where Alicia was before she moved here?"

"Nah. She never talked about it. I never asked." He went to shove his hands in his pockets, remembered he was wearing big rubber gloves, and stuck his hands under his arms instead. "Have you asked Karl? He's the one who would know."

"The manager," Bailey said, in case Casey and Eric had already forgotten.

"We'll ask him next." Eric pushed himself off the counter. "Thanks a lot, man. Appreciate it."

Sam shrugged. "Whatever. I hope you find whoever did it." He gave Casey one last glance and trudged back to his soggy corner.

Eric indicated the cook, who was busy scraping something around on the grill. "Think we can talk to him now?"

Bailey rolled her eyes. "You can try, but he is in a mood this morning."

"You can tell by the burned eggs," Casey said.

Bailey laughed. "Like that's any different from usual."

A man's voice came from outside the door, and Bailey jumped. "Okay, you guys go talk to Doofus over there. I'll try to keep Karl out." She swung through the doors, and was gone.

"After you." Eric swept his hand toward the kitchen.

Casey wrinkled her nose, but stepped forward, her shoe making a terrible ripping sound as she pulled it off the sticky floor.

Doofus—or whatever his real name was—had moved away from the grill and was slapping butter on some toast. He glanced up as they approached, but didn't speak.

"Spare a minute?" Casey said.

He threw the toast on a plate with a glob of egg and slid it onto the warming shelf beside a bowl of what looked like it might be oatmeal. "Order up!" he yelled.

Bailey's face appeared in the opening as she grabbed the plates. "New order." She shoved a slip through the slot, then disappeared.

The cook grabbed the paper, glared at it, then stalked back to the double-doored refrigerator. He pulled it open, yanked out some more eggs and a carton of milk, and slammed the door. "Don't know nothing 'bout Alicia."

"What's your name?"

"What's yours?" He cracked two eggs into an already eggy bowl, dumped some milk on them, and went at them with a fork. Once he'd poured them onto the grill, he took the milk back to the fridge and shoved two pieces of white bread into the banged-up toaster.

Bailey was right. He *was* in a mood. "I'm Casey. That's Eric."

No manly nods this time. Just a scowl to prove he *didn't want to talk*. He flipped the eggs, transferring some of the blackened eggs from earlier onto the fresh yellow ones, and grabbed a handful of shredded cheese from a bowl beside the grill. He tossed it on top of the disgusting mess and set a saucepan lid over it all.

Casey glanced at Eric. He was obviously trying not to laugh. Casey was trying not to whack the guy over the head with his own spatula. "And you are?"

He lifted up the lid and flipped the eggs again, this time transferring cheese to the burned patches on the grill. "Why do you care?"

"Oh, for heaven's sake, just tell us your name."

He waited several seconds, then grunted, "Pasha."

"Okay. Pasha. What can you tell us about Alicia?"

"I already said. Nothing. We weren't exactly friends."

"You didn't like her?"

"Didn't feel any way about her. She worked. I worked. This ain't exactly a social club."

The toaster popped, but Pasha ignored it, instead dividing the egg pile into two revolting mounds, scraping them up, and slopping them onto plates. He yanked the bread from the toaster, buttered it, and threw it beside the eggs.

"Order up!" he yelled, and slid them into the opening.

Bailey appeared and lifted a piece of the toast. "Toast is supposed to be unbuttered. And whole wheat."

"Oh, for—Do we even have whole wheat?" He grabbed the plates, threw the toast into the trash, and rummaged through the bags of bread on the counter. He found two pieces that looked like they might be wheat, and pushed them into the toaster. He looked up at Casey like he'd forgotten she was there. "I didn't know her except to give her plates of food, okay? We never talked. She was all thinking she was better than me, so I didn't give her no time."

"Did you know Ricky?"

"Who's that?"

"Her boyfriend."

"Saw him a few times. Hear he's the one who done her." He shrugged. "Don't make no difference to me if it was him or that other guy."

Casey went still. "What other guy?"

"The one who was here the same week she got killed."

"Who was he?"

The toaster popped and Pasha snatched the bread out and threw it on the plates. He grabbed a knife, stuck it in the butter tub, and pulled out a glob of butter. He stopped suddenly, knife in the air, then shoved the knife and the butter back in the tub. "Order!" he yelled, and Bailey came back just long enough to take the plates.

"*Who was he?*" Casey said again.

"Don't know. He came up the alley out back when I was out for a smoke. Said he was looking for Alicia, and showed me a picture, but it didn't hardly look like her, like it was from a long time ago. I told him she wasn't here. I asked him should I give her a message, but he said no, he'd find her himself." Regret filled his eyes for a moment. "Maybe he did."

"Did you tell her about him?"

"Soon as he left I forgot he'd even been here."

"Remember now. What did he look like?"

"I don't know. Older guy."

"Fifty? Sixty?"

"How should I know? It's not like I asked how old he was."

"Gray hair? Wrinkles? Glasses? Nice clothes? Nasty clothes?"

He held up his hands. "Lady, I don't know. I didn't notice. I told you he was old, that's everything I remember."

"Everything?"

"I guess his hair was gray, okay? And when he left he said, 'Ya'll have a nice day,' or something lame like that. Happy?"

Happy? Hardly.

But suddenly Casey saw a speck of light at the end of what she'd thought was a very, *very* long tunnel.

Chapter Nineteen

"Hey, you two." Karl followed them out to the parking lot, and they stopped by their car. He poked a finger at them, his entire body stiff with anger. "What's your business here? Why do you keep coming back?"

"Alicia."

His eyes narrowed. "What about her? She was a legitimate employee of this restaurant."

And suddenly Casey got it. "Look, Karl, we're not here to bust you for hiring her with fake information."

"Who said it was fake?"

"Seriously. It doesn't matter. We don't care. All we want is to find out who killed her."

"Well, it wasn't me. And it wasn't anybody here."

"Never said it was."

He glared at her for a few more moments, then relaxed his stance enough he didn't look like he was going to explode. "You find out anything?"

"Nothing for sure. But maybe something. If it pans out, you'll be one of the first to know."

Sorrow shone in his eyes. "I did like her, you know."

"Seems like most people did."

He took a deep breath and let it out. "So are you done here?"

"I think so."

"Give a call if you need anything else."

"Will do. Thanks."

He nodded shortly and headed back toward the front door.

"Hey, Karl," Casey called.

He looked back.

"You might want to think about hiring a different cook."

He shook his head. "You think I don't know that?" And he disappeared behind the front door.

"Come on," Casey said, jumping in the car. "We need to do some research."

"On what?"

"The South. That's where our killer was from. Maybe. If we're lucky. And if the cook wasn't making up that entire conversation."

"The *south*?"

"Of course, the south. Who else says, 'ya'll?'"

"Isn't that kind of stupid, though? I mean, to say something like that, if he's a killer and he's trying to keep a low profile. Somebody not from the South would remember that. Even somebody like Pasha."

They were driving back to Ricky's place.

"But the South is a big region," he said. "Knowing he's from 'the South' doesn't exactly help us."

"Just wait."

"What? You know something else?"

"Not yet."

She was out of the car almost before it was parked, and jogged into the house. Eric followed, catching up to her in the kitchen. She whipped open the pantry door and dug Ricky's secret stash out of the cleaning supplies. "This is the candy he was hiding. And the book about Carol Burnett. What do they have in common?" She scoured the small print on the Chick-O-Sticks wrapper. "There. Made in Texas." She tossed that aside and flipped through the biography. Eric read over her shoulder, and pointed at something on the inside flap. "Says Carol was born in Texas."

Casey couldn't breathe. "*Texas*."

"Is that our place?"

Casey dropped the book onto the counter and pulled Ricky's scribbled note of sayings from her pocket. "Turn on your Internet. See if either of these come up." While he set to work, she scoured the copy of the photo they'd gotten at the restaurant, but there was nothing that screamed "Texas." The license plate on the car was hidden by the man's body, and the visible background was made up of the sort of things one might see anywhere. Trees, sky, clouds. Nothing partial to any sort of specific geography.

Eric tapped on his screen and a web site came up. "Here it is. *Texas Monthly*. They have an article all about the things Texans say." He held out his iPad. "It's right there. *Fine as cream gravy.* It means you feel happy."

"And the other one?"

He scrolled down. "*Sharp as mashed potatoes.* Way of saying someone's not too bright. Hey, you okay?"

Casey sank onto one of the kitchen chairs. "I didn't really think we'd find anything. Especially not from some loser like that cook."

Eric watched her like he was afraid she was going to do something rash. When she stayed put he said, "So now what? Do we tell the police?"

"Tell them what? That this woman who isn't named Alicia McManus was maybe from the gigantic state of Texas at some point in her life?"

"I guess."

"But we don't even know that for sure, do we? Just because Ricky had these weird things hidden away. We don't even know they had anything to do with Alicia at all."

"You mean Elizabeth."

Casey looked at him.

"It's her name, right? We should probably use it."

"Not around here. We start calling her that, people will wonder how we know."

He looked at his iPad, then back at her. "And how exactly *do* we know her real name?"

"I thought you were going to wait until I was ready to tell you."

"Aren't you ready?" Casey jumped as Death's whisper froze her ear.

"What's wrong?" Eric's eyes went wide.

Death swooped to the other side of the table and swirled around Eric's head, stopping in front of his face. Eric shivered.

"Stop it," Casey said.

"What?" Eric said. "Shivering? It's cold in here."

"All of a sudden."

"Well, yeah. How come?"

Death reformed beside Eric and sat blinking at Casey, mimicking Eric's posture even though Death didn't have a chair. Didn't need one, apparently. "Are you going to tell him? Or are you still ashamed of me?"

Casey rubbed her eyes with the heels of her hands. "I'm sorry."

"You should be."

"It's okay," Eric said. "You've been under a lot of stress the past few weeks. Or, well, years."

Casey looked into his eyes and saw nothing but kindness and honesty.

"Oh, sure," Death said. "He wins you over because he's so *nice*."

"I'll tell you soon," she said to Eric.

He held her gaze for a few moments. "Okay. When you're ready, I'm here."

Death made a gagging motion and was instantly on the counter, holding the Droid. "Hello, suicide hotline? I'm about to slit my wrists. The reason? Excessive sappiness."

"So the cops," Eric said. "Are we telling them?"

Casey pushed herself from the chair and looked out the back window toward the mountains. "We should, I guess, but I don't know what I'd say. Telling them Ricky had a few Texas-themed items hidden away isn't exactly a smoking gun. I wish we knew what he was doing with those things."

Death laughed. "I guess the second Texas saying is supposed to apply to *you*. The one about being sharp as mashed potatoes.

Or how about this one?" Death pointed at the Droid, which now displayed a site on the Internet. "*If dumb was dirt, she'd cover about an acre.*"

Casey shook her head, confused.

Death huffed. "Come on. Ricky's not the *dead* one, remember? He may be in jail, but you can still ask him about the stash."

Casey closed her eyes and pushed on her temples.

"What?" Eric said.

"I've been an idiot. We need to go back to jail."

"Can we try something else first?" Eric poked at the iPad. "I want to see if Alicia shows up anywhere. Whoa. This says there have been hundreds of Elizabeth Mann's in Texas. Although this one died in 1828. And this one five years ago."

"Can we look at it on the way? Will the Internet work?"

"It's 4G. I can get Internet anywhere."

Death jumped down from the counter. "That is so *awesome*. Remember the old days when they used telegraphs? Or smoke signals? It took so long to forecast the weather that by the time they were done with the message a whole new front had gone through. Now—"

"—they're never right anyway."

Eric looked up. "One of them might be. But fine, let's go. You want to drive, or check these over?"

Casey chose to study the names, and was both amazed and frustrated by the wealth of information available. "There's no way to know which of these people is the right one. Except for the ones who are already dead, we know they're not her."

"Um, this Elizabeth Mann is dead," Death reminded her.

"A baby," Casey continued, "obviously not the right one. Old, dead, married to a Puerto Rican—although I guess we don't know she wasn't…nope, found a wedding photo. Definitely not her, unless her race has changed."

By the time they arrived at the jail she'd made a shortlist of seven Elizabeth Manns who could fit the profile but had no photos. There were still more Elizabeths to go, but she was out of time, and who knew if they should even be concentrating on Texas, anyway.

"Think I could take this iPad in to ask Ricky questions?"

"You can ask."

No go. Nothing but herself and the clothes she was wearing.

"I can show him mine," Death said. "Except that would be pointless, since he wouldn't be able to see it."

Casey took as many notes as she could, finishing them up while they sat in the waiting room. Not being on that day's visitor's list meant it took longer to get through the screening process, but since she was Ricky's sister, and she'd been there so recently before, they let her through after only forty minutes' wait. Eric had to stay in the waiting room.

"I don't like it," he said. He stood close, but didn't touch her. "You sure you'll be okay by yourself?"

"See," Death said, "he wouldn't have to worry if you'd told him about me. Then he'd know you weren't alone."

"I'll be fine." Those creepy-crawlies she was feeling weren't an indication that she *wouldn't* be fine, right? It was just the whole jail thing again. For once she didn't mind the idea that Death would be tagging along.

"Ask Ricky about the shirt, too," Eric said. "I mean, about the guy who was supposed to be fixing the bathroom. The one the neighbor saw."

"Right." Just because the cops had given up on that route didn't mean she should. Actually, it meant she should check it out *more*.

The guard called her name and she went back with her notes folded in her pocket, feeling Eric's eyes on her until the door closed between them.

"He still likes you, you know." Death had abandoned the heat sensor this time, choosing instead one of those new Smart Name-tags that syncs your interests and personality traits with whatever other technology you use. Death's name tag bore bright red lettering which proclaimed, *Hi! My name is GILTINĖ. I love clever conversation, tear-jerker movies, and long walks by the river Acheron.*

Death saw Casey checking out the tag. "I hate to think what yours would say. *Hi! Today my name is FILL IN THE BLANK, and I love running from the law, hitchhiking along the interstate, and keeping everyone at arm's length.* Don't think *Eric* would even want to date you if he saw *that*."

Casey bared her teeth with an audible growl. Death huffed and chose to walk up beside the female guard. "I wonder what *her* name tag would say? *My name is Bad-Ass Prison Guard and I'll happily whack you on the head with my baton?*"

Ricky was waiting, this time behind one of those plexi-glass partitions with the phones like Casey had seen on TV. The private room they'd had the other time was apparently an attorney-client bonus. Nothing they said this time would be privileged. Or anywhere close to confidential. A row of eight phones sat in the room, five of them in use. The one on Ricky's right was empty, but the other held a man on the prisoner's half, and a loud, under-age family on the visitor's.

Ricky was still pale and lost looking, and Casey had to rap on the window to get his attention. He jerked, then picked up the receiver. "Why are you back?"

"To see you."

"You have news?"

"I have a couple questions."

He winced, but kept the phone at his ear. "What?"

"First, did you hire some company called Hometown Interiors to do any work at your place?"

"The cops were asking about that, too. I've never heard of them, but they say I hired them to fix my bathroom. My bathroom doesn't need fixing."

She knew it. "I think he went into your house to plant fake evidence."

"The shirt."

"Exactly."

"That's what I keep telling them. The last I saw that shirt it was in the bottom of a drawer. I never wear it. I certainly never wore it around Alicia. Not with that stain on it. I mean the one from before, when you busted my face."

"The cops found emails and other correspondence saying you hired them."

"I *didn't*."

"I know."

"But why can't they ask them? They'll know nobody from their place was there."

"But that's the thing. They're saying they were."

A line formed between his eyes. "But…"

"So obviously it's a fake company, with fake employees answering the questions. We'll find them out."

"Whatever. I guess it doesn't matter anymore."

"Ricky…" But it was no use spending energy trying to pump him up, not when he was determined to be miserable. "Another question. Why were you hiding weird little things about Texas?"

He went completely still. "What do you mean?"

"Candy. Southern sayings. Carol Burnett."

He breathed through his mouth, then swallowed. "How did you find those?"

"Go on," Death said from the next cubicle, where a skinny black inmate had sat down to wait for a visitor. "Tell him you were snooping."

"I was looking for anything that might help get you out of here," Casey said.

"By going through my house? My private things?"

Casey gripped the phone. "How am I supposed to get you out of here if you don't tell me what you know?"

He looked away, dropping the receiver to his shoulder.

Casey banged on the window. "Ricky. Come on. Talk to me!"

The family to Casey's left stopped their yammering and looked over, all eyebrows raised, as if they were attached to a string.

"Sorry," Casey said.

They lowered their eyebrows and went back to their conversation, except for the youngest boy, who still peeked out from under his older sister's arm. Casey decided he'd get bored eventually, and rapped on Ricky's window again, more gently this time.

Ricky lifted the phone, but stayed silent.

"Come on, bud. What's the deal with Texas?" And then she understood. "Alicia was talking in her sleep again, wasn't she?"

He closed his eyes. "It's like I'm betraying her. Telling her secrets."

"It's her secrets that got her killed, Ricky."

He blanched. "You mean if I would have betrayed her before, she might still be alive."

"I didn't say that."

His arm drooped again.

"Ricky," she said quickly, before she lost him. "Tell me about Texas. Please."

"It could help?"

"Yes."

He let out a breath and shook his head, face toward the ceiling, like he was arguing with himself. He didn't look at her when he spoke. "She was sleeping. Real restless, you know? She never slept peacefully, at least not the few times I was with her. It was hard to understand exactly what she was saying, but it was something about not wanting to go to Texas."

"So you started collecting Texas knick-knacks? That's kind of a big leap."

"It was just—I wanted to know more about her. And when she'd mention something that seemed unusual I wanted to check it out, and then I kept the stuff so I wouldn't forget. Those expressions she used that people around here don't say, like the one about cream gravy, she wouldn't do it real often, but when she did I wrote them down. They were cute, you know? Then she mentioned that candy one time, those Chick-O-Sticks? They're pretty good, actually, and she said something about liking Carol Burnett—we were watching a birthday party for that old lady, Betty White, and Carol Burnett was there. When I asked Alicia why she liked her she just said she was funny, but I could tell it was more than that. So I got the biography so I could try to understand, but realized it was just about her being from the same place as her." He shrugged. "At least, I thought it was. Maybe I'm taking the whole thing out of context and she was talking about something else altogether and it had nothing to do with her being from *Texas*." He practically spat the word, then sagged. "I didn't know her at all, did I? Was anything she told me true? Her birthday? Her favorite color? Her *name*?"

Casey kept her face neutral and put her palm against the window. "Hey. We can't know everything about anybody. Especially if they don't want to share it. I'm sure you did your best."

"Like that did a whole lot of good."

"Ricky. Even when you do know a lot about someone, it doesn't always stop bad things from happening."

He looked at her, his eyes dark and wet. "I know. I'm sorry." He put his hand on the other side of the glass, his fingers only slightly longer than hers.

"We'll find who did this, Rick. I promise."

His lips twitched, like he was trying to smile. "Sure. Because that's what big sisters do, right? Get their little brothers out of messes."

"That's right."

"Only thing is…when you do get me out of here…what will I do then?"

Casey flexed her fingers against the plexi-glass, wishing she could interlace her fingers with his. "You'll just have to do what I've been doing for the past couple of years."

He shook his head. "I don't want to live on the road, Casey."

"Of course you don't. You'd be miserable. What I meant was you'll just have to go day to day, trying to make sense of it all. It *won't* make sense, but you have to try, anyway. That's just the way it is. You'll…exist."

He nodded, then took his hand off the window and set it in his lap. "Now I have a question for you."

"Sure. Anything."

He gestured toward the cubicle where Death sat across from the other prisoner. "Who's your friend?"

Chapter Twenty

"I don't want to talk to you!" Casey stomped down the hallway toward the waiting room.

"It's not my fault he could see me!"

"That's my little brother!"

"Who is not a kid anymore, in case you haven't noticed."

Casey stopped to get herself together before having to appear normal in front of Eric. She was just glad the guard had left her after the second barred door so she had a chance to let off some steam.

Death pointed back toward Ricky. "He's been through a lot, Casey. The woman he loved is dead. *Tortured* and dead. It wasn't an accident. Do you really think he's immune to guilt?"

"Guilt shouldn't mean he's not afraid of you."

"Who are you kidding? Guilt has been making *you* want to die for the past two years."

"It's not guilt."

"No? Then what is it?"

Casey went quiet.

"Well?"

"I'm thinking."

"Right. Because there's nothing else to say. You want to die because you feel *guilty*. You know that line you gave Ricky about bad things happening even when you know someone well? It's about time you believed that yourself."

"It's not…what about *grief*? Remember that? How people feel sad when they lose their husbands? Their *children*?"

"Oh, please. If everyone who lost a loved one suddenly became fearless, the entire world would see me 24/7. I would no longer be, as they say, rare and exotic."

"Exotic, my ass. More like a disease."

"Whatever. No matter what you think, what you're dealing with is not grief. Or not *solely* grief. It's guilt."

Casey gritted her teeth. "So what am I feeling guilty about, exactly? I didn't build the car that killed my family. Pegasus hadn't been in the national news, so I didn't know about the mechanical issues. I wasn't even *driving*."

"So you think your guilt should only come if the accident was your fault?"

"What else would I be feeling guilty about?"

Death gave a short laugh. "You really are as sharp as mashed potatoes."

"What? Wait! Where are you—"

Death disappeared through the waiting room door, waving serenely, like a 4-H dairy queen.

Casey whipped the door to the waiting room open, ready to pounce on Death and demand an answer. Several people close by jumped and instinctively grabbed their purses and children. The guard at the front desk stood, hand on his holster. Casey froze, arms half-raised. "It's okay. It's all right. I'm just…upset. That's all."

Eric stood in front of her, shielding her from the rest of the room, like he'd done at the restaurant only an hour before. "You okay?"

Casey took a shuddering breath that felt more like a sob. "No. I'm really not."

"Okay. It's okay. I've got you. Come on."

And with the gentlest of touches, he led her outside to the car.

Chapter Twenty-one

"Ricky couldn't tell *anything* from those notes about the women?"

Casey slouched in the passenger seat. "I didn't ask him."

"You didn't—why not?"

She didn't answer, still thinking about the bombshell Ricky had dropped at the end of their visit. If he was seeing Death, she couldn't let him stay in that jail any longer. He was going to do something stupid, or else just wither away to nothing.

"Casey, why didn't you ask him? I thought that was the whole point of seeing him. That and to ask about the Texas stuff. You did ask about *that*, didn't you?"

"Of course I did."

"*And?*"

"Look, Eric, I'm sorry about the names, but he was already stressing about not knowing much about Alicia, and he was questioning everything he *thought* he knew. Showing him a bunch of stuff about women who may or may not be his dead girlfriend wasn't going to solve anything except freak him out even more. So give me a break."

The silence in the car was palpable, Eric's hurt feelings like another passenger, ready to go where Death often sat in the back seat. Fortunately, Death had taken off after their little tiff in the jail, so there was no third person—or supernatural entity—to take sarcastic notice of this awkward conversation.

Casey let her head fall back against the seat. "I'm sorry, Eric. I'm *sorry*, okay? I'm just…" She rubbed her forehead. "The Texas stuff was what we thought. Only guesses. Alicia talked about Texas in her sleep, so he thought she might be from there. He didn't want to tell us before because he thought he was betraying a confidence. You weren't there. You didn't see his face. So don't give me a hard time for giving my little brother a break."

Eric looked straight ahead.

"Eric, come on…"

He gripped the steering wheel so tightly his knuckles were white. "Do you want me to go home? Because if you don't want me around, I'll leave. It's not like I don't have responsibilities back in Ohio. The soup kitchen, my mother, my *job*. As you said, this is your brother, not mine, so if you think you'll do better without my help, I'll just go."

Casey went to snap back that he should probably just go home then if that was the way he was going to be, then realized she didn't want to say that. She didn't *want* him to go home. It was nice having a companion who was actually a person, and not some horrific afterlife character from legends. "I don't want you to go."

His expression remained stony.

"Please, Eric. I said I'm sorry. I am. I'll be nicer, I promise."

His mouth twitched.

"What?"

"You just said you were going to be nicer."

"So? Isn't that what you wanted?"

"I just never put you and 'nicer' in the same sentence."

Great. Now he was doing the thing Death was always going on about. "I'm not always…Okay. As long as you've known me—" three whole weeks, if she was correct "—I haven't exactly been nice. But I can be."

"All right."

"Really."

"I'll take your word for it."

Casey shook her head. She could be nice, couldn't she? Whatever. It didn't matter. Eric was staying, so that was good. She could at least *pretend* to be nice.

"I checked out Hometown Interiors while you were in there," Eric said.

"He never hired them."

"Not surprised. They're a small, start-up company out of Boulder. Only a few employees, only a few jobs done. Only things I can find are on paper—on the computer, I mean. No people who have actually hired them."

"Sounds fishy."

"Of course it does. Because it's a fake company."

"But the cops can't see that?"

"It seems all they see is your brother and the evidence against him."

"*Fake* evidence."

They drove for a while, Casey fuming, Eric concentrating on the traffic.

"So what now?" Eric said.

Casey pulled out her notes on the women. "We figure out which, if any, of these women is the one we're looking for, and continue going through the lists of Texas women until we find the right one. And we figure out who we can call who can find out about this stupid home renovation company."

"Leave that to me," Eric said. "As it happens, I know a few people in the business world, even if my family is now officially out of it." His father had run a big business back in Ohio until he was arrested for fraud a few weeks earlier. Now, Casey hoped, those connections could be used for something positive.

They drove to Casey's house, where Eric made a few calls to get that ball rolling. They then went on-line, paid the fee to belong to some People Search database, and began looking for the right Elizabeth Mann. After forty-five minutes they were left with five possibilities, having eliminated the Elizabeth Manns who a) had non-Colorado address and phone information as recent as June, b) had current employment information that was not at The Slope, or c) had indicated their race as African-American, Asian, or "other."

"Think we should take out the ones with husbands and children?" Eric asked, looking at the five. "She wouldn't take off without at least one photo of her kids, right?"

Casey thought of her own travel bag, which hadn't included any photos until Ricky had sent her one the week before—probably only a day or two before his own life had been destroyed. Death had always given her a hard time about not carrying pictures. But it was just too difficult. "Can't count those out, Eric. What if it's her husband she's running from? Or if she's afraid for the lives of her children? She wouldn't want any sign of them. Or maybe it was just too painful to have the daily reminder." As if she would have needed photos to remember. As if there weren't enough images in her head.

"You didn't have any pictures." He had gone through her bag a few weeks earlier, when she'd run from Ohio, leaving her bag behind as she'd desperately put distance between herself and the man she'd killed. That was the reason she had her things back—Eric had followed the information on her driver's license and returned her stuff to Ricky. He knew more about her than she'd shared with anyone else in the past two years. "And there aren't any pictures here in your house. Not ones that I've seen, although I guess I haven't seen every room." He hadn't seen the bedroom.

Casey looked away, just the thought of him in her bedroom making her hot. "Ricky took the photos out when he got the place ready to sell. Most people don't want to see family shots on the walls of a house they're looking at—they want to see the place as their own. So do you want to make the calls to these women?"

"What about your bag?"

"What about it?"

"Casey. You weren't running from your husband. And you weren't afraid for your son's life. Why didn't you have any pictures?"

"The question I've always asked."

This time Casey didn't jump when Death joined the conversation, standing along the wall and holding up a computerized frame with Casey's family photo inside. It was informal, with Reuben in a Rockies jersey, Casey's hair back in a messy ponytail, and Omar wearing only blue knit shorts over a bulky diaper. His chest was slick with drool, but his smile more than made up for it.

Casey looked away, focusing on the view outside the window instead of the squeezing of her heart. "Why do you think I didn't have any?"

Eric didn't speak for almost a minute. Neither did Death, which was practically a miracle.

Eric cleared his throat. "I can call. I've got the phone. Unless you wanted to?"

She shook her head.

He hesitated, his fingers on the keypad. "If none of these women are the right one?"

"We start over."

"And if I do find the right one? I mean, find someone who knew her? Are we going to the police?"

"I don't see how we could. We aren't supposed to know her name."

"I guess it would have to be anonymous."

"They might not take it seriously then."

His hand clenched around the phone and his nostrils flared, like he was trying not to throw it across the room. At her. When he spoke, his voice was measured, and quiet. "Why don't I just see what I find, and then we'll decide."

"Sounds like a plan." It wasn't necessarily a *good* plan, but then, none of this could be placed in the 'good' category.

Eric began phoning Texas. When he reached an actual Elizabeth Mann he thanked her and hung up, saying he was looking for a different person, then moved on to the next one. Once he got a voice mail saying that that particular Elizabeth Mann worked for a place called Sunrise Technologies, and he should leave a message. He found the business, and then found the woman, so one more could be crossed off the list. He left messages with two others, one in San Antonio, one in a tiny town called Angus.

As Eric called, Casey grew increasingly restless, pacing the floor, looking in the empty cupboards, brushing at hard-to-reach cobwebs above the ceiling fan. Death ignored her and swiped at the screen of a Nook, proclaiming "A-*ha*!" and "Slice faster, nasty fruit slicer!" Finally, Casey left Eric waiting for return calls and went upstairs, where she put on her *dobak*.

"Seriously?" Death said from a seat on the bed.

"You know he's waiting for me." Her *hapkido* master.

"So what? He hasn't called."

"My answering machine isn't hooked up."

"So he could Facebook you."

"On what computer? Do you see a computer around here? And even if you do, do you see me on social networks?"

"Fine. He could use his incredible mental telepathy and contact you, or maybe he could just transport you to the *dojang*."

"He's not a magician."

"Could've fooled me. Anyway, if he's that anxious to get you over there, he could…gee…come by and ask, maybe?"

"I'm not making him do the work."

"Of course not. Because he's a *god*."

Casey laughed. "For heaven's sake. Are you *jealous*?"

"Of what?" Death frowned. "You mean of the fact that he's somebody you actually want to see? As opposed to your mother, Eric, the neighbors, *photos*? Or…even me?"

"You know there's one situation where I *would* want to see you."

Death's shoulders sagged. "Still, Casey? You *still* want me to take you?"

She tied her belt tight around her waist and pulled her hair back, securing it with a band. "How many times do I have to ask?"

"But you have…" Death stopped, poking at the Nook in that way people do when they aren't really doing anything, but want to avoid a conversation.

"What? I have what?"

"Never mind. If you need me to tell you, it's pointless to even bother."

"But—"

Death disappeared so suddenly it was like Casey had been alone all along.

"Casey?" Eric was calling up the stairs.

She grabbed her sneakers and headed down.

"Going somewhere?"

"Out." She walked past him, toward the front door.

"Do you want me to come?"

"No."

"Okay. So I take it this is you being nicer?"

She stopped, her hand clutching the doorknob. Nicer. Right. "I'm sorry, Eric. I guess I'm not used to…people…anymore." She let go of the door and turned around. "I'm going to work out. Would you like to come?"

He gave a tight smile. "If it's all right, I think I'll stay here and wait for a call from one of the Elizabeth Manns. But thanks for asking."

Not sure whether to say it was all right, sorry, you're welcome, or anything at all, Casey kept her mouth shut and walked out the door.

She really needed to go kick some ass.

Chapter Twenty-two

The *dojang* was housed in an old warehouse almost three miles from Casey's place. She left the bike and Eric's car at Ricky's house and jogged over. She could feel the miles she'd run in the middle of the night, but it was a good burn. It had been too many days since she'd had a chance to exercise properly.

The building looked the same as it had the last time, except for a fresh coat of blue paint on the door. The parking lot was half-filled, but that would represent rides for the different businesses housed within.

Casey walked up the stairs, passing the ground floor pottery, the family counseling center on the other half of the floor, and the second-floor dance studio and dancewear boutique—along with the dance moms and girls Casey had always tried to avoid. Avoiding them was always pretty easy, as the moms kept their precious darlings far away from the martial arts thugs. Casey always thought it ironic that the children—and their mothers—would be far safer with the martial artists than just about anybody else in town, and the crazy moms chose to alienate them. It was just as well. Casey had never been sure how to respond to all the ribbons and lipstick.

The door to the *dojang* was open, releasing the humid workout air into the stairwell. Casey stood for a moment just outside, breathing in the smells and sounds that instantly found a home in her body. Apparently you could take the woman out of the *dojang*, but couldn't take the *dojang* out of the woman. Wasn't that how the saying went?

Casey went left in the hall, toward the workout room, away from the lockers. A class was in session, and she could hear someone calling out instructions. Not Master Custer. Someone younger, most likely one of the current black belts. It was what she used to do, back when she was the highest-ranking belt, other than the master.

She checked in the small room that served as the office—windowless and damp—but no one was there except the very out-dated computer, so she made her way to the open door of the workout room. An array of students stood barefooted on the mats, ranging in age from young teens to thirty-somethings, men and women. A black belt stood at the front of the classroom facing the students, who displayed every color belt, with the lower belts in the far back corner. Two other black belts worked out in the front row, one a dark-skinned woman about Casey's age, the other a white guy younger than Casey, and the thirty-year-old at the front.

Casey's teacher stood only a few feet from the doorway, his back to her, arms crossed as he surveyed his class. His gray hair was pulled back in a ponytail, and his posture was straight, but relaxed. His feet were bare, and his own black belt had been tied around his waist. The gold bars on the edge of the belt, indicating his rank, gleamed against the black fabric. Three on each end, showing he was a sixth-degree black belt. As always, Casey felt a little in awe just to be in his presence.

She watched from the doorway as the class finished the *kata* and the black belt resumed his place in the front row.

"Casey," her teacher said without turning around. "Sword Form Number Two. Everyone else clear the mat."

Of course he knew she was there. Of course he knew she was already warm from jogging over.

She slipped off her shoes and socks, bowed to the mat, bowed to the Korean flag, bowed to him. The black belt who had been calling orders brought her a sword and handed it over with a bow to her. She didn't know him, but somehow he knew her. Her teacher said nothing else, just stood there with his arms crossed and his expression unreadable, his eyes the only thing moving as they followed her to her beginning position.

Casey focused on the far wall and breathed deeply, centering herself. For one moment she allowed herself to be thankful she had kept up with her training as she'd traveled, making use of hotel rooms, empty fields, deserted roads, and the occasional athletic facility. She was in shape physically. Now she just had to prove she could also perform mentally.

Casey bent her knees, held the sword straight in front of her body, and began. She stabbed, blocked, swung, kicked, circled, knelt, and did a one-handed cartwheel. It felt good. Her speed was fast and consistent, her feet were grounded, and her center held rock-steady. She thought of nothing but the movement. Nothing but the slap of her feet on the mat, the twirling of the sword in her hands, and her breath coming full and even. She finished with a complex series of swordplay, crouched in a defensive stance. After a few beats she straightened, put her feet together and the sword down, and bowed.

"Critique," her teacher said. "You." He pointed at a blue belt who was probably about sixteen.

The kid's jaw shook, but he replied, "Her speed was steady, Master, and she seemed focused."

The Master's lips twitched. "Correct. But I meant for her to critique you. On the mat. Hapkido Third Form."

The kid swallowed and his eyes flicked to Casey, then back to Master Custer. "Yes, Master."

Casey bowed to her teacher and left the mat, turning to watch the young man as he went through the form. Part of her felt sorry for him for being singled out, but that was the type of thing that made a strong, confident fighter out of a spindly teenager. So Casey kept her feelings in check. When he was finished and had bowed to both her and the master, her teacher, still not looking at her, said, "Critique."

Casey looked directly at the boy, but he kept his eyes on her belt. His clenched fists pushed against his legs. "His movements were sharp, with good form. He over-rotated on the kicks, and his center of gravity often seemed to shift forward. Focus was split between his movements and the room, but he kept his shoulders straight, and he used the space well."

"Do you hear the critique of your better?" Master Custer said to the kid.

"Yes, Master."

The teacher nodded. "Good work. Much improvement from last time."

"Thank you, Master." The boy bowed again, and strode from the mat to join the others.

Custer nodded at the female black belt. "Lead the class in cool down. When you are satisfied, class is dismissed."

"Yes, Master."

When she was in front and the others had lined up and begun their stretching, the master turned to Casey. "Come."

She followed him not to the dingy office, but down the hall and up another flight of stairs, which led to the roof. They stood, facing west, toward the mountains. He didn't speak. Casey didn't feel like talking, either, so they stood in companionable silence for quite a while, until they heard footsteps behind them.

The oldest black belt stood there, his face reflecting his discomfort at interrupting. "I'm sorry to disturb you, Master, but there is a phone call for Ms. Maldonado."

Custer's eyebrows rose, but he remained facing the mountains. "I guess someone knows how to find you, after all."

Casey excused herself and followed the black belt down the stairs to the little office. He handed her the receiver and left her alone.

"It's me." Eric.

"What is it?"

"We struck out."

"What? *None* of them?"

"I'm sorry."

Casey sat in the desk chair and stared at the trophies crammed on a shelf above the computer. There were others in the big room, the locker room, and on stands in the hallway that had been won by the *dojang*. But these were the master's personal stash. "We can't be done."

"I have an idea."

"Which is?"

"I'll just start calling Manns in Texas and see if I find anything. Because think about it. She came here during the summer, but this might not have been the first place she ran to. She may have been on the run for years. So she wouldn't even have—"

"—a home phone number in Texas."

"Exactly. But we had to call around to all of these Elizabeths to make sure."

"So you're just going to start calling. That will take forever."

"What else am I going to do with my time? I'll see you later."

"Eric…"

But he'd hung up. Casey sat there for several seconds, then stepped out of the office. The black belts were in the workout room, preparing for the next class, which was apparently for kids. One had already arrived, and was fitted out in a helmet. More were coming up the stairs. Casey escaped to the roof.

The master was standing in the same place as when she'd left. He said nothing.

"I'm sorry," Casey finally said.

He didn't respond.

"I should have called. I should have written. Something."

He looked out at the mountains. "You mistake my silence for criticism. Or anger. I feel the need for neither one."

Casey waited, and her teacher finally turned toward her and studied her face. "I feel nothing but sadness for what you have been through. Nothing but concern, and the desire to help. But I believe what you need must come from inside you."

It was Casey's turn to gaze at the mountains. "I don't recognize what's in there anymore. Who I even am. Who I'm supposed to be."

"I know. It is a journey, and you alone are able to find your destination. Your way may twist and turn, but eventually you will find what you are looking for."

The same thing she'd been told by a sensei in Florida only days before. These centered, disciplined, wise people were all the same.

"I've been trying to follow the path," she said. "But I have no idea if I've made any progress. It's all so pointless."

"I understand," he said. "Life has changed your course, and it's hard to find your way."

They were quiet again, while Casey stewed about her teacher's idealistic philosophy. Easy to say "follow the path" when you weren't the one trying to beat back the brush to find it.

"You say you have been following the path, and I believe you," the master said. "But there is one thing I learned long ago that helped me find peace along my own journey."

"Oh, did you lose your entire family in an explosion, too?"

"There are other journeys, Casey. Other ways pain forces itself into a life. Yours is not the only story. Your brother is living in a rather sordid story of his own right now."

Casey's face burned. "Of course. I'm sorry, Master."

"I don't want you to be sorry. I want you to hear what I say."

He waited for Casey to tear her eyes from the mountains and fix them on his face.

"You must make this journey, and you alone can discover exactly what it is you need. But that doesn't mean you must *be* alone."

Casey heard his words, but they didn't sink in. Not until he said it again.

"Casey, my friend. There comes a time when you need to realize that a journey is not a solitary experience. You must allow others to aid you along the way. The grief is yours, and the heartache, but it is something that only lessens when you share it." He smiled gently. "Do you understand what I'm saying?"

"That I need to let someone else travel with me." She gave a little laugh. "But who else wants to spend life on the road?"

He shook his head so subtly Casey almost missed it.

"What?"

"You're listening to my words, Casey, but you're not hearing what I'm saying."

"I am. I hear you. You're saying I need to let someone else travel with me."

He watched her for a few more moments with his piercing blue eyes, then went down the stairs to join his class.

Chapter Twenty-three

"Any progress?"

Eric was still in the kitchen when Casey returned. Papers with scribbled notes lay scattered on the kitchen table, and his eyes were bloodshot and watery.

"My ear is numb, and I've lost the ability to explain who I'm looking for, and I think I might have forgotten why I'm making all these calls in the first place."

"Maybe you're confused because you're hungry."

His jaw dropped. "I forgot all about lunch."

"Which is why I got some."

"You?"

"Yes, me. I do have the ability to walk and carry a bag at the same time."

"I didn't mean—"

"I know what you meant." She pushed some of Eric's papers aside and distributed two large salads, two carry-out containers of chicken noodle soup, and a loaf of French bread.

"This can't possibly be from the gas station."

She laughed. "Not a chance. But grocery store delis, now, *they* are a wonderful thing. Do you want to eat here, or should we take it outside?"

"Definitely outside. I think I'm suffering from cooped-up-ness. And yes, that is an actual medical term."

They sat on the back steps and ate, only inches from each other. Casey was aware of the heat of Eric's leg, even though they weren't touching, and the brush of his arm against her sleeve. She ordered herself to remain where she was, and to act like a grown up about it.

"So, how was the *dojo*?" Eric said.

"*Dojang. Dojo* is Japanese."

"And *dojang* is…"

"Korean. I study hapkido, which is a Korean martial art. If I studied aikido or judo, or if I wanted to be a ninja—" she grinned "—I'd go to a *dojo*."

They ate quietly for another minute.

"So, how was the *dojang*?" Eric said.

Casey stirred her soup. "Humbling."

"Forgotten how to do things?"

"Apparently."

"You look in shape."

"I am. Physically. It's the mental part the master seems to be worried about."

Eric nodded. "I can see that. But did you tell him you were committed to being nicer now? Maybe that would help."

Casey sipped her soup. "Didn't get around to that. Guess I should have, since he's convinced I don't know what I'm doing."

"About what? Ricky?"

"Life."

"Ah."

Casey tossed a bread crumb to a squirrel, who took it and scampered away, like Casey was going to change her mind and try to steal it back. "You would get along with him well."

"How come?"

"You both think I'm hard to be around."

"Maybe he and I should get together and talk. Except I'd be afraid of him."

"Why?"

"Isn't he the one who taught you to…do what you did?"

"In Ohio? You mean, kill people?" Eric had been there. He'd seen her fight, had seen the man die.

Eric looked deeply into his soup. "That's not exactly what I meant."

"Of course it is." She gazed up into the trees, where the rusty leaves let patches of sunlight through in moving patterns. "I wish you hadn't seen that. I wish it hadn't happened. But it did, and we probably ought to talk about it sometime."

"I don't need to. It's over. I told the police it was self-defense because I really believed it was."

"You were right. It definitely was. I never...I didn't want to kill anyone. Ever."

"Then why the hapkido? Isn't that basically training you to... well, kill people? Or at least fight them?"

"No, it's a defensive art, not an offensive one. And seriously, how many people—Americans, especially—do you see going around using it in bars or whatever? And I don't mean in the movies. It's more an art form—or an exercise. It's great for getting in shape, and for your frame of mind."

"Then why not just do aerobics? That's exercise. That should release the seratonin—isn't that what's supposed to be released?—and make you a mentally healthy person."

Casey shuddered. A week earlier she had been the aerobics instructor at an exclusive club, and the seratonin definitely hadn't been flowing there. "Hapkido isn't *just* an exercise. It's a way of life. A way of looking at things. Awareness. The ability to see the whole of something and not just a small part. Stability. Self-assurance."

"You have all those things?"

"I used to. That's why today was so humbling. As soon as I stepped on the mat I felt focused, but the moment I was off and it became about life I lost it all." She shook her head. "I've failed my master and hapkido as a whole. Or hapkido has failed me."

"Maybe not. Maybe you would be a complete loss if you hadn't had your training. Maybe hapkido really did save you, after all. Did your teacher tell you to stay away?"

Casey remembered Master Custer's back as he left her on the roof. "No. But he didn't encourage me to return anytime soon, either."

Eric put his empty dishes aside and stretched out his legs. "Looks like you're stuck with just me, then."

"Yeah, looks like it." Casey stabbed some lettuce with her fork and took a bite because she felt like she might laugh just a little. Or maybe cry.

Eric's phone rang in his pocket and he took it out, looking at the screen. "Texas area code. Hello?" He listened for several seconds, then said, "And how long ago was this?" He made a motion like he needed a pencil. Casey hopped up and ran into the kitchen, returning with paper and pen. He scribbled madly, saying, "Uh-huh. Uh-huh. Okay. And what was his name?"

Casey tried to read over his shoulder, but she couldn't see around his arm, and he waved her out of his space.

"And you were his what? Cousin? Niece. *Her* cousin. All right."

Casey stuck her nose over the paper and he shoved her aside.

"I'm just trying to find her family. No, I'm sorry, that's all I can tell you for now—"

He listened for a bit, biting his lips together.

"I'm in Colorado, and a woman with that name died and we're trying to find out about her family. Actually, the woman was using another name entirely, but there seemed to be a connection with an Elizabeth Mann."

He listened some more.

"I know. It could easily be someone entirely different. No, no, I don't think you should come up. At least not yet. I'll send you a photo."

She squawked on the phone.

"No, no," Eric said, "I have a nice picture from before her death, so it will be….Good. Do you have an email account or something where I could send it? Right. Got it. I'll be in touch when I find out more. You have my number. And I'm sorry. Good-bye."

He hung up and took a shuddering breath. He'd gone pale.

"What is it?" Casey said. "What's wrong?" She grabbed the paper, but couldn't make sense of his handwriting.

He took the paper back and laid it on his thigh, smoothing his hand over it. " At least one Elizabeth Mann grew up in a little town called Marshland, Texas. This woman—Betsy Lackey—was her cousin."

"Lackey? How did you know to call her if her last name's not Mann?"

"I didn't. I left a message on her father's phone, and he gave her the message."

"Did she know why Alic—Elizabeth came here?"

"She didn't know she was even in Colorado. Had no idea where she was. If this really is her. We have to remember that. We could be talking about someone completely unrelated to Alicia."

"What about the guy? You were talking about a guy."

"This Elizabeth Mann's father. Cyrus Mann. If we have the right person, it could be the man in the photograph we got at the restaurant."

"Is he still there in Marshland?"

"No." Eric let out a breath and shook his head. "He hasn't been there for over seventeen years. And neither has Elizabeth."

"Seventeen—Why so long ago? What happened back in the early nineties?"

Eric lifted his eyes from the paper, and Casey winced at the pain she saw. "Cyrus Mann was murdered," he said. "On the same night his teenage daughter disappeared."

Chapter Twenty-four

"So who murdered Elizabeth's dad?"

"Lots of theories," Eric said. "No certain answers."

"What do we know?"

"It was bad. An execution, really. Shot in the head. Left to die."

"What do the cops think?"

"This woman didn't get into it all, but basically it sounds like his murder has never been solved, and the police have stopped trying to solve it."

"Do you think the cops had something to do with Elizabeth disappearing? I mean, do you they think *she* killed him?"

Eric shrugged. "You heard my side of the phone call. We didn't talk that long."

"So let's see what we can find out."

They went back inside to use Eric's iPad. Death sat at the table in Eric's chair, looking over the scribbled notes from the morning.

"The murder was so long ago," Casey said, "I wonder how much will even be recorded."

Death looked up. "How long ago? And who are we talking about?"

"About seventeen years, right, Eric? What was his name? Cyrus Mann?"

Eric looked at her curiously, and sat down in his chair, right on Death's lap. Death squeezed out from beneath him, and Eric shuddered. "Does your heat work? Can we turn it on? And yes, his name was Cyrus. I told you all this."

"I wanted to be sure."

Death was visibly trying to call up the information, finger tapping on chin, eyes unfocused. "Ah, yes. Cyrus Mann. I remember. Not much to go on. You know with these violent, spur-of-the-moment deaths I'm not always there in time to see the cause. Or the perpetrators, anyway."

"Any witnesses?" Casey asked.

"Haven't found anything yet," Eric said. "Give me a minute. It's not coming up under just her name…"

"Only one other person there," Death said. "A girl. Fourteen years old. She was holding him when he died."

"Didn't he die immediately?"

Eric glanced up. "Why are you asking me these weird questions I don't have answers to? Oh, here we go. I had to put in everything I knew in order to find it. 'Man found dead. Daughter missing.'"

"It's not like the movies," Death said. "People don't die instantly, even when they're shot in the head. Well, if their head is completely blown off I guess they do, but this guy hung on a few minutes. By the time I got there, the girl was the only one—Wait. Are you telling me that girl was Alicia McManus?"

"Elizabeth Mann."

"Right." Eric sat up. "'Cyrus Mann, forty-two, died of head wounds on March 11, 1995. No witnesses, no evidence suggesting who might have done it. His daughter, Elizabeth, fourteen years old, went missing that same night. No clue as to where she went." He tapped on a later article. "Looks like they did consider her for the murder for a while, but eventually gave up. There were a few other leads, but none of them panned out."

"What kind of leads? And where was her mother?"

"Didn't see a mother," Death said.

Eric flipped through a few screens. "Nothing about a mother. Just stuff about—" His eyebrows rose.

"What?"

"They lived in a car."

"*What?*"

"Elizabeth and her dad were homeless. They slept and kept their stuff in a 1973 Chevy station wagon. Says here that first he sold off a woodworking business that he owned, then was hired by a houseboat manufacturer. That job didn't last very long, and he lost his house in December. Oh, here it says the mother died. Cancer. So she was out of the picture. The townspeople knew him and his daughter, let them keep the car in the local park. The cops left them alone."

"So generous of them. I don't suppose any of them had spare rooms Elizabeth and her dad could actually stay in?"

"Oh, you mean like in this house?" Death said. "It's only been sitting empty for two years."

"Does it say—what did Elizabeth do before this all happened and she disappeared?"

"Went to school, I guess. Says here she was enrolled at Marshland High School. Hardly ever missed a day until her dad died and she disappeared. After a while people just assumed she was dead, too." He sat back. "Here's a photo. That look like our girl?"

Casey studied it. "Hard to tell. She's so young here." With innocence in her eyes, instead of haunted sorrow. "I guess it could be."

"The lady I talked to today was surprised to get my message. She'd assumed that whole thing was over and done with, and her cousin's disappearance was one of those events that would always be a mystery."

"Does she think Elizabeth killed her dad?"

"Not from what she said. She'd always thought Elizabeth was a victim, too." Eric set down the iPad. "You do realize who would be good help with this."

"The cops. I know. But how do I tell them?"

"You need more, unless you do it anonymously," Death said. "Attach all these articles to a throw-away email address and send it in."

Eric put a hand on Casey's arm, and she jerked, but didn't pull away. "Maybe it's time you tell me how you know her name."

Casey looked at the tabletop. "I'll tell Detective Watts I found out from Ricky."

"But then Ricky would get in trouble for not telling them first."

"How else could I know?"

"You found something in her apartment? At work? Maybe in another hidden place?"

"But I'd have to show them what it was. And I don't have anything."

Eric was quiet. "You're not ready to tell me."

"I'm sorry."

"You know where you might be able to find more," Death said.

Casey shook her head, too exhausted to consider it.

Death pushed the button on a small digital projector, and a map of the United States covered the far wall. Texas was highlighted.

"I know," Casey said. "I *know*. We have to go."

"Go where?" Eric said.

Casey sighed. "Where do you think? Marshland, Texas."

"Without telling the cops?"

"Why would we tell them? They don't know anything about this."

"Because…I don't know. It just seems wrong to sneak away."

"We're not sneaking. We're traveling."

"And Ricky?"

"I'll tell Don. He can let Ricky know if he needs to."

"Are we driving?"

"You and I may not have a lot of things, but there's one thing we seem to have plenty of."

"What's that?"

"Money. We might as well use some of it. It's not doing anyone any good sitting in the bank."

Death made a noise. "Just like this house, sitting here empty."

"So can you buy plane tickets on that thing?" She gestured to the iPad.

Eric nodded. "Sure."

Death grinned and held up a Nook. "Quicker than you can say *the porch light's on, but nobody's home.*"

Casey left them to it and went upstairs to pack.

Chapter Twenty-five

"First class?" Casey said to Eric. "Really?"

"I know, it seems extravagant, but, as you said, between the two of us we've got more than enough money, plus—" he held up his hand to stop her from arguing "—I couldn't really see you sitting knee to knee with some annoying businessman from Boulder, wanting to sell you life insurance. Violence is usually frowned upon when flying commercial."

He had a point.

"I'm going to see if the flight attendant has an extra blanket," Eric said, standing up. "I can't get over this chill." He moved down the aisle, toward the attendants' supply area.

"You could've reserved one more ticket." Death remained in Eric's seat, which Eric had unknowingly been sharing. "Where am I supposed to go?"

"Baggage? Overhead compartment? Hell?"

"I don't spend time in Hell, and you know it. It's very... unpleasant. And hot."

"You have to take people there, don't you?"

"Way out of my job description, my dear. You know that. My thing is to pick up and deliver to…you know who. After that they're on their own. Or not."

She looked out at the clouds, floating far below them. "So tell me, is Saint Peter really guarding the gate?"

Death grinned. "Come now, you don't really want me to spoil the surprise, do you?"

"Got one for you, too." Eric was back, and handed her a folded blanket. "She's also going to bring me some coffee. I need something. I hope I'm not getting a cold."

Casey looked at Death, who grudgingly gave up Eric's seat. She smiled. "I think you'll be warmer now."

Eric sat down in his empty place, and Death hovered for a moment in the aisle. "Fine. See how you feel when someone leaves *you* out." The attendant was coming down the aisle with a tray of hot drinks, so Death gave Casey one more glare and disappeared, sucked up into the neighboring row's air vent. The older couple in those seats shivered, fiddled with the knobs, and went back to what they were doing before.

Eric warmed up eventually, then wondered why he'd even worried about body temperature once they hit the ground in Dallas. "It must be eighty-five degrees down here."

"At least." Casey enjoyed the sun on her face as they walked out to their full-size rental car. "You driving?"

Marshland, Texas, was a sleepy town literally, as well as in a manner of speaking. It was past midnight by the time they had stopped for a very late dinner and pulled up in front of the only motel in town, which was a one-story, park-at-the-door type place. Eric wrinkled his nose, but Casey had slept in worse. Far worse.

"I got this." Casey went into the office and asked for two rooms.

"How many nights?" The kid behind the desk was probably in high school. He wore a Skillet T-shirt and jeans that hung off his practically nonexistent butt. His hair was sandy brown and hung in his eyes, making him look young and sort of clueless. What he was doing manning a night desk was a mystery, but also not any of Casey's business, so she didn't ask.

"Not sure how long we're staying. Can we let you know day by day?"

He shrugged. "Don't matter to me. It's not like we're full up." He took her cash and handed her two keys. "Rooms are around back. Quieter back there."

"Thanks." She put her wallet away. "Any chance you know Betsy Lackey?"

He nodded as he put her money in the cash drawer. "Sure. She's Billy's mom."

"Know where they live?"

"Right downtown. Blue house on the corner by the stoplight."

The stoplight. Not a specific stoplight. Just 'the' stoplight.

"She work days?"

"At the pharmacy, last I knew. Not sure exactly what she does there."

"Married?"

"Well, yeah. He's the physics teacher at the school."

Again with the singular 'the.'

"All right. Thanks."

"How come you're looking for Mrs. Lackey?"

"We called her today about her cousin."

"Which one?"

Casey deliberated, then finally decided there was no reason not to tell him. "One from way back. She disappeared in the nineties."

He went still, and his eyes opened wide. "Seriously? That one? She went to school with my dad. Did you find her?"

"So you know about her?"

"Do I—I mean—Sure. She's the local legend. Well, her and Cyrus, you know, her old man. There's all kinds of stories."

"Like what?"

He leaned forward, his fingers spread on the counter. "They lived in a car, for one thing. And they were mixed up with bad folks."

"What kind of bad folks?"

"Depends who's talking. Drugs. Smugglers. Weapons. Slave traders."

"Slave traders? What slaves?"

"You know. People from Mexico. They want to come up, they got to pay some guy, and they end up working for him forever for nothing. It's messed up. I wrote all about it for my government class. Been going on for ages."

"What about Elizabeth? Your dad know her very well?"

"Yeah, I guess. This size town, you pretty much know everybody. But it's not like he talks about her a lot, or anything. I think they were friends back then, or maybe even more than that, you know? But he married my mom, and, well, it's not a subject that comes up too much."

"Think he'd talk to me?"

"Probably. I can ask."

"I'd appreciate that…what's your name?"

"Robert. You can call me Robbie, if you want. Everybody does."

Casey smiled. She was liking young Robert. "Well, thanks a lot, Robbie. You can call me Casey."

He shook her hand formally. "Nice to meet you, ma'am."

Ma'am. Somewhere along the way she'd turned into one of those. Or maybe it was Texas manners.

"Um, did you find her, or something?" He didn't want to let her go without an answer.

He was going to have to. Casey smiled, but didn't tell him anything more.

She and Eric found their rooms and paused to say goodnight under the awning that went the length of the building.

"Any certain time in the morning?" Eric asked.

"Don't think there's a rush. It'll be better if we catch people once they're up and around. No use spoiling anyone's morning."

"All right, then. See you whenever."

"Yeah."

They stood there awkwardly for a few moments until Casey turned and went into her room, locking it and leaning against the door.

"Two rooms?" Death said from a seat on the bed. A projector beamed a Houston Texans game onto the wall, and Death was texting someone with one eye on football and one eye on the phone. "Waste of money."

"Like we've been worried about that today. First class plane tickets. Big car. Eating out."

"Whatever. You're scared."

"I'm not scared."

"Are too."

Casey slammed the door of the bathroom and took a very long, very hot shower. When she came out, Death was still there, although now instead of football the projector was showing "No Country for Old Men."

"Seriously?" Casey said. "Could you be more depressing?"

"It's the real Texas."

"I don't think so. How about something uplifting, like 'Apollo 13?'"

"That was Texas?"

"*Houston, we've had a problem.*"

"Oh. Right."

"Anyway, no matter what state it's about, you have to turn it off. I'm going to sleep."

Death pouted. "You're never any fun."

"And you're a barrel of dead monkeys."

Death harrumpfed, rolled off the bed, and was gone.

Casey fell asleep fast, but was wide awake by six, without a prayer of drifting off again. She got dressed and went out for a run.

The town was as small as she had imagined. "The" pharmacy, school, and bank were all quiet and dark, with no sign of life except the digital clock hanging on the corner of the bank. The gas station-slash-convenience store was open, making Casey think of home, but she didn't stop. She passed the stoplight—one of those blinking red ones, not even a full-fledged green-yellow-red—which meant she was passing Betsy Lackey's blue house. She saw a light in what was probably a bathroom, with a frosted glass window, but decided against a spur-of-the-moment visit. Pulling someone out of the shower wasn't exactly a way to get off on the right foot.

The streets were neat and clean, and the houses well-cared for. She didn't see anyone sleeping in a car or in a doorway, and saw nothing that said there was a bad part of town. By the time she got back to the hotel, she was convinced Marshland was much more an "Apollo 13" kind of town than a "No Country for Old Men" town. Thank God. The last thing Casey needed was some creepy guy coming after her with a handmade airgun.

Eric was sitting outside reading his iPad. "So you're not even in there. I was afraid to make any noise since you were being so quiet."

"Couldn't sleep any more."

"Want to grab some breakfast? The kid in the office told me there's a good diner on the opposite edge of town."

"Robbie?"

"You mean the kid? I guess. Same one as last night. He was getting ready to head out for school. Not sure how he'll function, since he was working all night."

"Teenager." That description would account for many things people could do that seemed superhuman. "Give me a few minutes, okay?" She showered and went back out to find Eric still sitting there.

"Forgot to tell you," Eric said. "The kid said his dad will talk to you, if you want. He works second shift, so the best time to catch him is early afternoon."

They found the diner, had a good breakfast, and were in the middle of "downtown" by eight-thirty. The pharmacy was open, so they walked down the street and into the store.

"Can I help you?" a woman said.

Casey turned to reply, but was struck dumb. The woman at the counter was the spitting image of Alicia McManus.

Chapter Twenty-six

"Can I help you?" the woman said again.

Eric glanced at Casey, then stepped forward. "Yes, you and I talked on the phone yesterday. I'm Eric VanDiepenbos. This is Casey Maldonado."

The woman's face went blank for just a second, until recognition hit. "About Lizzie? But…weren't you in *Colorado*?"

"Yes, we flew in late last night."

"You didn't email me the photo you promised."

"Sorry, we headed out as soon as we could get plane tickets. We thought we should come and see what we could find out."

"But what if it's not even Lizzie? You made the trip for nothing."

"We didn't." Casey found her voice. "You look just like her."

Betsy Lackey paled and sat down on a high stool behind the counter. Her mouthed worked, and she pressed her hand against it.

"I'm sorry," Casey said. "Here she is." She pulled out the picture of Alicia, and Ricky and laid it on the counter.

Betsy's eyes filled. "Oh, God. Even after all these years." She touched the photo gently. "She looks the same. She looks…like me." Tears dribbled down her cheeks. Eric found a tissue carton on the counter and handed her a Kleenex. She held it scrunched in her hand as she stared dumbly at the picture.

"Betsy?" An older woman appeared in one of the aisles, and walked toward the counter.

Betsy slid the photo into her lap and turned it over.

The woman looked from Eric and Casey to Betsy. "Is everything all right?"

"I…" Betsy shook her head. "May I have a few minutes?"

"Of course. Do you need me to do anything? Are these people bothering you?" She looked suddenly afraid. "It's not Billy, is it?"

"No, no, Billy's fine." Betsy managed a wobbly smile. "It's something else. Can I talk with them somewhere?"

"Use the lunch room."

Betsy nodded and came out from behind the counter. Eric followed. Casey felt the woman's eyes on her, and hesitated. "I'm sorry to disturb her."

The woman's concern seemed genuine, her eyes reflecting only care for Betsy, plus maybe a little anger that Casey had caused her pain. "Is there something I can do?"

"I'm sure she'll let you know." Casey followed the others to the back of the store, into a cheerful room with a table, refrigerator, and sink. Betsy was already sitting, and she looked up as Casey closed the door. Finally, she wiped her face, and sat straight.

"Tell me, please."

Eric looked at Casey, and she sighed. It really was her story to tell, more than his. Casey sat down across the table and explained that her brother had been Alicia's boyfriend, and that's how she'd gotten involved. She recounted what she knew about Alicia's death—downplaying the torture and rape—and everything she and Eric had found out about her life, including the fact that Ricky was in jail for her murder even though nobody in her personal life believed he could be responsible. She left out the part that that circle of people could be counted on one hand.

Betsy listened with obvious confusion. "She was using the name Alicia McManus? Why?"

"Weren't the cops looking for her in connection with her father's death?"

"Not for years, and never really seriously. She was a kid, not a killer. A sweet kid, too. Funny, smart. She always got good grades, even though—" She made a face.

"I was wondering about that," Casey said. "How you could be so close to her, and yet she and her dad lived in a car."

Betsy's eyes flicked up to Casey's. "Listen, we offered lots of times. Told Uncle Cyrus we had plenty of room—he was my dad's brother, you know. He knew they were welcome in our house. My dad used to say at least Uncle Cyrus should let Lizzie stay, even if he didn't want to. I think he would have let her, but Lizzie didn't want to leave him."

"Why wouldn't he just move in?"

"Pride, I guess. Didn't want to take *charity*. Not even from his own brother. My dad about went crazy trying to convince him. After he got…after he died, my dad couldn't forgive himself for not insisting. We kept telling him he'd tried. He'd done everything he could. Uncle Cyrus was just stubborn. Flat out refused to let us help him. Wouldn't even park on our property. Had to find other places to stay where he thought it wasn't because someone felt obligated. They ended up with a sort of permanent spot at the park."

"And you couldn't convince Elizabeth to stay with you?"

"Like I said, she didn't want to. Felt her place was with her dad, even if it was in that dumpy old station wagon. He tried to convince her, too. Even moved her stuff into our house, but she moved right back out again."

Eric pulled the photo of the man out of his folder. "Is this your uncle Cyrus?"

Betsy's eyes filled again, and she took the photo. "That's him. And the stupid car. Lizzie took this with my camera. She had it because she was supposed to take a picture of him for some job prospect. I guess she was just messing around." Her voice had gone quiet, and she took a shuddering breath before looking up, steel having replaced the tears in her eyes. "How can I help?"

"If you could just tell us whatever you can remember. Was Cyrus mixed up with bad people? Were there any rumors after his death? Had Alic—Elizabeth ever said anything about being afraid of anyone? "

"Like who?"

"Men, I guess."

Betsy shook her head. "Can't think of anything like that. But as far as after his death…" She chewed on her lips, deep in thought, then stood abruptly. "I'll be right back."

She left, and Eric took a seat at the table. "Well, what do you think?"

"She's the best lead we've got. Maybe she can tell us something useful, even if she doesn't know it is."

Betsy came back. "I got the afternoon off. We'll go to my house and I'll show you some things."

They walked with her several blocks to the pleasant two-story house Casey had seen on her run. Flowers bloomed in beds around the foundation and at the end of the walk, as well as in hanging baskets on the porch. A bicycle leaned against the house, and a well-used basketball hoop was attached to the garage. A porch swing hung beside the front door, a perfect place for looking out over the pretty neighborhood and tidy lawns. Oaks and elms spotted the yards, now in riotous red and orange, and Casey couldn't help but notice that even with the warm weather, it still looked like autumn.

"Come on in." Betsy led them into a large living room, with a huge flat-screen TV on the wall, and multiple wires and game controllers snaking across the floor. Shoes and sweatshirts and various plastic cups littered the floor and end tables, but rather than looking dirty, it made the house seem lived in. Casey wanted to sit on the puffy couch and curl up with a bag of chips.

"House with teens," Betsy said. "No getting around this stuff anymore."

"Looks familiar." Eric grinned. "Wasn't too long ago I was the one throwing stuff all over my folks' place." He blinked, then went quiet, probably thinking about the fact that his parents weren't together anymore, and his father was actually in prison. Not too much opportunity to leave stuff lying around there.

"Have a seat here in the dining room," Betsy said. "We'll use the table. Do you mind waiting a minute? I'll get the stuff from upstairs. I pulled it out of the attic after you called yesterday."

While she was gone, Casey looked around. Another room that was lived in. More formal, of course, being the dining room, but the sideboard was covered with books and magazines and school papers, and even a few empty bowls and a half-filled glass of something that was probably orange juice. The table itself didn't look like it was actually used for family dinners, but served as a catch-all for whatever didn't have a home elsewhere.

Casey stepped into the kitchen and took some time study-ing the collage that was the refrigerator: school menus, report cards, church calendars, grocery lists, magnets that took many forms—owls, motorcycles, pharmacy information, Garfield—and, of course, the gamut of photos. Those ranged from senior pictures to Christmas cards to casual family shots. Again, Casey was shocked at how alike Betsy and Elizabeth were, and she was taken aback even more at the photos of a girl who had to be Betsy's daughter. She was in elementary school, but already looked like a younger version of Elizabeth.

"That's my daughter," Betsy said at Casey's shoulder. "Junie, we call her. Born in the summer. She's nine. Cutest thing ever, of course." She smiled. "Third grade and giggly as anything. Billy is seventeen. Not exactly a giggler. I was still in high school myself when he was born. Got married when I was eighteen, but we'd already had him before then. He's a good boy. Gets good grades, plays soccer. Worst thing he's ever done was to be late for school once last month. He's kind of moody, especially this past month, but that's to be expected with a senior, right?" She cleared her throat. "Sorry. You probably don't want to know all about their lives. That's my husband, Scott." She pointed to the man in the family picture, a nice-looking guy with a cheesy grin, messy black hair, and wire-rimmed glasses. Casey liked him on sight.

"I didn't mean to snoop," Casey said.

"It's no problem. We don't have anything you shouldn't see. Or, if we do, it's buried under piles of laundry." Which could easily have been the case, seeing how the small sitting room across the kitchen's island had clothes mountains to rival the Rockies.

Betsy tipped a Marshland Elementary lunch calendar to the side to show a picture underneath—the same one Eric had found when they'd looked up Elizabeth's disappearance on the Internet. "Lizzie's last school photo." Her smile faltered. "We used to pretend we were twins sometimes." She looked at the photo for a few more seconds before allowing the menu to hide it again. "Come see what I found."

Betsy and Eric had moved the mess on the dining room table to one side, and Betsy placed two boxes on the cleared end. "This box is just photo albums and stuff from when I was little. Lizzie would be in there, especially before high school, when her mom was still around. After she died, well, it seems like they would have come around more, doesn't it? But Uncle Cyrus sort of …I don't know…it was almost as if he thought he and Lizzie had suddenly become this burden on us. And he was so *angry* about it all. About Lizzie's mom dying. I still saw Lizzie at school, and at church when they'd show up, but it wasn't like it had been."

Casey looked at a photo Betsy put on the table. Elizabeth appeared just about as she did on that last school photo. Cyrus seemed healthy and happy, and the woman—"What was her name?"

"Vivian. Vivvie, Cyrus would call her. To me she was Aunt Viv."

"How did she die? Cancer?"

"Pancreatic. It was like one day she was fine, and the next she was dying. It was terrible. You can't see it in this picture, even though five months later she was dead. I remember, because we all got our family portraits done at the same time, at church, you know, when we made a new directory. The pictures were taken in the fall the year before everything happened with Cyrus and Elizabeth. By the time Christmas came around they didn't even send out the photo with their cards because Aunt Viv looked like a different person by then." She rubbed her finger gently across the photo, then heaved a huge album out of the box. "These are just random shots from when we were kids. This and that. But here—" she turned to the back pages "—this is the nineties, when we were teens. There's Liz and Wayne Greer and me and Scott. I had just found out I was pregnant. I hadn't told Scott yet, but Lizzie knew. She was younger than the rest of us, but she was my cousin, so she hung out with me and my friends."

Betsy looked remarkably carefree in the picture, for having such a heavy secret. Perhaps it hadn't quite sunk in yet. Or perhaps she really didn't care that her "innocent" teenage years were about to come to a crashing end.

"What about Elizabeth and Wayne?" And why did that name sound familiar?

"They weren't actually an item, at least, not yet. If he'd had his way they would've been married already." She laughed. "Not really, but he had it bad for her. I'm pretty sure she was in love with him, too, but you know how it can be when you're teenagers and friends and you don't want to mess things up. This was taken just before her dad lost his job. Aren't too many pictures after that." She paged through. "Look, there's a copy of the one Lizzie took of Uncle Cyrus for that job application."

Cyrus Mann looked serious, but not unpleasant. His hair was slicked back, and he'd shaved, so it must have been after the casual shot by the car. He wore a clean, button-down shirt, and he smiled gently, showing no teeth. His eyes were deep and dark, and revealed a depth of sorrow with which Casey could relate. "Did he get the job?"

"Never found out. It was soon after that he was—he died. It became a nonissue, especially since Lizzie disappeared." She sat down, the enjoyment she'd shown at seeing the old pictures draining away. "So she's really gone? You finally found her, and she's...gone?"

"I'm sorry."

She didn't speak again for a few minutes, while she warred with her emotions. She idly paged through the album, her jaw set in that way people do when they're trying not to cry. Suddenly she stood, put the album back in the box, and pulled the other box closer. "This is what I really wanted you to see." She reached in and took out a folder, which she laid on the table.

It was fat and tattered, with papers sticking out the sides, and scribbled notes on the cover. "I kept a whole file of everything from after it all happened, along with whatever else I could find. It was so…I felt guilty, of course, and sad." She swallowed. "And also scared. If it could happen to Lizzie…" She let out a breath and picked at the folder before finally opening it, revealing a stack of newspaper clippings, hand-written notes, photos, and scrap bits of paper. She held out the top one, and Casey took it. Eric looked over her shoulder. It said simply, "Dad call," along with a number.

"That's my handwriting," Betsy said. "A cop left a message on the answering machine, asking my dad to call down to the station. Didn't say why. I didn't really take any notice. I was a teenager, you know?" She sniffed. "That piece of paper changed my life. Changed all our lives. I dug it out of the trash because, well, I'm not sure why. It just felt wrong to throw it away, like it was any old message."

She took back the paper and laid it face down on the open side of the folder.

"This is the very first news article. *The Denver Post*. First time Marshland had made that paper in ages. Usually they pretend we're not here, since all we have is your usual small town kind of news, but this…I guess it was going to sell papers."

The headline screamed, MAN MURDERED, TEENAGE GIRL MISSING, which was a minor variation of the article Casey and Eric had found earlier.

"If you read it you'll see they make a big deal about the fact that our cops aren't big town, like if only they had been, the murder would have been solved overnight, and Liz would be back home. Or Uncle Cyrus wouldn't have been killed in the first place." She shook her head. "Our cops may work in a small town, but they're smart. And they care about us." She smoothed her hand over the paper, then turned it over to join the scrap message. "It wasn't until the next day that the papers said anything that might have actually been true." She handed Casey another article, and Casey read it.

"It says here he was involved with some shady people," Casey said, referring to a quote from someone who said she saw some people hanging around Mann's car during the previous week. "Do you know who they might be?"

"No idea. But I don't believe it. Uncle Cyrus may have been stubborn, and maybe a little stupid for living in that car, but he wasn't a bad guy. He wouldn't have done anything dangerous. Not with Liz around. He knew if he got desperate he could come to us."

"This person still around?"

"Nope. Died several years ago. I never was quite sure if she was telling the truth, anyway, or just wanted the attention."

"How about your dad? You think he would know who these bad influences were?"

Betsy sat back and pushed the folder toward Casey, who kept it going toward Eric. He pulled up a chair and began going through the stack.

"Dad's around, sure, but I doubt he knew anything. Uncle Cyrus and he really didn't talk much. Dad tried, but…I didn't even tell him about what you said during our phone call yesterday. He gave me the message, and I said I'd take care of it. I was waiting to see…I was hoping…No point in hoping now, is there? I mean, I'm assuming Lizzie didn't have any family we should know about?"

"Not as far as we know. Or my brother knows."

"Your brother?"

"Her boyfriend. The one who's in jail but didn't kill her. The one in the picture."

"Right." She looked at Casey briefly, then stood up. "I guess I should call and tell my father. Or maybe I'll just go over. He's working. The bank." She hesitated. "Do you want to stay here?"

"If you're comfortable with that."

She lifted her hands, then let them fall. "It's fine. Go ahead and look through the box. I'll be back to help with whatever I can."

"Betsy. Thanks."

She nodded. "Whatever I can do for Lizzie."

The door closed behind her, and Casey stood to look in the box. The first thing she saw was a school paper, an essay about "My Dream: Finding a Cure for Cancer." The name on the top was Elizabeth Mann, and the grade was an A+. The teacher had written a note in red, which said:

"Wonderful paper, Elizabeth! Your mother would be proud. It is easy to imagine you being successful in this goal. You will change the world!"

A prophet, she was not.

Chapter Twenty-seven

Casey and Eric sat quietly going through the box contents, speaking only when one of them found something new and interesting. Most of the items were yellowed articles rehashing the bloody facts, delving into Cyrus and Elizabeth's private lives ("What kind of a father has his daughter living in a Chevy?"), and making much of the fact that this "small town" police department hadn't found either the killers or the girl. There weren't even suspects discussed, other than the brief flirtation with Elizabeth. As far as anyone was willing to say, it was someone with a big gun. That about summed up the communal knowledge. Not exactly inspiring. The papers were much freer with the death itself.

"It really does sound like an execution," Eric said. "Shot in the head. Nasty. Think Elizabeth was watching?"

"God, I hope not." It was horrible enough seeing your family die in a flaming car wreck, but at least that wasn't done with evil intent. "If she was, she had to be hiding. They wouldn't have let her live if she'd seen their faces, and they knew it." She stopped.

"What?"

"The Three." Casey shuffled quickly through the remaining papers and photos, looking for anything that might relate.

"Three what?"

"Men. When she was dying she talked about three of them." She pulled out a birthday card, to Betsy, signed by Lizzie, a

Marshland High T-shirt, a bank book, and, finally, a stack of photos. Casey was so busy going through them she didn't realize that Eric had gone still.

"How do you know that?" he said.

"Know what?"

"What she talked about when she was dying?"

"A fair question."

Casey blinked and looked up, surprised to see Death sitting across the table.

"Yes," Death said. "Exactly how *do* you know that? Oh. Right. *I* told you."

"I thought there weren't any witnesses," Eric said. "That they didn't find her until she was dead. *Completely* dead. Not *almost* dead. How would you know what she said when she was dying?"

A sharp pain began behind Casey's eye. Or, actually, it was already there. Now it worsened. "Did I say that?"

"You did."

She and Eric stared at each other, neither one willing to say any more.

"You're going to have to tell him sometime," Death said. "Oh, look, this guy had a mullet."

Casey snatched up the photo Death was indicating. "Who are these guys?"

"Casey." Eric grabbed the photo from her hand. "What aren't you telling me?"

"Nothing. I mean, it's nothing. Really. It's all…in my head."

"Excuse me." Death's voice rose. "In your head? Seriously?"

Eric's jawed worked. "What, exactly, is in your head? How you imagined her death to have happened?"

"Yes. That's it."

"And not how she died after Ricky attacked her and you showed up to clean up his mess?"

"*Eric!*"

"Well, what am I supposed to think? I came along here—and to Colorado in the first place—because I believed in you. I trusted your judgment about your brother, and I really thought you'd killed that guy in self-defense, so I didn't want you to go to jail for it. But you know Alicia's real name, even though the cops don't. You don't go to the police with information. And you claim to know what she said *as she was dying*. How am I supposed to believe anything you say anymore?"

Casey grabbed the photo back. "Whether you do or not isn't what's important right now."

"It's not?"

"It's not?" Death echoed.

"I mean, of course it's important. You know it is. I'm very glad you're along and helping me and everything. But look at this." She shoved the photo in his face. "Who are these men?"

Eric's nostrils flared, and he stared through the doorway to the kitchen.

"Oh, you've done it this time," Death said. "He may not come back from this one."

"Eric." Casey gritted her teeth. "Eric, I'm sorry. I'm an ass, I know I am. It *does* matter what you think, and I appreciate that you came with me, and…"

Death leaned forward. "And?"

"And please forgive me, all right? I really will try to be nicer, just like I said."

Eric's mouth twitched, which Casey chose to take as a good sign. Finally, he let out his breath, rubbed his forehead, and looked at the photo. Cyrus Mann stood with two men outside a restaurant. They stood close together, their expressions serious. Actually, Casey could only see the faces of the other men, one of whom looked at Cyrus, while the other gave a profile shot, looking up the street. Cyrus' back was toward the camera. The photo must have been taken with a telephoto lens, because if the photographer had been close enough to take it life-sized, they would have seen her. The way they stood, sort of tense and secretive, they had no idea their photo was being taken. Plus, the image was a bit grainy, like photos get when magnification is used.

"There are only two of them," Eric said.

"Right."

"You were talking about three."

"So this could be two of the three, couldn't it?"

"I guess. Anything that might identify them?"

Death studied the men with no sign of recognition. "Complete strangers to me, which is odd, if these guys go around killing men and their daughters. You'd think I would have seen at least one of them before. But I guess there's a first time for everything, unless they're always sure to leave their victims alive."

"Dark clothes, dark shoes, dark hair," Casey said. "Pretty nondescript. Could be anybody."

Eric shrugged. "Put it aside. We'll ask Betsy if she knows."

Casey pawed through the rest of the photos, but there were no more of the men. Just shots of Elizabeth with Betsy, with Cyrus, with her mom. A few of school friends, which often included the two teenage guys from the earlier photo Betsy had shown them. Betsy's boyfriend, and Wayne, the kid with Elizabeth.

"Wayne," Casey said suddenly.

"What about him?"

"That's the name she called the dishwasher kid at The Slope. Something about Sammy reminded her of this old boyfriend."

"He's a teenager," Eric said. "And I guess their coloring is sort of the same."

"She slipped. Must have been thinking about him for some reason. But it proves he was someone who mattered to her."

Casey pulled a Marshland High yearbook from the box. "I wonder why Betsy kept this in the box?"

"Why do any of us keep them at *all*? It's not like high school is the time *I* want to remember."

"Because life since then has been so grand?"

He gave a little laugh. "You said it. Do you have yours?"

"Probably. Somewhere in the attic."

"Mine was called, 'Building for the Future,' or something close to that. Had nothing to do with our mascot or anything. But the sponsor was a sap."

Casey laughed. "Ours was something like, 'A Year to Remember.' It's hard to be creative when you're a high school senior—you just want something sentimental, because you think those are the best days of your life."

"Pretty sad."

"I never had a yearbook," Death said. "It's fun to think about, though, even though it would have been a small class. I wonder what Pestilence looked like as a child. Or Famine. Jesus wouldn't be in it, because he actually *was* a child at one point, and would have had his own class. As would Mohammed and Sidhartha—Buddha, I mean. War would be there, I suppose. And I guess..." Death winced and pointed up. " I guess You Know Who would be the principal."

Eric opened the yearbook's cover and looked inside. "This is Elizabeth's book, not Betsy's." He looked up. "Have you noticed that?"

"I see it now. Everything is written to Lizzie."

"No, I mean, do you think Betsy's name is *also* Elizabeth?"

"I guess it could be."

"I'm guessing it probably *is*."

"So?"

"So I wonder why."

"Family name, probably. Nicknames would be a way to keep them separate. Lizzie, Betsy."

"Still seems like it would be confusing."

Death groaned. "Don't even talk about nicknames. I am the victim of a million nicknames, and none of them are nice."

Casey scanned the page. "What year is this? It has to be before high school, if Elizabeth disappeared when she was fourteen."

Eric turned the yearbook over. "1995. The year she went missing. Look, if you read these you can see that all of the notes were people saying they hoped she was all right and she'd be back. It was signed *after* she was gone."

Casey shuddered. "Creepy."

"Or nice. Betsy's way of keeping hope alive."

"Think that's what this was about, too?" She held up some dried flowers and a statue of Saint Anthony.

"Except if she put him in the box it must mean she thought he wasn't doing his job. And now…Elizabeth is finally found, but not really."

She set the statue aside, and Death took a good look at it. "Nope. Not a good likeness. Nose is too small. I tell you, Tony has got quite the honker. Not that there's anything wrong with that. I always marvel that he can find anything, because I can't believe he can look past his nose." Death chortled.

Casey pulled out the last thing in the box, which was a canvas bag, zipped shut. It was filled with things you might expect a teenage girl to have—lip gloss, a brush, a well-worn teenage romance novel—plus some simple necessities, like deodorant, maxi-pads, toothbrush and toothpaste, and even a Walkman, with a Cars CD in it.

"I bet this is Elizabeth's stuff," Casey said. "Think Betsy cleaned out the car afterward?"

"Someone did. But where are all their other things? Clothes, shoes, you know. And when they lost their house, did they lose *everything*?"

"What in the world is this, though?" A cardboard cylinder, like the kind you mail posters in, was stuffed in with the toiletries. Casey pulled out the papers, which turned out to be blueprints. "Looks like cabinet designs."

"Why would Elizabeth have them?"

"Don't know. Maybe she was just holding them for him, since they lived in a car? Or it could be they just got stuck in here afterward, when everything was chaos."

"Someone's coming," Death said.

The front door opened, and Betsy rejoined them. "I told Dad." She sat heavily in a chair. "He didn't want to talk about it."

"Shocked that she was still alive?"

"Stunned. He never said, but I always thought he believed she was dead way back then. That she'd died the same night as Uncle Cyrus."

"Did he say why he thought that?"

"No, but I guess because it was too painful to think otherwise."

"You mean that she'd killed him herself?"

Betsy blinked. "We never thought that."

"Never?"

"No!" She brushed something from her pant leg. "There were always some people who did, but not us. Not her family."

"So what didn't your father want to face?"

Her head snapped up. "What do you think? That she'd been kidnapped, raped, murdered." Her eyes filled again. "Which is what did finally happen, didn't it? Not the kidnapped part, but the other. Why would anyone—" She closed her eyes and pressed her fingers against her mouth, like she had before.

Casey tipped the canvas bag so the opening was toward Betsy. "Elizabeth's belongings?"

Betsy sniffed and opened her eyes. "It's all they would let me have. They took all her clothes, I don't know what they did with them. The car, her schoolbooks, whatever there was in the station wagon, that was all gone, too. Evidence, they said. This was in her gym locker at school, so I guess they sort of forgot about it. Once the teacher found it at the end of the year, the cops had basically given up, so she just gave it to me." She fingered the material. "It's really all I have left of her."

"Know what these are?" Casey showed her the blueprints.

"Uncle Cyrus was working for a houseboat manufacturer when he got laid off, so I guess those are some of his designs. Lizzie was probably keeping them safe in her locker since the car wasn't exactly secure. Not like a house. They'd be for his portfolio, I imagine."

"Speaking of houses, what happened to everything else when they lost theirs? Did they store it somewhere, one of those storage units, or something?"

"Nope. All gone. What wasn't sold in the auction to pay off debts went to Goodwill, if it was worth anything. Or else Uncle Cyrus just got rid of it."

"No pictures? Toys? Nothing?"

"He said it was too painful to see things from their old life."

Eric waved a hand at the photos. "But living in a car was better?"

"It could have been." Casey understood. She'd spent the past few years living as far from her old life in ways much deeper than simple geography. She'd spent nights in train cars, run-down farm sheds, even cornfields. Sometimes that was easier than even the thought of sleeping in the same bed she had shared with Reuben. "Can you tell us who these people are?"

She slid the photo of the two men across the table, and Betsy frowned at it. "Never saw them before." She looked at the date stamped on the back. "Lizzie must have taken this when she had the camera."

"Is there anyone who might know who they are? What about your dad?"

She frowned. "I told you. Uncle Cyrus would never tell him anything. Dad was always complaining about it. So if Cyrus knew these guys I think you'd be better off talking to somebody else. Maybe Wayne."

"The guy from the photo of you four?"

"Yeah. Wayne never let the whole living in a car thing change how much he saw Lizzie, so he knew more about her life than I did after a while. Plus he was a guy, so maybe Uncle Cyrus told him something. Or Lizzie did."

"Think you could get us in touch with him?" It would be good to talk with the one person they knew Elizabeth remembered.

"I can try." She went in the other room, and they could hear her talking. She came back, looking amused. "He says he was already planning on meeting with you."

"What?" Casey looked at Eric. "Did you set something up?"

He was shaking his head at the same time Betsy said, "No, it was his kid, Robbie. He works at the motel. Says you talked to him last night."

Robert. The nonsleeping high schooler. "Right. His dad went to school with Elizabeth. Wait—Wayne is Robbie's dad?

The guy in the picture with the four of you just so happens to be the motel kid's father?"

"I told you it was a small town." Her eyes went distant. "It about crushed Wayne when Lizzie disappeared. He held out for her a long time, but then…" She shrugged. "We all had to go on, didn't we? I mean, that's life. I really thought he'd give up sooner than he did, but I guess some guys can surprise you. I don't think he ever really did let her go. Not all the way."

"*Ahem*," Death said, and pointed at Eric. "Think you've got one of those here, Casey. He's put up with your BS for the entire time he's known you—which, granted, is only a few weeks—and is still here. That's saying something."

"So when are we meeting him?" Casey asked Betsy.

"How does right now strike you?"

Chapter Twenty-eight

"It's been a long time since I've thought about her," Wayne Greer said. He was a good-looking thirty-something man wearing jeans and an Astros T-shirt. Casey could see Robbie in his face, and in the wavy brown hair. He gripped his glass of Coke so hard Casey was afraid it was going to break, and he swiped his other hand across his head, so some of the hair stood up, making him look younger, more like the boy Elizabeth had been falling in love with back in the nineties. Betsy sat next to him in the booth, looming over him in protective woman mode, like this news was going to make him crack.

The photo of Elizabeth—Alicia—and Ricky lay on the table, and Wayne apparently couldn't decide whether to look at it or pretend it didn't exist. "I can't believe she's dead."

"Didn't you already think she was? After all this time?"

"I don't know, I guess I'd always thought she'd made it out somehow. It just didn't feel right that she could be so alive one day and then…it sounds stupid, I know. But they never found her body, and I just didn't *feel* like she was dead. Does that make any sense?"

"Not really," Death said from the next booth over. "But then, I don't make sense to most people, especially when they're in love, or think they are. Did you *see* these cool miniature juke boxes? Right on the tables? Do you have a quarter?"

"You never heard from her?" Casey asked Wayne.

"No." He ran his finger through the condensation that rimmed his glass.

"What about these guys? Do you recognize them?" Casey put the photo of the strange men on the table.

Wayne glanced at it like he couldn't really care any less. "Sure. What about them?"

Eric's knee knocked Casey's, but when she looked at him it seemed he hadn't done it on purpose.

She returned her attention to Wayne. "Who are they?"

Wayne shrugged. "Some guys Cyrus knew. He worked with them, maybe. Liz didn't like them, said they were bossy, and pretty rude to her dad. And she said they always came sort of secret and quiet, like they didn't want anyone else to see them. They got all hinky when I was there once."

"Was there another man who hung out with them?"

"Yeah." He made a face. "Pretty creepy. Never said anything, but was always around when they showed up. Liz couldn't stand him. Actually, if she saw him coming she took off. Said he scared her."

"So were these guys Cyrus' employers?"

"I guess. Not sure, though. Never even heard their names. Or what they did."

"Robbie was telling me about 'bad guys' Cyrus hung out with," Casey said, "but that no one knows for sure what they were doing that was bad. Would he be talking about these three?"

"Robbie?" He gave a half-laugh. "That boy sees criminals everywhere he looks. He'd have half the town in jail if we believed everything he suspected. And that's just the stuff happening now. The town's history is apparently an open booking session."

The waitress came with their lunches, hamburgers and fries for everyone but Betsy, who got a small salad that she didn't even touch. Wayne picked up his burger, then set it down and wiped his hands absently on his napkin.

"So you don't think Cyrus was into anything illegal?" Casey asked.

"I can't imagine it. He was a straight shooter. Wouldn't take charity—wanted to pay his own way, which is supposedly why they lived in a *car*. He didn't drink, didn't do drugs, there weren't any other women…" He looked down at the table for moment, but then shrugged. "Liz didn't seem to mind too much, about the car. She'd spend nights at Betsy's sometimes, and I know he and Liz went to the church to sleep when it got super cold that one week."

Betsy started. "Really? I didn't know. Oh, *why* wouldn't they come stay with us?"

"You know why. And like I said, I think Liz was okay with 'camping out' most of the time. She used the showers at school, and only slept in the car. She could study at one of our houses, or the library. She was okay. I think she felt like she sort of had to take care of her dad, ever since Vivian died. That pretty much destroyed him."

Betsy frowned and crossed her arms, shaking her head.

"Back to these men," Casey said. "Any idea what work Cyrus was doing for them?"

"Something temporary. He kept telling Liz it was just for a while, then those men would be gone. It was something he was good at, probably to do with woodworking. He was a master craftsman, people were lucky if they got something built by him."

"Woodworking? That doesn't sound criminal."

"I told you, it wouldn't have been. Not with Cyrus."

Casey spun the photo around and looked at it again. Elizabeth—Alicia at the time of her death—had said it was the Three. It had to mean these three men, didn't it? "Were these guys questioned after Cyrus was murdered?"

"Maybe. I hadn't seen them around for a while. Cyrus went out of town sometimes, I guess to work, and Liz seemed to think Cyrus' time with them was almost done. I've never seen them since Cyrus died."

"She'd stay with me those nights Uncle Cyrus was gone," Betsy said. "He told her she wouldn't be able to hang out at the work site. I was always glad when she came, but it wasn't often enough."

Eric pulled out his notes. "We didn't see anything in the newspaper articles about these guys, or about the cops even questioning anybody but Elizabeth. In fact, the media got on the Marshland cops for not knowing what they were doing."

"Yeah, well." Wayne frowned. "That was the big time folks thinking they knew more than people they considered hicks. The cops here did everything they could. They knew Cyrus and Liz, so it's not like they didn't want to catch whoever did it. They talked to all of us, all of their family, everyone Cyrus ever worked for. But there was nothing to go on. Forensics weren't the same then as they are now, and the stuff they had just took them nowhere. The bullet couldn't be matched to any guns, there weren't any unknown fingerprints on the car—"

"How do they know that?"

"We all got fingerprinted," Betsy said. "All their friends and family. And there weren't any prints they couldn't match to people who had a reason to be in or around the car."

"Like people they knew couldn't have done it," Death said. "You humans are so loyal. Or stupid. Any luck finding that quarter?"

"There were tons of calls from people who thought they saw Lizzie after that," Betsy continued. "You know, like on cop shows when they set up a line for information. But none of them ever panned out. They were mostly cranks. After a few months the calls stopped coming, and the cops stopped looking."

"They didn't stop look—"

"Wayne, they *stopped.*"

He picked at the placemat that was now sodden from his glass. "What else were they going to do? They put her photo all around, all over the Internet, you know, at least as much as there was. Facebook wasn't around yet—there really wasn't anything like social media, unless you count faxing her picture to cops all over the country. But what else were they going to do? They couldn't buy space on milk cartons for the next however many years it's been since she left."

Like he didn't know the exact number of years—or perhaps months, or even days. The knowledge was there to read in his eyes, and in the lines beside his mouth.

"But that begs another question," Casey said. "She wasn't here, but she was obviously alive."

Wayne looked from the photo of Alicia and Ricky to Betsy. "She really did look just like you."

"Yeah, I know."

They had a sad moment together as they gazed at the picture.

"So where would a fourteen-year-old go?" Casey said. "She would have no license, no vehicle, probably not much money." It sounded, in fact, a lot like Casey's first days on the road, before the settlement had loaded her bank account. Except she'd been a grown woman with resources no teenager would have. "Relatives? Friends somewhere else?"

"They would have told us," Betsy said. "You don't take in a girl and not tell her family where she's gone. Especially not when her father has just been murdered."

"Or maybe that's exactly why they didn't tell," Casey said.

"What do you mean?"

"We don't know where Elizabeth was the night Cyrus died. What if she saw the whole thing? What if Cyrus' killers knew she was there? She wouldn't be safe anywhere. She would have to stay completely hidden. Even if that meant someone not telling."

"But after all this time? Surely they would have said something by now."

"Because the danger had passed? Somehow I don't think it had." She met Betsy's eyes, and Betsy stifled a sob. Obviously the danger hadn't passed. Not if Elizabeth's death was connected to whatever had happened in Marshland back in the 90's.

"We don't know that her...her murder had anything to do with this," Wayne said. "It could have been something else. Some random killer. After this many years she couldn't have been afraid of them anymore. Why would they still be looking for her? It's been so long."

"So why didn't she come home?"

"Any number of reasons. She'd found somewhere better. She'd found some*one*." He used a finger to flick the photo of her and Ricky across the table. "I don't know. Maybe she just didn't want to come back to the place where her father died. Or maybe she was glad for a new start and was happy to be rid of us all."

His voice rose, betraying his anger and hurt. His old girl-friend, whom he'd been grieving for years, had been alive and well—and hadn't told him. Casey could only imagine how much that would sting.

Eric broke the awkward silence. "Betsy, would you have a list of family or friends she might have run to after Cyrus' death?"

She nodded, her face white and tired, as if the past few hours had aged her. No doubt she was feeling the same betrayal as Wayne.

"What about the police who worked on the case?" Eric asked. "Are any of them around anymore?"

Wayne and Betsy looked at each other. "I suppose," Wayne finally said. "Not all of them, of course. I guess the chief was here—but was just an officer. And there were only a few others. Like the papers made very clear back then, this isn't a huge department."

Betsy got up. "I'll go home and see what I can find. Should I call you at the motel?"

"My cell phone," Eric said. "Do you still have the number?" He wrote it out for her, just in case, and also for Wayne. Wayne reciprocated with his own, then scooted out after Betsy, leaving his hamburger and fries. "I should go to work in a couple of hours, but I can skip if there's something I can do. Want me to go by the police department?"

"No," Casey said. "Thanks. What is the chief's name, though?"

"Kay. Chief Kay. Been around since I was a kid. What else?"

"Not sure at this point. We'll be in touch."

Betsy was standing quietly beside the table, almost as if she were in a trance. Wayne touched her back, and she jerked, instantly alert. "Sorry. Sorry, I'm just…" She stopped talking and walked out the door.

Wayne watched her go. "It's been hard on Betsy. She waited for Liz for a long time, they were best friends, you know, besides being cousins. She always believed. Never could quite accept that Liz was gone for good." He tapped the table with a finger, and followed Betsy out the door.

"Well?" Eric said.

Casey waited until Wayne had walked past the window, head down, hands in pockets. "I guess I believe them both. Betsy acted like the three men were complete strangers, and Wayne didn't seem to think much of them." She paused. "They're both hurt and angry."

"That's what happens when people you love disappear with no explanation."

Casey scooted sideways. "I had an explanation."

He looked at her innocently. "Oh, were we talking about you?"

Casey shook her head and finished up her food. When they were both done they eyed Wayne's burger. "Want it?" Eric asked.

"I already feel like a bucket of grease."

"Yeah, me, too."

Casey looked around, expecting Death to put in the usual whining bid for food that was earthly and unattainable, but the booth behind them was empty. The mini juke box, however, was lit up, playing Sarah McLachlan's song *I Will Remember You*. The song wasn't even on the playlist.

Chapter Twenty-nine

Eric paid the bill, beating Casey to the punch, and they left the little restaurant. The heat hit them like a wave, and Eric pulled his shirt from his stomach. "You didn't want Wayne to give us an introduction at the police station?"

"We go in there, they're going to contact the police in Colorado. Then what happens?"

They meandered down the street, discussing their next move.

"We need to let the cops in on it sometime," Eric said. "They have resources we don't. They could make these connections. They might even be able to find those men."

Casey stopped and watched a mockingbird pecking at something in the grass. "I know you're right. It's just, cops and I, we haven't exactly…"

"Been on the same side for a while?"

"Well, yes."

"Do you feel the same about retired cops?"

"What do you mean?"

"If one of the cops from back then became chief, that must mean—"

"—*that* chief would be retired. Unless he's dead."

"Nice."

Casey looked around, hoping to be able to ask Death if the former chief had crossed Death's path, and she went still. She'd seen a man just for a moment before he'd ducked into a doorway.

He wore jeans, a gray sweatshirt, running shoes, and sunglasses. He was about Eric's height, fair-skinned, with blond hair, and he was trim. Late twenties, maybe. And he was obviously spying on them. She turned back toward the mockingbird, although she was not really interested in watching it, anymore. "Don't look around, Eric. I mean, act normal, all right?"

Eric tensed. "Why? What's wrong?"

Casey turned up the sidewalk and resumed walking the way they'd been going. "Come on."

Eric trotted to catch up. "I'm not looking. What is it?"

"We're being followed. *Don't look.*"

"Followed? How do you know?"

Casey didn't answer, instead taking Eric's elbow and leading him down the street that headed to their motel. She tried to make it look like they were just out for a walk, with her hand on the crook of his elbow, but in reality she had an iron grip on his arm so he wouldn't be tempted to turn around. It wouldn't be a secret where they were staying, not in a town that size, so having someone follow them to the motel wouldn't matter.

"Who is it?" Eric's voice was tight.

"Don't know."

"But what if it's one of *them*? One of those three men?"

"Don't worry."

"Seriously? Don't worry? That's why you're cutting off the blood circulation in my arm?"

"It will be fine."

The pharmacy where Betsy worked sat at the end of the block. A safe place. Casey eased Eric in that direction, and they went inside.

The woman who had given Betsy the afternoon off was behind the counter. It took her only a second to recognize them. "Is Betsy with you?"

"No, she needed to go home and check something."

The woman frowned. "Is there anything I can do?"

"Maybe, thanks. We'll let you know."

Casey pulled Eric down an aisle, and heard the woman greet someone else and start talking. It was a one-sided conversation. Casey peeked back and saw she was on the phone, probably calling Betsy.

"Stay here a minute," Casey told Eric. She snuck back toward the front of the store and looked out the window from a protected space in the aisle. No one passed the window or entered the store, so Casey figured whoever was following them had settled in to wait. Casey went back to Eric. "Distract the woman when she gets off the phone, okay?"

"What are you going to do?"

But Casey was already walking to the back of the store. She made sure to keep shelves between herself and the cashier, and looked for another way out. There had to be a second door for fire codes, even if it wasn't used as a public entrance. A tall counter ran the width of the store at the back wall, with a gate to the skinny hallway on the far right side. A man with white hair and a lab coat peered over reading glasses at a computer screen, holding a medicine bottle in one hand and poking at the keyboard with the other. He gave a little grunt, then swiveled the other way and disappeared behind a rack of bottles and boxes.

Casey stepped over the gate and walked quickly back the little hallway, past an empty office, a tiny bathroom—"Employees Only"—and the break room where they'd sat before. Beyond that was an exterior door that said, "Emergency Exit." She pushed the bar, and went out. No alarms sounded. Typical.

She eased the door shut and walked down the alley, back in the direction they'd come. The pharmacy was part of a bank of brick buildings with no opening between them to the street, so hopefully no chance of being seen by their stalker. When she got to the end of the row, she looked around the corner, but the side street was empty except for two moms talking to each other while one toddler pulled on her mom's hand and another leaned over to spit very slowly onto the sidewalk. Casey didn't want to take a chance of still being in front of whoever was following them, so she continued across the street, walked behind a row of houses, and cut back up to the street at the next crossroad. She hoped the women hadn't noticed her, or, if they had, they hadn't wondered too much about what some strange woman was doing in the alley.

A man was standing in front of the bank, not moving, not looking like someone with a check to cash. Casey spotted him immediately, even from that distance. He stood across from the pharmacy in the lee of the bank's awning, facing the big front window of the bank, holding a phone to his ear. The pharmacy would be reflected in the glass. He was very obviously—to Casey, anyway—using the phone as a prop, because he wasn't talking into it, and from his expression he wasn't listening, either. Casey moved closer, wishing she had a phone of her own, so she could call Eric and have him come out so the man would follow him, and Casey could follow the man. But maybe the man would wait for her, instead of going after Eric. No telling. It was irrelevant, anyway, since she *didn't* have a phone.

The man switched his phone from his left ear to his right—his arm was probably getting tired since she and Eric been in the pharmacy so long—which partially hid his face. When Casey got to the crossroad, the two women with the toddlers were walking away from the main street, so Casey didn't have to worry about them giving her away. She used the man's new hand position to get closer to him, crossing the street when she arrived at the angle at which she would start to be reflected in the bank's window.

She walked up behind the man and grabbed his upper right arm, pinching a pressure point to keep him from moving. "Looking for me?"

He jumped, fumbling the phone and dropping it onto the sidewalk, where it landed with a loud crack. His voice was tight with pain. "What do you want?"

"I think I should ask you that."

He glanced around, as if afraid someone would see them together. Or maybe afraid they wouldn't.

"I'm not going to assault you," Casey said. "I just want to talk."

"You *are* assaulting me."

"No, I'm keeping you from reaching for your gun."

"What gun?"

"Please. Who wears a sweatshirt in Texas on a day like this?"

"Don't take it."

"I'm not going to touch it. Like I said, I want to talk."

"About what? I don't know you."

"Exactly."

"What?" He licked his lips and glanced at his phone, where it lay on the ground.

"No one's there," Casey said.

"What?" He was like a broken record.

"You weren't really talking to anyone on the phone. So there's no one there."

A flush crept up his neck, and blotchy red spots stained his cheeks. Up close he looked younger than Casey had originally thought. His lips were a dark pink, and pale freckles were scattered across his nose and cheekbones. He blinked rapidly and straightened his shoulders as much as he could while she still held his arm. "Who are you? What do you want?"

"That's really the way you want to play it?"

He glanced around again, shifting from one foot to the other. "I don't understand."

Casey sighed. "Look. You were following us. I caught you. Now is the time when you tell me why you were doing that."

"I don't have to tell you anything." He clenched his jaw, reminding her of those toddlers she'd seen.

"I could make you." She squeezed harder.

He winced. "You can't. And you'll get in trouble." Again with the toddler thing.

"Who are you going to tattle to?"

His chin trembled. "My boss."

"Your boss? Who's your boss?"

He pinched his lips together.

She moved forward so he could see into her eyes. His were unreadable behind his sunglasses. "Look, I'll let you go, but if

I see you reaching for your gun it won't be pretty. Trust me on that."

He hesitated for only a few seconds before nodding.

She allowed him to yank his arm away, and he rubbed it.

"Yes, my boss sent me. And now I see why."

"Look, I didn't want to hurt you. But I also didn't want to get shot, and didn't want some weirdo catching me at a bad time."

"I'm not a weirdo."

"So who are you?"

He made a slight move, and Casey grabbed his arm again.

"Hey," he said. "I just want to show you something. *Not* my gun."

She narrowed her eyes, but let him move.

He pulled up his sweatshirt to show her a badge clipped to his belt.

Great. "You're a *cop*?"

He nodded, and gave her a very toddler-like smirk. "Which means *you* are in very big trouble."

Chapter Thirty

"I didn't know he was a cop," Casey said for the fiftieth time. "All I knew was he was following us, and I didn't want to get shot."

The woman on the other side of the table, one Chief Rose-anne Kay, watched Casey with flat eyes. She wore a police uniform, dark-blue-rimmed glasses, and a hairstyle that could only be described as, well, *short*. What there was of her hair was salt-and-pepper, with just a little more salt. She finally blinked. Once. "You assaulted a police officer."

"Well, he hadn't introduced himself, had he? In fact, he was going out of his way to *not* look like law enforcement. Jeans, sneakers, sweatshirt. If anything, I guess the sunglasses should have given it away, but you can't blame me for assuming regular Texan citizens might actually use those to block the sun. You can't charge me for something I wasn't even aware of."

"Actually, I can. But the question is, do I want to?"

She had the power. She was the chief. Which meant she'd been on the job when Elizabeth Mann had disappeared.

"What I want to know, Ms.—" The chief made a show of looking over Casey's license yet again. "—Kaufmann, is it?"

Casey hadn't corrected the information printed on the license. She was too annoyed.

"—is what you are doing in our little town."

"You know," Casey said, "you could've just asked, instead of sending a child to spy on me."

The chief's mouth twitched, but Casey wasn't sure if that was from humor or irritation. "Or you might have just come to us."

"Is that the law now? You visit a town and have to check in with the cops before doing anything else?"

"It's not the law. But it might make things easier if you're looking up an old crime. The police do try to protect and *serve*."

"How do you know what I'm looking up?"

"Little birdies told me."

Uh-huh. "I had my reasons for doing this on my own."

"I'm sure you did. Wondering about those reasons was what made me seek you out." She tapped the computer tablet in front of her on the table, on which Casey could see her own picture. "Detective Watts was very helpful, informing me of your recent brush with the law, as well as your proper name, which seems to have missed getting changed on your ID. An oversight, I'm sure. He was also very interested in what you were doing here in Marshland, since the last he'd seen you was in Colorado, where your brother is in jail for the murder of a young woman who looks remarkably like one of my town's citizens. When I told him I believed you were checking out a murder and disappearance from more than fifteen years ago that involved that very family, he became *extremely* interested."

"Look." Casey passed a hand over her eyes. "I've been in here a long time. I've answered all your questions. Do I need to call my lawyer? He'll come if I ask." Actually, she didn't know if he would or not, but it sounded better to be confident.

"You *haven't* answered all my questions, because I haven't asked them all yet. So far I've just been concentrating on the fact that you assaulted one of my officers." She held up a hand. "I know. You didn't realize he was a cop. That's our mistake. Perhaps he should have been in uniform."

"Or perhaps he shouldn't have been stalking me in the first place."

"He wasn't stalking."

"You say armadillo, I say…"

Kay leaned on the table and clasped her hands. "Ms. *Kaufmann*, you're not under arrest. We don't even suspect you of anything criminal. We just…want to help. And if you can help us solve an open case from a past decade, then, hey, we'll take it. But you need to do it without any one else's bodily harm. Or even the threat of it."

Casey sat back and looked at the ceiling, with its old-fashioned, pock-marked tiles. She was tired, hungry, hot, and they hadn't let her call Eric. Not that she knew his phone number. Or had any idea where he was. When she'd realized the man following them was a cop, she knew the only option was to cooperate and go with him to the station. She suggested it, and even began walking that direction. The cop was so taken aback he seemed to forget all about Eric, and was going to leave him there at the pharmacy, even when Eric came out onto the sidewalk and tried to accompany her. The cop was surprised to see him, and refused to let him in the car, which had arrived to pick them up and deliver them the whole four blocks to the police station. The cops had not told her anything other than that Eric was fine, and she'd be seeing him soon enough.

Kay was waiting, her gray-blue eyes not moving from Casey's face.

"Where's my friend Eric?"

"He's fine."

Casey shot up from her chair and paced around the room. She stopped at the far end, her back to Kay. "If I answer your questions, will you let me go?"

"As long as you don't implicate yourself in anything criminal."

"So I *should* call my lawyer."

"If you want to wait till tomorrow for him to get here."

"Just answer the questions, sweetheart." Death sat beside Chief Kay, syncing Kay's computer notes onto an iPad. "She's got nothing to hold you here, but she really would like to get Cyrus Mann's murder out of her in-box. It's been cluttering up the place forever and has gathered a lot of dust."

"You have Mann's folder on your desk?" Casey said, spinning around.

"Well, I do now. We had to dig it out of storage when you started nosing around this morning. We're pretty organized, actually, so it wasn't that hard to find. It's like a historical document, though. I thought it might evaporate when I touched it."

"I'll go scan whatever's visible," Death said, and was gone.

"But now I guess we have something new to add to it," Kay said. "The missing daughter has now been found."

Casey thought about that, about Elizabeth Mann lying dead in her Colorado apartment under someone else's name, with no one to say where she'd been, what she'd seen, or who she had become during the past decade. About all of that lost time. Were those years as empty as they appeared, or had Elizabeth somehow made a life for herself amidst the running?

I was here.

A lonely cry, pressed onto a bathroom mirror. A sentiment she thought no one else would understand. Or even see. Casey sat down and looked Chief Kay in the eye. "All right. What do you want to know?"

Chapter Thirty-one

"What I still don't understand is how you knew to come to Marshland."

Casey had already told her everything else she knew, which wasn't much. She explained about Ricky, and the things he'd said, how he'd figured out Alicia was from Texas. She'd mentioned the way the man had said, "Ya'll" to the cook at the Slope. And she'd showed her the photos, of both Alicia and Ricky, and Alicia's dad.

"That is Cyrus Mann, right?" Casey pointed at the one of him and the car.

"Of course it is. But I don't see how that—"

"And what about this?" She'd saved the one of the other men talking to Cyrus, for last. "I have a feeling if we showed this to the cook, he might recognize one of them."

Kay looked at the photo with surprise. "Where did you get this?"

"Betsy."

"You think these men are somehow responsible for Liz's death?"

"Could be. She didn't like them back when she was a teenager; the one guy she avoided at all costs, apparently. They haven't been seen since Cyrus' murder, but we know he was into something with them around that time. Wayne seems convinced Cyrus wouldn't have done anything criminal, but people have been wrong before."

"Wayne Greer?"

"You know we talked to him. Your officer followed us from the diner where we had lunch with him."

Kay nodded, with what might have been the beginning of a smile. "Just making sure." She took the photo. "You know the name of the cook?"

Doofus. "Pasha. Don't know the last name. Terrible cook, though."

"Very important information, I'm sure." Kay took the photo. "Anyone else see this guy?"

"Just the cook."

"What about Circus Lady?" Death had returned. "You know, Ricky's neighbor, who saw the guy with the shirt?"

Casey kicked herself. She had forgotten all about the planted shirt.

"See if Watts can ask my brother's neighbor. Her name is Geraldine, don't know her last name. She lives across the street."

"She saw him?"

"Maybe." Casey explained what Geraldine had told her about the man from "Hometown Interiors," and how she caught him coming from Ricky's house. "The cops think he was legit, but my brother said he hadn't hired anybody to do anything."

Kay considered it. "All right. I'll be back." She left, shutting the door firmly behind her.

"She's not going to let it go," Death said, "the question of why you're here. Not forever. She's going to keep asking about your source until you tell her something."

"I guess I'll have to be creative."

"Because God knows you wouldn't want to tell her the truth."

"And end up in the loony bin? No, thank you."

"I'm just saying…Anyhow, here's what I found on her desk. There were stacks of papers I couldn't go through, but these photos were on top."

Casey cringed. The first shot was of Cyrus Mann's body with a hole through his cheek. His eyes stared up, the light gone from them. The second was of the car, blood splattered all across the side panels and windows. Mann lay on the ground, his arms flung out, one of them resting against the front tire. His legs were bent, as if he had collapsed right where he'd been standing when he was shot.

"God, I hope Elizabeth didn't see this."

Death pulled the iPad back and looked at it sadly. "Casey, honey, you know she did. She was holding him when he died."

"Wait. So whoever killed him shot him, then left him for dead—did they realize he was still alive?"

"It didn't matter. They knew he didn't have long. You don't live long when you have a hole in your head."

"Which really has to mean Elizabeth *was* there when it happened. There was no time for her to arrive from somewhere else and find him alive. So the question becomes not whether or not she was there, but whether or not they *saw* her." She couldn't believe that. "It seems impossible. If they saw her, how did she possibly get out of there alive?"

Death shrugged. "Fast runner?"

Kay returned without the picture, but with a stack of fat files. "We're faxing the photo to Detective Watts. He'll take it over to the restaurant and see if the cook can recognize the man, even though he would have aged a lot by now. And he'll run over to your brother's neighbor." She sat down. "You realize you still haven't told me how you knew to come to Marshland. Or even what Elizabeth's real name was."

"Here we go," Death sang.

"Lucky, I guess," Casey said.

Kay nodded. "Um-hmm. And how is that?"

"Ricky had already figured out the Texas part."

"Right."

"We have the photo of Cyrus and his car."

"Which has nothing on it to indicate it was even in Texas, let alone a specific location."

"We searched for missing women from Texas."

"Of which there are thousands if you go back that far."

"I don't know, Casey," Death said. "I think she's got your number."

"It was everything together," Casey said. "And my lawyer and I were talking about how her false name—you can ask the cops, they thought it was a false name, too, since they couldn't find anything on Alicia McManus—and how people often choose something sort of like their real name. When we saw the name Elizabeth Mann, it sort of stood out."

"Wow," Death said. "That's actually a pretty good argument. But at the same time it's a bit lame."

Kay looked steadily at Casey. After a while she said, "Okay. I'll accept that for now."

Casey tried not to look too relieved. "So can I ask some questions?"

Kay gestured for her to go ahead.

"Why were there never any suspects, other than Elizabeth?"

"We talked to a lot of people."

"But no one seriously."

"Who's to talk to? People in this town? Nobody here would shoot down someone they know. They aren't like that."

"Kay, this is *Texas*. Everybody has a gun. Or two. You telling me they aren't going to use them?"

"Yes, of course our citizens own guns. But these are law-abiding neighbors. We don't have gangs or the mafia or even drugs, other than the random weed. Our folks aren't resolving their differences by shooting each other. They have guns in their houses to protect their homes and families from outsiders."

"By owning deadly weapons that can be turned just as easily on them?"

"Oh, boy," Death said. "Are we really going to get into this argument? I don't think you can win it. Not down here."

"You were asking about suspects," Kay said. "And there just weren't any to be found. The gun forensics didn't match up with anything we have on file. No one saw strangers that day, certainly not these men on the photo, and there wasn't anybody in town who wanted Cyrus dead. We may have wanted him locked up, but not dead."

"Locked up? Why? From how Wayne talked, Cyrus was a straight arrow."

"From a hormonal teenage boy's perspective he might have been. He put up with Cyrus because he was in love with Elizabeth. Even sixteen-year-old boys get snookered when they're horny. Or maybe I should say *especially* sixteen-year-old boys."

"But what was Cyrus into? If you had reason to lock him up, why was he still free?"

"It wasn't that he was a criminal. But he was living in a *car*. A lot of us wanted to lock him up for child endangerment."

"Betsy said he didn't want to take charity. And that Elizabeth was the one who chose to live in the car instead of with Betsy."

"I'm sure that's what Betsy's father told her." She rested her elbows on the table. "Cyrus was a woodworker. A good one. Just the year before he'd had his own business, making custom furniture, but apparently he was never good with the money end of things, so he ended up selling out right in the middle of his wife's illness. I'm sure the stress did him in. He got another job right away, over on the Gulf with some people who built luxury houseboats—"

"As if there's any other kind," Death said. "You ever see a poor person with a houseboat?"

"—and that was a good start, but he lost that job within a few months. It was like something had switched off in his head. His bad business decisions expanded into bad personal decisions, and the next thing we knew, he and Elizabeth were living on the street, and he was working shady jobs."

"Couldn't you do something about their living arrangements? Aren't there laws—child services, or whatever?"

"Believe me, we did our best. Chief Zinn, who was here before me, he was friends with Cyrus, with his parents, actually, and he did everything to get him to be sensible, but there was something about it…" She shook her head. "Elizabeth didn't help. She said she was staying with her dad no matter what, and she didn't mind living in the car."

"So you let a fourteen-year-old make her own housing decisions?"

"You weren't here!" Chief Kay clenched her fists, then opened them as she breathed out a steady breath. "It wasn't cut and dried. They needed each other. What it really boiled down to was taking Elizabeth away from Cyrus, and no one was prepared to make that choice. Not even his brother. So don't judge us. It's a small town and we take care of each other. Or at least we try."

"Who exactly is she trying to convince?" Death said.

"So again," Casey said, "back to the whole no suspects thing. You're saying no one in town would want him dead, but at the same time you're questioning what he was into. Makes sense to me that it could have been people from that part of his life."

"We checked it out, but as I said, we had no hard evidence of anything he was doing, and nobody was seen here that day. No one knew the names of people he was associated with—including these men—and Elizabeth wasn't around to ask. Nothing in Cyrus' car gave us any names, and forensics turned up nothing but locals. That's why I was interested to hear that Wayne was talking about the men."

"He didn't give us names, and he only mentioned them because we found this photo in the middle of Betsy's stack of mementos. All he said was that Elizabeth didn't like them, which I would assume he'd have told you folks back when this all happened."

Kay flipped through some pages. Each time she turned one over, Death snapped a picture.

"Just because Elizabeth didn't like them didn't mean they were killers," Kay said.

"True. But it could have been a clue."

Kay's nostrils flared, but she kept looking through the pages. "We aren't complete idiots, you know. The papers aren't always right."

"I know. I'm sorry. Is there any chance Elizabeth contacted anyone over the years and they didn't tell?"

"Can't imagine who that would have been. Betsy would have been the one, and if not her, Wayne. Either one of them would have told *someone*."

"Unless they had something to do with it all, and they didn't want Elizabeth to bring it all back up again."

"Her cousin and her boyfriend? Please."

"Betsy says he wasn't her boyfriend."

"Maybe not officially. But they were together all the time. He spent a lot of time in that car."

"So his fingerprints would have been all over, and no one would have questioned it."

Kay stopped with the pages and looked up. "You think Wayne Greer killed Cyrus?"

"It could explain a lot."

"Like?"

"Like why Elizabeth was at the crime scene but didn't get killed. Why she ran away and didn't tell. Why he's only now telling about these men."

"But what reason would Wayne have had to murder his girlfriend's—or even just a good friend's—father? And why on earth would Elizabeth let him get away with it?"

"She's too close to it," Death said. "She can't see the forest for the very prominent trees."

"I think everyone in this town is overlooking what could be a huge issue," Casey said.

"And I suppose you are going to enlighten us?"

"What if something really did switch off in Cyrus Mann's mind? What if he really had gone over to the dark side one way or another? Maybe Elizabeth was ready to take charge of her own life."

"By killing her own father?"

"No, I don't see that. What I do see is her talking to her boyfriend about it. He could see how it would bother her, living in a car, or seeing her father fall apart. You called him a hormonal teenager. You don't think he'd do whatever he could to protect her? Or at least get in her pants?"

Death *tsked*. "We're getting a little crude, aren't we?"

Casey leaned forward. "It could have been an accident. Did Cyrus own a gun?"

"No."

"You sound very certain."

"I am. When he died he had no guns registered to his name. And no unregistered ones in his car."

"So being a completely sane and law-abiding citizen there would be no way for him to have one that was off the record."

"You think he had a gun?"

Casey threw up her hands. "How do I know? I'm just throwing out possibilities which apparently you people were afraid to look at all those years ago. Or too blind to look at."

Kay stood up so suddenly her chair tipped backward and fell onto the floor with a *crack*. "I think we've talked enough for today."

"Thank God." Casey stood, too.

"You think you're leaving?"

"I know I'm leaving. Unless you're going to arrest me."

It was obvious that the thought wasn't an unpleasant one, and for a moment, Casey was afraid the chief was actually going to do it.

Instead, Kay said, "Rules." She held up a finger. "No more assaults."

"Fine."

Second finger. "I want to be kept informed. If you find out anything new, no matter how small, I want to be told."

"Okay." How was Kay going to know? Easy promise to not keep.

Third finger. "No harassing the citizens. If I find out you're bothering people I will put an end to it."

Casey held up her hand, as if she were swearing in. "I promise to be a good tourist."

Kay shook her head. "Now get out of my house before I change my mind."

So Casey fled.

With dignity.

Chapter Thirty-two

"I thought they'd never let you out." Eric was waiting in the lobby on the other side of the bulletproof glass, and put his iPad aside.

"You and me both." The sight of his smile gave Casey's weary heart a lift. How had this man, whom she'd known for less than a month, become someone who could set her pulse racing? She wanted to press up against him right there in the police station, and feel his strong arms around her back. It was crazy. Where was any sense in that? She stood in front of his chair, looking down into his face. "Did they question you, too?"

"Only for an hour or so. Apparently you get treated differently when you assault a police officer."

"I didn't—" She cut off when she saw his grin.

"Come on." He stood. "Let's get out of here."

They were on the opposite side of town from their motel, but seeing how the entire town was only a few blocks long it wasn't a hardship.

"All that questioning made me hungry," Casey said as they walked. "But I don't think I can stomach that diner again."

"Great minds, and all that," Eric said. "I found us a place a few miles down the road."

"You know they're going to be watching. Some infant cop will probably try to stop us from leaving town."

"And you're going to let him?"

Casey looked back as they left, only to see Death gesturing frantically toward the police station. "I'm going to stay. See if

I can get photos of the rest of the file. Now that you've asked those questions, she's got to go through it all again. I'll be in touch. Yikes! She's starting!" And Death was gone.

Casey and Eric got back to their rooms, washed up, and headed out in the rental car. He made a detour down a side street and parked at the edge of a community park. Parents were out playing with their kids for this last hour before bedtime, and the air was filled with shrieks and laughter. To one side a small group of boys, from about nine to thirteen years of age, were arguing, one of the bigger ones holding a football, with one of the smaller boys in his face. As Casey watched, they worked out their differences, as boys will do, and began to play.

"What are we doing here?"

"You know that photo of Cyrus with his car? This is where he parked it."

"I hadn't even thought to check it out. It's not like there will be anything left to discover."

"Still. Want to take a quick look?" He led her down the path to the far corner of the park, which was wooded, with a moss and birdpoop-covered picnic table, alongside one of those grills that was more rust than metal, and which no self-respecting cook—or person who wanted to avoid tetanus—would ever use. On the edge of the trees was a scraggly lawn, and beside that was a small, unused parking lot, whose asphalt had become more a mine of cracks and weeds than an actual level slab. Casey pulled the photo from her pocket and tried to line it up with landmarks.

Eric pointed to the left, where the grass met the pavement. "The cop I spoke to said Cyrus was killed right about here. He and Elizabeth would park the car in the corner spot, use the picnic table for eating, and those restrooms." A still-used, and probably updated, building sat across the park. From that distance Casey could just see the "Boys" and "Girls" signs above the opposite sides.

"Cyrus was found half-on, half-off the asphalt," Eric continued. "As far as the cops knew, the car hadn't been burgled. His and Elizabeth's supper still sat on the picnic table."

"What about her things? Did she take anything with her?"

"Apparently not. When the family went through the car they couldn't think of anything that was missing."

"So when she ran, she was really doing just that. No coming back for stuff." It wasn't hard for Casey to imagine the fear, or the grief. Watching her father die, knowing her own life was at risk. Running away with his blood on her clothes. "I wish we could go back. Protect her. Protect them both."

"World would be a different place if we could do that."

Casey felt suddenly chilled, and slipped her hand into Eric's. If he was surprised, he didn't show it. He squeezed her hand, and his warmth flowed up her arm, until she was ready to leave that place. Soon, without having to discuss it, they let go of each other and walked back to Eric's car.

Nobody tried to keep them within the town limits, and no one followed as they drove. Eric's phone stayed quiet while they had a pleasant dinner at a family seafood restaurant, and they didn't talk much until they'd finished eating and were back in the car.

"Now what?" Eric pointed the car back toward Marshland. "Nap?"

"I wish. Bed sounds good." He immediately went red, and Casey felt herself go hot, as well.

"Sleep will come soon enough," she said, trying not to show her discomfort, and failing miserably, she was sure. "How about Betsy? Should we go by her place and see if she was able to get a hold of any relatives?"

"Sure. Sounds great."

They drove in silence until they parked in front of Betsy's house.

"Casey—"

But she couldn't talk about what was happening between them. Not then. Maybe not ever. She got out of the car and walked up to Betsy's door. Once she rang the doorbell she heard Eric's car door close, and his footsteps come up the walk.

A man answered the door. "Oh, you must be Casey and… Eric, is it? It's them, honey!" he called toward the back of the house. "I'm Scott, Betsy's husband. Well, that's kind of obvious, isn't it?" He laughed. "Kind of weird if I wasn't, huh? Come on in." He wore khakis, a light blue, button-down shirt, and slightly crooked wire-rimmed glasses. He was in stocking feet, and his dark hair stuck up in the back, cowlicks gone wild. "We're just finishing up dinner. Are you hungry?"

"Just ate, thanks."

"Come on back, if you don't mind watching us eat. It's not always pretty." He grinned and led them back through the dining room to the kitchen. Amusement lit Eric's eyes, and Casey herself found it hard not to laugh. It didn't seem exactly kosher to be giggling, what with Betsy's long-lost cousin being dead and all, and Casey's brother in prison, but Scott exuded a cloud of good cheer. Her heart lightened—in a completely different way from when she looked at Eric—and she wondered what Scott would be like on a normal day. They'd probably all be on the floor, clutching their sides.

Betsy sat at the table with a teenage boy and a young girl. Casey couldn't remember their names, but just from looking at them it was obvious they were related to Elizabeth. The girl looked just like her mother—and, therefore, her aunt—and the boy was basically a younger version of Cyrus. It was eerie how familial characteristics could hop from great-uncle to great-nephew, and she wondered if Betsy even saw it.

Scott pulled a couple of chairs in from the dining room and made room at the small table. The remnants of baked spaghetti and garlic bread looked good, even though Casey was full, and she wondered how long it had been since she'd had an actual home-cooked meal.

"So you're the ones who found Aunt Lizzie?" the boy said.

"Billy!" Betsy went to touch his arm, then jerked her hand back and clenched her hands in her lap.

Billy. Casey remembered now. And the girl's name was something different. Julie? Janie? *Junie.*

Casey looked into the boy's face and saw some of the same strength—and uncertainty—she'd met in a whole group of teens a couple of weeks earlier. Those strong-willed Kansans had proven to her that young people deserved answers. And truth. Even if they were a mess of rampaging hormones. "We didn't actually find her, Billy. Her landlord did. But we figured out who she was."

"And she's dead?"

"I'm sorry."

He shrugged. "She was gone before I was born."

"Yes, I know. I never met her, either."

"Then why do you care who killed her?"

Junie was listening with wide eyes, her mouth slightly open, as if it was taking all her concentration to follow along. Casey wondered about continuing with the conversation in front of her, but figured her parents were sitting right there, and they should be the ones to put a stop to it, or send her to her room. Perhaps they figured the whole answers and truth thing extended to pre-teens, as well.

"My brother Ricky loved her," she said. "They were seeing each other. Romantically." What did teenagers call it anymore? Dating? Going out? Hooking up?

"So why isn't he here? Or is this him?" He gestured at Eric.

"Sorry," Eric said. "I'm here for Casey. We're…friends."

Billy looked at them knowingly, so Casey rushed to continue before he had a chance to remark on what he'd already figured out, which was apparently more than they had. "The cops think Ricky killed her."

Billy took in this information stoically, working at something in his teeth with his tongue. "You don't think he did?"

"I *know* he didn't."

"Because he's your brother?"

"Well…yes."

"And you're trying to find out what happened so you can get him out of jail?"

"Yes. He's a mess. He loved her a lot, apparently, and this is all just—" She was going to say, killing him, but stopped herself in time. "It's been really hard for him."

Billy watched her a little longer, then nodded. "Okay."

Okay. Law enforcement, Elizabeth's co-workers, the media, they all doubted Ricky's innocence. This kid in Texas, who didn't know Ricky from Adam, but could see how his mother was hurting from the final loss of her cousin, believed it instantly. Casey wanted to hug him.

"You think she was killed by somebody from here." He was watching her closely.

"That's my guess. She was obviously in hiding. I guess she could have been running from something that happened later, but this is where it all started."

"You think somebody here found out where she was."

"It looks that way."

"How could they have? I mean, if Mom didn't know, after all this time. The cops, the papers, no one knew, no one could find her."

Casey glanced at Betsy, then said as gently as she could, "I think people had pretty much stopped trying, Billy. It's been a long time."

Scott rubbed Betsy's shoulder. "Tell them what you found out today, hon."

She sat frozen for a moment, then patted her mouth with a napkin and pushed herself back from the table. "I'll show you."

Billy followed them into the dining room, where the boxes of memorabilia still cluttered the table. Junie stayed behind with her father, and Casey soon heard the clanking of dishes and silverware.

"I called everyone I could think of who Elizabeth might have known." Betsy handed Casey a handwritten list of names and numbers, all checked off, some with numbers crossed out, and new contact information noted beside them. "Grandparents, aunts and uncles, family friends, her folks' college roommates, even kids we met at summer camp…I couldn't find anyone who took her in or who she even approached for help."

"Or who would admit it," Casey said. "It might be embarrassing now to say after all these years that they knew she was alive, when they know her family had been wondering all this time."

"No, I believe them. No one heard from her, no one saw her, no one had a *clue* where she'd gone. It was like she completely disappeared off the face of the earth. Until now."

"How could that happen?" Eric said. "How could a teenage girl—and a *young* teenager, not like eighteen or nineteen—hide out that well and for that long? Don't shelters and hostels and things like that have to report runaway teens, or wouldn't they watch the news? Even bus drivers, cops in other towns, you know. Isn't there a network?"

"Sure, there's a network," Casey said, "but this is a huge country, and there are thousands of homeless teens. Cyrus probably had some cash in the car, or had hidden some in another place. Especially if he was mixed up with some folks who weren't exactly above-board. Elizabeth could have grabbed the money when she ran, and used it to hop a bus or train or something that would take her far away from here. It's not that hard to disappear if you really want to, and back then they wouldn't have insisted on ID like they do now. But even today, use a fake name, lie about your age, it's amazing what you can get away with."

Eric looked surprised for a moment, then smiled gently. "Fake names. I remember those. And it's not like fake IDs are that hard to come by, even for kids."

"She was only fourteen!" Betsy said.

"I'm seventeen," Billy said. "You don't think I could disappear if I wanted?"

"I certainly hope not!" She grabbed his arm. "What are you talking about?"

"Mom, don't freak out." He pushed her away. "I'm not going anywhere. I'm just saying. Sometimes people have reasons. Sometimes things aren't what you think. Sometimes people just want…" He shrugged. "Never mind."

Casey watched the panicked mother, and the son. Something about the son…

"Billy," Casey said, "what is it?"

He chewed his lip, looked back at the kitchen, and shoved his hands in his pockets. Emotions ran crazily across his face—stubbornness, anger, fear, and finally worry, or was it sorrow? His eyes shone with tears.

"Billy?" Betsy placed her hand on his arm again, this time with gently. "What is it, honey?"

"It's my fault." His lips trembled.

"What is?"

"That Aunt Lizzy's dead."

"Honey, it couldn't possibly be—"

"What happened, Billy?" Casey saw it in his face. He really thought he was to blame. "What did you do?"

He hesitated, then lifted his eyes to meet hers. A lone tear escaped and dripped down his cheek. "I saw her. I saw Aunt Lizzie. And then I sort of told them where she was."

Chapter Thirty-three

The room went still.

"You saw Lizzie?" Betsy whispered. "*My* Lizzie?"

He nodded miserably.

"Where? When?" She shook him, and her voice rose. "Why didn't you tell me?"

Scott came from the kitchen and gently pried her away. "It's all right, Bets, come on, now."

"It's not all right! He saw her! He saw Lizzie!"

"I'm sorry, Mom. I'm sorry." Billy was crying openly now. "I should have told you, but she said not to. She said I should just leave things like they were, and it would be better for everybody. Better for you. I didn't know she was going to *die*!"

"Where did you see her?" Anger flashed from Betsy's eyes. "She came here? She approached you, and not…not me?"

"I don't think she meant for me to see her."

"Oh, that's even *better*."

"Betsy…" Scott spoke quietly, but firmly. There was no hint of his inner child now. Betsy opened her mouth to say something else, and then her face crumpled, and she leaned forward, burying herself in Scott's shoulder.

Eric had found a tissue box somewhere, and held it out to Billy. The boy grabbed one, and rubbed his face and nose.

"Can you tell us about it?" Eric asked.

Billy sniffed and backed up against the wall, crossing his arms over his chest. Scott was rocking Betsy, and Junie stood in the doorway, her eyes even wider than they had been at the dinner table.

"I was at school," Billy finally said. "It was the end of the day, like a couple weeks ago, and I was walking out. I thought I saw you, Mom, and I wondered what you were doing there. But you turned and walked away, and you were wearing this dark trench coat kind of thing that I know you don't have, and that was really weird, and I wondered—" He made a face. "I wondered if you were spying on me, or something, so I followed you."

"I wasn't spying on you—"

"Well, I know that now, don't I?" He shoved his hands farther into his armpits and stared at the floor. "I followed her down the sidewalk toward our house, and there were a lot of us around, you know, since school just let out, so I don't think she saw me at first, but she kept looking back, and when it was pretty much just us left, after most everybody else went to their cars or down their streets or whatever, I couldn't really hide. She stopped a little bit, then turned and walked faster. I tried to keep up, but she went around a corner, there by the pharmacy, so I ran, but when I got there, she was gone. I was going to ask you about it, but I don't know, I felt strange about it, so I didn't."

"Oh, Billy, I wish—"

"I wish, too, Mom, okay?"

"No, I mean—"

He held up his hand. "Let me finish. So I come home and we have dinner and whatever, and I have soccer practice, and I come back and shower and do homework and you go to bed and it sort of became this thing that I was probably just imagining, so I sort of, well, forgot about it." He licked his lips. "But then the next day I was on my way to school and it was like I knew someone was watching me. When I got to town I went around the corner at the bank and went into the little entryway there, you know how it juts back? They weren't open yet, so nobody was in there to ask me what I was doing, so I waited, and next thing I knew she was coming around the corner. She was wearing that same black trench coat, and she looked just like you,

Mom. I stepped out in front of her. I thought she was going to take off, but she just stood there, staring at me."

He swallowed, and looked past us all, out through the dining room door to the front room.

"What happened then?" Eric asked.

"I knew who it was. I mean, it had to be her, right? I've heard about her my whole life, not just from family, but from other people, too. Even at school, sometimes, our own town's unsolved mystery, you know? Plus, I've seen that photo on the refrigerator. Who else looks that much like Mom? But before I could say anything, she goes, 'You look just like him.' I'm like, 'Who?', and she says, 'My dad. Your Uncle Cyrus.' I'm starting to say, 'I don't have an Uncle Cyrus,' but then I stop, because I know who she's talking about, and I say, 'I do?' She looks around, like she's worried about somebody seeing us, you know? And she pulls me farther back, sort of behind one of the pillar things, and she looks at me like she can't believe I'm standing there. I ask her why she's here, and where she's been, but she shakes her head and says it doesn't matter and all that matters is that I'm safe and my mom is safe, and do I know who Wayne Greer is and if he's happy."

"Wayne?" Scott sounded surprised. "Why was she asking about him?"

Betsy gave him a sweet, sad smile and patted his cheek. "She was in love with him, honey."

"But I thought…"

"She wasn't sure yet, but Wayne had it bad for her—"

"Well, I knew that."

"—and she was afraid."

"Of Wayne?"

"Of losing their friendship."

Scott rolled his eyes. "I *hate* it when girls say that."

"Anyway," Casey said. "What then?"

Billy blinked rapidly, like his brain was clicking back to that spot in the story. "I told her what I knew about Wayne. I'm friends with, I mean, I know Robbie, so I know who his parents are—and about Mom and Scott, and how they got married young because of me and how we have Junie, too." He glanced at her in the doorway and gave her the sweetest smile that about broke Casey's heart. "I asked her what she was doing back home, and why didn't she come over, and said that in a few minutes Mom would be just across the street in the pharmacy and she could say hi. But she said she couldn't, it wouldn't be safe, that it wasn't safe for her to be talking to me, and that I shouldn't tell anybody, not Mom, not Wayne, not anybody, that it would have to be a secret, but she had to come home and see it for herself one more time. I asked her why it wasn't safe, and she got all sad and said she was sorry, and that she loved me, and that I should be happy and be kind and…" He shrugged. "She got all choked up. I asked again where she'd been, and she just said, 'Around.' I asked her where she was living now and she said it was beautiful, and the sky was bluer than blue, and there were mountains that would take my breath away, and she wished she could take me skiing, but she couldn't afford it, and it wouldn't be safe, even if she could. Somewhere…somewhere in Colorado." He stopped suddenly, like he'd run out of breath, or words, or both.

"She told you where she was?" Casey was surprised. So either she was planning to move on soon, so the information wouldn't be relevant anymore, or she really was going to stay and make a life there. One way she had lied to Ricky, and the other way she was ready to give up the fear.

"What else did she say?" Betsy asked. "Did she give you a message for me?"

He looked at his mother. "She said I couldn't tell you that she'd been here or where she was living. She said she never should have told me that. That if I told anybody it would put us all in danger; her, too. She hadn't meant to talk to me, at all, but maybe it was meant to be, for her to have contact with at least one person in her family. She made me swear I wouldn't tell, and she looked so scared I promised."

"You're not supposed to keep secrets from us." Betsy broke away from Scott. "We're supposed to be the ones you tell everything to."

Casey held in a laugh. What teenager told his parents everything? She certainly hadn't. "Was that it, Billy?"

He turned toward her quickly, glad for the reprieve. "She grabbed me, gave me a big hug, told me again to be happy and love my family, and then she left. I mean, she looked around some more, like she was all worried about somebody seeing us, then practically ran away." His lips trembled again. "And now she's dead, and it's all my fault." He curled over, like he was trying to protect himself.

"Come here, Billy." Eric pulled out one of the chairs at the table. "Sit down, bud, before you keel over." He led the boy to a chair, where Billy sat down and put his hands on the side of his face, hiding himself from the rest of the room.

Eric sat next to him, a hand on his back. "It's not your fault. She's the one who came here. You didn't ask her to."

He shook his head, still looking at the floor. "No, it's not because she came here. It's because of me. If it hadn't been for me she'd be fine."

"Billy," Eric said. "Tell us what happened."

Billy shuddered, but didn't take his hands away from his face. "It was last week sometime. This guy found me at school. They called me to the office and said he wanted to talk to me."

"At school?" For the first time, Scott sounded alarmed. "Who was he?"

"He said he was a cop and he was there about Aunt Lizzie. That he had some information that there were people after her, and he was wondering if I could help by telling him where she might have kept her things before she died. I told him that anything she had was my mom's now, but he said there must have been somewhere else."

"What day was this?" Casey regretted the sharpness of her voice, but this was a whole new ballgame.

"I don't know. Monday, maybe. Yeah, just this past Monday, because it was the start of the week and I was tired."

So he had come after Elizabeth was already dead.

"Did he give you his name?"

"I guess. He showed me a badge, but I don't remember. I didn't want to tell him about her being here, so I said Aunt Lizzie had disappeared before I was born, so why would he come to me for information, but he didn't go for it. He said he knew I'd had contact with her just the week before, and that she was in danger, and he wanted to help her. The only way he could was by finding something she'd lost. I asked him what it was, but he said I didn't need to know. I'm not sure how I was supposed to help him find it if he wouldn't tell me."

All of the adults started to speak, but Eric held up his hand and leaned toward Billy, speaking calmly. "How did they know you'd seen her?"

"I don't know." He shook his head. "I don't *know*. Maybe they saw us?"

"Did you tell anybody?"

"She told me not to—"

"Billy, it's important. *Really important.* We're not going to be angry. It's not your fault, okay? Elizabeth's death is *not your fault.*" He paused, then asked again. "You didn't tell him about seeing her? Or anything she said?"

His whole body shook with his response. "I didn't tell him anything. I said I didn't know her. That I'd never known her. He said he'd be back to talk to me if he couldn't find out from someone else. That maybe I'd know something, even if I thought I didn't."

"Why didn't you tell us?" Betsy demanded. "If cops come talk to you, you need to tell us!" She turned to Scott. "Why didn't the school at least call us? They should inform parents if cops pull our children out of class!"

"The guy told me not to tell anyone," Billy said. "He said it would just worry you, and if I hadn't really seen Aunt Lizzie, then there was nothing to worry about. Maybe he told the people at school, too."

"How did he know to talk to you?" Eric asked him. "Why did he think you'd seen her?"

"I don't know. Maybe he saw us? Maybe somebody else did?"

Or…"I know you didn't tell him," Casey said. "And you didn't tell your parents. Did you tell *anybody* about your meeting with your aunt?"

Billy dropped his face into his hands, and his body shook with sobs. "I didn't mean to. I wasn't planning on it. But he was talking about it, and I just wanted…I just wanted to…"

"Who did you tell, Billy?"

He gulped, and wiped his nose with his arm. "It was just one person. Just one. And he swore he wouldn't tell."

"Billy, *who was it*?"

"It was Robbie. Robbie Greer. I told him."

Chapter Thirty-four

"You're sure it was this man?" Casey held out the photo of Cyrus and the two men.

She hadn't believed the story Billy had been given about the guy being a cop, and thought she'd take a chance that it was Cyrus' old cronies who had been back in Marshland, on the hunt for Elizabeth. Billy couldn't say for sure that the man was the same as one of the guys on the photo with Cyrus, but he thought it might have been. He was so upset, however, she wasn't sure he was seeing anything clearly, and a lot of years had passed since the picture had been taken.

Now, she was showing the photo to a different teenager. Robbie Greer studied the photo for the tenth time. They were in the dingy motel office, so the lighting wasn't great, but it was good enough if Casey tilted the photo to the right, to catch both lamps in the room. Robbie himself looked different from the evening before. Tonight he was nervous, biting his fingernails and tapping his knuckles on the counter. His eyes jumped around from thing to thing, and he didn't call Casey "ma'am."

"I think it's the same guy," he said. "I mean, like I said, he's older now. His hair had gray in it."

"And what *exactly* did he ask you?"

"I already told—"

"Again, Robbie. Tell me."

He sighed, like Casey was asking for him to recite all the presidents. In order. "He wanted to know if I'd heard anything new about Elizabeth Mann. I like that kind of stuff, I mean, mysteries, or whatever. There's her, and then there's that guy from down the road, who took off one night in his truck and never came home, and that ranch where they think the ghosts of cowboys are coming back to haunt them." He chewed on his thumbnail.

"And? What did you tell him?"

"He didn't actually want to know about all the history. I guess he knew that. He just wondered if I had any idea where she was."

"And did you?"

He shifted his feet. "Not for sure."

"Robbie, Billy told you something. He admitted that. Did the guy ask you what he said?"

Robbie paled. "Why would he?"

"Because you're one of Billy's friends, and because, according to you, you're the town expert on Elizabeth's disappearance."

"But no strange men have ever asked me before."

"Then something must have happened. Something to tip them off that new information had come to light."

Robbie's tapping became more frantic. "I didn't mean anything. I didn't want to get her in trouble. I thought it was *good*. Billy was so happy, you know, but also freaked out, because he'd seen his aunt, and he wasn't supposed to tell his mom, but he wanted to tell somebody, so…so he told me. He knew I would be interested, wouldn't think he was weird." He squeezed his eyes shut.

"Robbie, what did you *do*?"

He scratched at his forehead.

"*Robbie.*"

"I had a web site, okay? I talked about the unsolved crimes around here, in all of Texas, really, but this case—Billy's aunt—she's special, you know? Because she's from here, and Billy's my—" He choked, and cleared his throat. "—my friend."

"So when Billy told you about Elizabeth, and that she'd been here, you put it on the *Internet*? Even though he told you it was a secret?"

"I didn't know it was going to get her killed! It seemed like no big deal, I mean, Colorado's a big state! She could've been anywhere! I didn't think…" He slumped. "I just didn't think."

Casey wanted to reach across the counter and shake him, but it wouldn't change what he'd done, and really, what had he done that every other teenager on the planet wasn't doing? Tweeting and blogging and…whatever else they did that had a weird name. Well, every other kid except for Billy, who had a personal stake in it all.

"Okay," Eric said. "So he found you because of Billy, and your web site. Did you tell him anything new, that you hadn't already posted?"

"I didn't *know* anything new. Only what Billy told me."

"But you did report Elizabeth's description of where she was living."

If anything, he looked more miserable. "Word for word."

"Does Billy know this?"

He shuddered. "Yes. He knows."

So much for that friendship. Casey couldn't imagine how betrayed Billy was feeling. "Did the man tell you who he was?"

"I told you—he said he was a cop. I don't remember his name. He called me to the office at school, so I figured he was for real."

Apparently the school administration thought so, too. They'd called both boys down to the office that same day, except they'd called them separately. Too bad the boys hadn't confided in each other that time.

"Why didn't you tell Billy the guy was here asking questions?"

"Seriously? Because I didn't want him to rip my head off for posting what he'd said. And because the guy told me not to tell anyone."

So *now* he can keep a secret?

"But he found out, anyway."

Robbie nodded miserably. "He saw the blog and figured that's why the guy came asking for us."

Casey was confused. "Did you use Elizabeth's name on your blog? And the name of this town?"

"Sure."

"Then why didn't we find it when we were doing Internet searches for Elizabeth Manns from Texas?"

Robbie hunched over. "When were you searching?"

"Couple days ago."

"Yeah. You wouldn't have found it anymore. I deleted it."

"You deleted her name?"

"No. The entire web site. Billy was so mad. It was the only thing I could think of that might make him not hate me anymore." He sniffed, and wiped his nose with his arm.

Eric shrugged. "You had to do something, man. That was a start. Now, anything you can remember that could help us find this man?"

Robbie plopped down on the chair behind the counter. "You think he did it, don't you? You think I gave her away on my web site, and this guy saw it, and then he went and killed Billy's aunt."

Casey leaned over the counter. "*Can you remember anything.*"

He shied away, then looked at his shoes for a long time, muttering things like, "He was dressed like a cop," and "He spoke like us," and even, "He just looked *like a guy.* There was nothing special about him, or anything that screamed where he was from or…" He sat up.

"What?" Casey could see a new light in his eyes.

"I don't know if it means anything."

"*What is it?*"

"He called him Cyrus."

Casey and Eric just looked at him, not sure what he was getting at.

Robbie waved his hands, like he had something in his brain rushing to get out, but was stumbling over itself. "He didn't call him Mr. Mann. Or Elizabeth's father. Or even the murder victim. He called him *Cyrus.* Like he knew him."

"Not like Cyrus was just part of a case he was working."

"Right. And then…and then he asked where I thought it was."

"Where what was?"

"That's what I asked him. Billy said he asked him, too."

"And?"

"He wouldn't tell me what it was. Just said if I didn't know what he meant, then I wouldn't know where it was, and he wouldn't bother me any more. He told me to go back to class, and I never saw him again."

Chapter Thirty-five

"You showed remarkable restraint," Eric said. They were walking toward town, Casey moving so fast she was practically jogging.

"Yeah, well, the little twerp got lucky. And here I thought he was going to be a nice kid." He'd called her *ma'am*.

"He *is* a nice kid."

"Who ratted out his friend's aunt and got her killed."

"He didn't kill her. He was just being a kid."

"So that excuses his betraying a confidence? On the *Internet*? *Twice*?"

"Of course it doesn't excuse it. But he's not exactly the first person to post something they regret."

Another reason Casey was glad she was living far outside that whole cyber world.

Eric spoke from behind, not quite able to keep up with her pace without full-out running. "Where are we going?"

"Betsy's. If anyone would know what 'it' was, she would."

"I don't know. She seems pretty clueless about things."

Casey stopped so quickly Eric had to grab her so he wouldn't knock her down. They stood there for a breathless moment, faces inches apart, until Casey pushed away, brushing at her sleeves like he'd left something on them. "Do you have a better suggestion?"

"I think Wayne is the one who would know. He's the one who visited the car. He saw the men, and he even knew a little about what Cyrus was up to, with the woodworking and everything.

Betsy had her own stuff to worry about, being seventeen and pregnant. Plus, Wayne is Robbie's dad. The man at the school might have thought Robbie knew something because of that."

"But wouldn't he just ask Wayne?"

"Maybe he did."

"And Wayne didn't tell us he'd talked to a man who just might have come back from the past and killed his old girlfriend?"

Eric shrugged. "Maybe. Maybe not. But we won't know what 'it' is unless we ask somebody. And I don't know who else to ask."

"Certainly not the cops. They don't seem to know much of anything. Okay. You're right. Wayne is the best option. Anyway, I hate to bother Betsy's family again, what with Billy feeling responsible and Betsy blaming him."

"She doesn't—"

"Yes, she does. At least for now. Hopefully she'll get over the fact that her teenager kept a secret from her. Just like your argument about Robbie and the Internet—I hardly think Billy's the first teen to keep a secret from his parents."

Eric laughed. "Hardly."

Casey began walking again, this time headed for the Greers' house. "Betsy's sort of possessive about the whole event, don't you think? Like Elizabeth was hers and no one else's, except maybe Wayne's. I'm not sure Betsy has ever really gotten over it, at least not completely."

"The boxes were in the attic, not the living room."

"True. But she is kind of freaking out, you have to admit."

"Of course she is. A tragic event from her past has come back to haunt her. People have to move on from grief, but that doesn't mean they've forgotten, and if it returns like this…"

Casey walked a little faster, and they didn't speak again until they reached the Greers' front door. A woman answered. She was short, with a plain, pleasant face, and hair that had obviously been dyed and styled at a salon. "May I help you?"

"Yes, is Wayne home?"

She looked behind them, like she was expecting someone else. "Who are you?"

"Sorry, I'm Casey, and this is Eric. We've been talking to him about Elizabeth Mann."

Her face fell. "Why? She's been gone for years. Since high school. And why would you talk to Wayne about it, anyway? She had lots of other classmates."

Uh-oh.

"We're talking to a number of different people, Mrs. Greer. Wayne's name came up, and we thought we'd check in with him."

She glanced back into the house, then said, "He's not home."

"Oh, that's right, he's at work, isn't he?"

"How would you know that?"

"Your son. We met him at the motel and got to talking. He mentioned that your husband knew Elizabeth, so we thought we'd see what he might know."

It was all true. Casey just hoped Wayne's wife didn't get too hung up on the actual chronology of when these things had happened.

Mrs. Greer gripped the doorframe. "They called me. His employers. He wasn't home when I got here, so I figured he was at work, like usual. But he's not there, either. They called, asking where he was." She looked like she was going to cry, which was a look Casey was becoming far too familiar with in the past twenty-four hours.

"Any idea where he went?"

"I called his cell phone right away, of course, but he didn't answer. I texted him, too. His family, his mom and dad, I mean, they say he's not there, and I called the diner. He doesn't seem to be anywhere in town."

"I'm sure he's fine." Casey wasn't sure of that at all, but it seemed like the thing to say. In fact, Casey was a little worried. It seemed risky for the murderers to come back to town *again*, but if they hadn't found 'it' before, and they somehow knew that Casey and Eric had figured out Elizabeth's identity, they might take their chances and return to see if there was new information. Wayne would most likely be one of their first stops.

"I don't suppose Wayne has told you anything about something Elizabeth or her dad might have hidden back before he was killed?"

Her face got all pinched. "We don't talk about her."

"You *never* have?"

She put a hand to her forehead, like even thinking about Elizabeth Mann was giving her a headache. "We may have long ago, but I never knew her. Just heard about her. From everyone. I moved to town after she was already gone."

"But you didn't talk specifics."

"More specifics than I cared to know. But nothing about any hidden documents or whatever you're talking about. She was… it took Wayne a long time to get over what happened. I don't want to bring it all up again. Not now."

Casey didn't bother telling her it was a little late for that. "When he comes home, can you please have him contact me at the motel?"

"I hardly think that would be appropriate."

"He can contact me, then." Eric scribbled his phone number on a scrap of paper from his wallet.

Wayne's wife looked at the piece of paper he was holding out, but didn't take it. "I know the phone number for the motel. He can call there if he wants to."

"You'll tell him we were here?"

She stepped backward, into her house and shut the door halfway. "Please go now. I don't know where my husband is. There is nothing to find out from him about her. Not anymore. She's been gone a long time, and he's moved on." She closed the door, and the locks shot home.

"Well," Casey said as they made their way down the front walk. "I think we just met a woman who's a little bit insecure."

"And a little bit scared."

"What do you think she's scared of? She apparently doesn't know anything that's been going on around here today."

"Or she doesn't want to acknowledge it. There's obviously some history with the whole Elizabeth story."

Casey tried to think, but her brain felt sluggish. "So Elizabeth, who's been gone for seventeen years, has somehow frightened this woman. She's never met her. Why would she be scared of her?"

Eric looked at her sideways. "You're not really that dense, are you?"

Casey considered it. "No. But this woman—we never did get her first name, did we?—has Wayne *now*. They have a home, at least one kid, a *life*. They're married, for heaven's sake. Have been for quite some time."

"That doesn't necessarily solve everything, Casey. You know that. Not when there's another person—another *absent* person—who remains a part of their lives. A part of *his* life."

"But after this many years?"

"It doesn't matter how long it's been, Casey. Twenty years, or two. Elizabeth will always remain, in Wayne's mind, how she was back then. She won't grow old. They won't have fights, or stop being friends. She won't do anything except just…be. And I gotta tell you, Casey, I feel for Wayne's wife. Because no matter what she does, she's never going to quite live up to the woman that *could* have been. It should be in every self-improvement book that's ever been written, in order to avoid heartbreak—it's practically impossible to compete with a ghost."

Chapter Thirty-six

It was completely dark by the time they got back to their rooms. They didn't talk much the last ten minutes of their walk. When they arrived at their doors, Eric looked at the sky. "Lots of stars out tonight."

Casey stood beside him, close enough to almost touch, and gazed heavenward. "Pretty."

Eric kept his face pointed up. "You're pretty, too."

Casey laughed. "Yeah."

"I'm serious."

She could feel him watching her, and she turned and looked into his warm, kind eyes. "I don't get it, Eric."

"What? Why I think you're pretty? You're fit, your hair's a nice color, your smile's amazing when you ever use it—"

"That's the thing. I don't use it. Not very often."

"So?"

"You're going on about ghosts and competing and everything. But I just don't get it. Why do you even want to be with me? You and I both know there are other women who would take you in a heartbeat. You're younger than me—"

"By what? Five years? Please."

"—and far nicer. Look how you were with Robbie, and Billy, and even the lady at the pharmacy. And lord knows you don't go around assaulting police officers."

"You didn't know he was a cop. Casey—"

"I don't think this is a good idea."

"Talking?"

She shook her head.

He stepped closer. Casey stood her ground, but closed her eyes so she wouldn't see how close they were standing. "Eric, please." He brushed some hair from her forehead, and she shuddered, wanting him to touch her some more. Wanting to run screaming into her hotel room.

"Casey, if you'd just give us a chance, I know we'd be good together."

"How do you know that? From our four days of running around Clymer watching people die?" She felt him move away, and opened her eyes. "Eric, you hardly know me. I've got tons of emotional crap I'm lugging around, I'm no fun, and I don't even live in a house."

"You *have* a house."

"In Colorado. What is that? A thousand miles from Ohio?"

"A little more, actually. But I don't care. I can leave Ohio."

"To live with a crabby, damaged woman you've known for less than a month, and who you had to get out of police custody? *Twice.*"

"Yes."

She stepped back. "You're crazy."

"Maybe. But I'm also right."

"About what?"

"You could be nicer, sure. But that's fixable. You need me to tag along." His lips tightened, like he wanted to smile but wasn't sure he should. Or even could.

"Eric…" Casey put her hand up, to rest it on his chest, but at the last second she dropped it and turned to her room. "I'm sorry. I'm just…I'm no good for you. Not long-term."

She unlocked her room, fumbling with the key and almost dropping it.

"Casey, please—"

"Goodnight, Eric."

She finally got the door unlocked and practically fell into the room, bolting the door behind her and leaning against it, pressing her hand against her mouth so she wouldn't scream.

"You really are a mess, aren't you?" Death turned on an old reel-to-reel projector. "Look. I got that whole scene on tape. You can analyze it and see where you went wrong."

Casey stared at the images on the wall, of her and Eric, standing so close together just moments before. She strode forward and thrust her hand through the projector, causing it and the image on the wall to waver.

"Can't you ever leave me be? Can't I ever have a moment to deal with my emotions on my own?"

Death looked at her, not without kindness. "Apparently not, my love."

Casey ran into the bathroom, where she locked herself in until she woke up on the floor several hours later, cold, and with a crick in her neck.

Chapter Thirty-seven

It was quiet in the bathroom, but really, really uncomfortable. Casey sat on the side of the tub, rolled her neck a few times, and decided she ought to find a better place to sleep. Her room was empty, thank God, and the stupid projector was gone. She undressed and climbed into bed.

And lay there, awake.

Where was Wayne? And why on earth did he disappear all day? Had someone taken him? Or worse? Or had this all become too much to deal with, the history, and his wife's jealousy, and now the death of someone he had once loved? Or perhaps still loved?

Casey squeezed her eyes shut and tried to force herself to sleep. Fifteen minutes later, she was no longer thinking about Wayne, but about Eric asleep in the next room. Or possibly not asleep. *That* certainly wasn't going to relax her.

She got up, put on running clothes, and slipped out into the night. She began jogging without a destination, glad simply to be on her own. Her feet pounded the pavement, and her body loosened up quickly in the warmth of the night. It had cooled since earlier in the day, but still she was slick with sweat within minutes. She ran up and down the residential streets, passing Betsy and Scott's, and then the Greers'. She wondered if Wayne had returned; there was a light on in an upstairs room. Either he was home and they were hashing out the implications of the past twenty-four hours, or his poor wife was waiting up. Casey considered stopping to check, but decided it really wasn't any of her business, and Wayne's wife—whatever her name was—was capable of calling the cops if she thought it necessary. She wouldn't welcome another intrusion on her life by people who were concerned with the fate of Elizabeth Mann.

Casey ran through downtown, past the pharmacy, the bank, the school. And then she found herself retracing the path to the park, where Elizabeth and her father had lived for those last months, before Elizabeth's life was turned upside-down and his had ended. The park was quiet now, no parents and toddlers, no dogs, no school kids arguing over who would be on which team. The lamps along the path shone brightly, and Casey felt almost like she was being followed by a spotlight.

She was glad when she neared the relative privacy of the spot where Cyrus Mann had bled out. She ducked off the path toward the broken-up asphalt, where enough light found its way through the trees that she could see at least the outlines of her surroundings. There was still no sign, of course, that the Manns had ever been there. No bloodstain on the gravel, no tire tracks, no plaque to commemorate Cyrus' passing. And still no smoking gun.

Casey meandered around the splotchy lawn where Cyrus and Elizabeth had spent so much time. Had he hidden something there? Were there still any secrets left to find? She poked in the crooks of trees, beneath bushes, and under rocks, hoping she wouldn't get bitten by any snakes or spiders, but soon realized that her efforts were pointless. Any cop—or criminal—worth his stuff would have scoured the place. Where else might Cyrus have hidden something important enough to get him, and now his daughter, killed?

A stick broke in the silence, and Casey darted behind a tree. She listened so hard her ears felt filled with static. Nothing happened for several seconds, until she heard another stick snap, and the rustle of dry grass. She peeked out from behind her tree to see a man come into view. His back was to her, and in the patchy light she couldn't see enough details to know who it was. Had the man who'd questioned the boys come back to hunt down the hidden object? Or had she been followed? What if it was Eric?

The man stood there for a while, as if he were waiting for something, and turned a slow circle. His face remained in shadow. Casey didn't see any point in a confrontation, so she decided to stay put until he left or did something incriminating.

He didn't leave. Instead, he brushed off a spot on the picnic table and sat on the bench backward, his elbows resting on the table top. He tilted his face up like she and Eric had done not long ago, toward what sky showed through the branches, and a slice of light hit his face.

It was Wayne. Whole and unhurt. And here in Marshland.

Casey stepped out from behind the tree. "Wayne?"

He jumped up so fast he almost fell backward when his foot struck a thick patch of weeds. "Who is it?"

"It's Casey. We've been looking for you."

"Here?"

"No." She walked forward and stood across the table from him. "I was just out for a run and stopped by."

"Why were you hiding?"

"I wasn't. I was looking for something."

"What?"

She sat down and waited for him to follow suit. He didn't. "Wayne. Please. Sit down."

He looked around, then sighed heavily and sat sideways on the bench, not facing her.

"What's going on, Wayne?"

"I don't know what you mean."

"Are you really going to try that? You've been missing all day—have you even told your wife you're back?—you didn't go to work, your son has admitted to exposing Elizabeth's secrets—"

"What?"

"And a strange man has been in town asking if anyone knows where 'it' is. I don't suppose he's asked you?"

He sat up. "He's here *today*?"

"No. Last week. You didn't see him?"

He was quiet for so long Casey thought he wasn't going to answer. But he slumped, hanging his head. "Of course I saw him. Do you really think he'd come and talk to the boys, but not me?"

"So what is it, Wayne? What is he looking for?"

"I don't know—"

"Will you *stop*? Of course you know. You know more than anyone else about this whole mess, and it's been eating at you all these years. The look on your wife's face told me that."

He flinched, as if Casey had struck him. Which she wouldn't necessarily have been opposed to doing.

"It's not important anymore."

"Not important? I'll tell you what's *not important*." She half-stood, leaning so far over the table that she was in his face. "*Not important* is you living your pathetic life down here, wishing you still had Elizabeth, wishing it all away, when my little brother is in jail for killing her. Which he didn't do, and you know it. And if I have to drag you all over this town, you will tell me what the man is looking for and where it is."

Wayne swung his leg over the bench to escape, but Casey grabbed his ankle. He stood hopping on one foot. "Let go! I'll tell you, okay? I'll tell you."

She glared at him for several seconds before throwing his leg down, cracking his ankle on the bench. He hesitated, rubbing his foot, then took off limping toward the main part of the park. Casey heaved a sigh and chased after him, dodging branches and rocks and tree roots. Wayne made it to the sidewalk, but Casey caught him, grabbing him from the back and pinning his arms to his sides. He tried kicking her, so she swept his feet out from under him and flipped him onto his stomach, grabbing his arm and twisting it straight out behind him, her hand on the back of his elbow.

"Stop!" He arched his back upward. "Stop! Please!"

Casey knelt over him until he let his head drop forward onto the ground, and his body relaxed. She let go of his arm, but stayed there, squatting beside him, one knee on his back, in case he tried to run again.

He turned his head to the side. "Can I get up?"

"No."

"I won't run."

"Uh-uh."

He closed his eyes. "Fine. What did you want to know?"

"You remember. What was the man asking about? What is 'it?'"

"Plans."

"Plans? What do you mean? Plans for what?"

"Can I get up?"

"No."

"Can I call my wife?"

"When we're done."

"Cyrus was a woodworker, right? He was really good at it, designed things, built them."

"I know, he had his own business, ran it into the ground. You told us all that already."

"Right, then he went to work for a houseboat business down in Whitley. Rich folks wanted boats as comfortable and luxurious as their houses. Maybe more. He was the go-to guy. But he got laid off, not sure why, and he couldn't find anything else."

"Why couldn't he? The early nineties weren't like now. There were jobs all over."

"Not that suited him, I guess. Elizabeth always said he was picky about where he would work. Wanted to be his own boss, pretty much, even though it didn't turn out so well when he was. Can you take your knee out of my back now?"

Casey eased off. "So what were these plans you were talking about?"

"I don't know for sure, but from what Liz heard it sounded like plans for a special houseboat."

"Wait, this was while he worked for the houseboat company?" Bells were ringing in Casey's head.

"I guess, but afterward, too, when they were living in the car. Those men, the ones in the picture, they came to him and he spent all this time designing something. I got to the park one time, and he had his stuff spread all over the picnic table. He had a big sheet of plywood he would use as his drafting table, and he had blueprint paper spread out on it. I walked up and surprised him. He got all mad and told me to go away. Liz wasn't there, so I didn't want to stay, anyway, but it was weird."

"What was on the blueprints?"

"What I told you. A houseboat. Or stuff he was designing for one, anyway."

"And you think those blueprints are what they're looking for?"

"I don't know. Maybe. I guess they could incriminate somebody somehow, or else whoever commissioned the boat is still after these men to get it done."

"That's unlikely. There's got to be somebody else who could design something. And after all this time they probably wouldn't need it anymore."

"Can I get up now?" Casey let him sit up, and he rubbed the elbow she'd overextended. "Liz swore me to secrecy about what I saw, because she didn't know what kind of trouble her dad could get in for whatever he was doing, and after he was killed and she disappeared, I didn't think it mattered anymore."

"You never thought it might have something to do with his death?"

"A houseboat? No. I never thought a houseboat was worth killing over." She watched him until he said, "What?"

"How long have you told yourself that?"

He ran a hand over his face and replied quietly. "Ever since that night."

"You never told anyone about them? Not the police?"

"I knew they didn't find any blueprints when they searched the car, so I figured they were long gone and out of the picture. That maybe the job was even done. So I thought it would just make Cyrus look bad if I talked about how he'd reacted when I'd seen them. I know, I know, it was dumb. I was a teenager who'd just lost his best friend. His *girlfriend*."

"But even now, as an adult, you never thought you should tell?"

"What good would it do? Cyrus is long dead, and until yesterday I thought Liz was gone, too. Not dead, necessarily, but just…gone."

Casey hauled him to his feet. "It's going to do some good now."

"Now? In the middle of the night?"

Would it really help anything to tell him about the blueprints she'd found in Betsy's box? Was it worth it to wake them all up and look? Casey wanted to do it. She wanted to wake up the whole town. But nothing could happen quicker than if she just waited until everyone was awake—Betsy, Chief Kay, her lawyer Don, even Ricky. "Okay, in the morning. I guess now you should let your wife know you haven't skipped town."

"She wouldn't think that."

"Great, so she thinks you're dead."

He yanked his arm from her grip. "Can I go now?"

"You need to tell the cops tomorrow morning."

"I will."

"First thing."

"I said I will."

Casey let him go, watching as he flickered from lamp to lamp along the path, until he was gone.

Chapter Thirty-eight

Casey ran back toward the motel, every fiber in her being wanting to make a detour past Betsy's house to scour the blueprints. No one had ever considered the blueprints, because no one knew they were there, except Betsy, and she just figured they were old portfolio type things for Cyrus. She'd gotten them after the investigation was over and had stuck them in the attic. Billy didn't know. Robbie didn't know. And, most importantly, the three men didn't know.

But Casey knew. And she was going to be at Betsy's door at the break of dawn, demanding to be shown the thing that could get her brother out of prison. She shook herself. No, the blueprints couldn't get him out of prison—they wouldn't say anything about the murder up in Colorado. But they were going to point her toward the people who killed Elizabeth Mann. She knew they would. Somehow.

With each footfall, Casey felt something within her rising up. Something foreign. Something new. Something almost like…hope.

No. It couldn't be that.

Could it?

By the time she arrived at the motel it was almost two. She remembered in time to be quiet so she wouldn't wake Eric, and shut her door quietly.

"Where have you been?" Death stood in the middle of the room, fists on hips.

"Like you couldn't have found me."

Death frowned. "I *couldn't* find you."

"What?"

"I was going to see what you were up to. Join you, hang out, help with clues, like always. But it was like…like you'd closed me off."

"Seriously?"

"Casey…" Death was like a statue. "Do you want to live?"

Casey took a long, deep breath. Did she? Did she really feel like living another day would be a good thing? Something she should look forward to?

"I don't know. I think…maybe."

"Casey…what does this mean?"

"You tell me. You're the supernatural being."

"*I couldn't find you.* How supernatural is that?"

"It's not. It's just weird."

Death flickered, like a bad hologram in a science fiction movie.

"Oh, God," Death said. "Are you deserting me?"

Casey stepped forward, reaching for Death.

And Death disappeared.

Chapter Thirty-nine

Casey woke Eric at six. He came to the door in a wrinkled T-shirt and shorts.

"Come on," Casey said. "We've got things to do."

He blinked. "Can I have a few minutes?"

"Make it quick."

Nine and a half minutes later, during which Casey was completely alone except for the cars passing on the other side of the motel, they were walking very quickly downtown.

Eric smoothed down his still-wet hair. "Where are we going?"

Casey explained what she'd found out the night before. Eric listened, then said, "What do you think we're going to find?"

"What could we find in designs for houseboats?"

"I think it's obvious. Hidden compartments for smuggling. We're right across the Gulf from Cuba, and that was the early nineties. All kinds of stuff went down then with smuggling. People coming over illegally, cops taking down boats full of drugs, causing tons of deaths on both sides, all sorts of violence and betrayal and theft. Nasty stuff."

Casey remembered Robbie talking about smuggling when they'd first gotten to the hotel, although he was talking partly about human trafficking. "I guess it depends how big the boat is."

"Or how big the inventory is. Could have been anything. Drugs. Cigars. Diamonds. Even cash. You could squeeze a lot of those things in small spaces."

"But don't they usually use speed boats to smuggle? Or bigger yacht-type things? Houseboats aren't exactly fast, or even seaworthy, not out in the middle of the ocean."

"Guess we'll have to see what's on the plans."

They arrived at the Betsy and Scott's house. A light was on in one of the upstairs rooms, so they wouldn't be waking everyone. Casey rapped lightly on the door, and listened for footsteps. When they didn't come, she tried again, a little louder.

The door opened, and Scott stood there, looking much like Eric had twenty minutes earlier, in shorts and a stretched-out T-shirt. "You're up already?"

"So are you."

He smiled. "True."

"Can we come in? Is Betsy up?"

"Sorry, of course, come in. I'm not quite awake. I'll go get Bets." He shut the door behind them and padded up the stairs.

Betsy came rushing down, tying her housecoat. "What is it? It's not Wayne, is it?"

"No, he's fine. But he gave me an idea of what the men were looking for. Can we have another look at your boxes?"

"They're still in the dining room."

Casey went right to the memento box and popped the end off of the mailing tube. She breathed a sigh of relief when she saw the blueprints right where she'd left them.

"Those?" Betsy said. "They're just some of Cyrus' old stuff."

Casey shoved the boxes aside and lay the blueprints flat on the table. Eric held down one half while she held the other.

"I guess it's a houseboat," Eric said. "But it kind of looks like a yacht."

The first drawing showed the dimensions of the outside of the boat, as you would see it from the side if it were floating up above the water. It was a typical pontoon-style houseboat, just like Casey had imagined. In the lower right hand corner was a logo which said simply, "Private Boats, Inc." Casey peeled that top sheet off and let it slide to the floor. The second drawing showed the same outside view, but from the front and back, while the third showed the opposite side. Each of them had the same logo imprinted on the bottom corner. Casey got rid of them, too, and finally saw the interior.

The top sheet was an overview of the entire layout. Kitchen, bar, lounge, bathroom, two bedrooms, and two bunk rooms. Lots of room, but then, if someone was really living on it, it would have to be somewhat sizable. All of the rest of the papers were individual sections of each room, as well as electrical, venting, and water pipe diagrams.

"Why is it important?" Betsy asked.

Casey didn't know. There was nothing obvious. Nothing saying, "Hidden compartment for smuggling drugs."

"Give me a minute," Eric said. He flipped back and forth between several sheets, muttering to himself, for several minutes. "Hand me those other sheets, will you?"

Betsy grabbed the ones on the floor and put them on the table.

"The dimensions," Eric said. "They don't add up between the outside and the inside."

"What else?" Casey was used to looking at set blueprints from back in her theater days, but that part of her brain had rusted, and these drawings just looked like a bunch of lines and angles with no real meaning.

Eric scanned the sheets again. "I need more time."

"Can I help?" Scott was standing in the doorway. He'd taken a shower, and was wearing khakis and another blue button-down. Things you'd expect a high school teacher to wear.

"Please." Eric stepped aside. "You're physics, right? Maybe your kind of brain could figure this out better. We think these are plans for some kind of smuggling boat. Cyrus drew them."

Scott leaned over the drawings, saying things like, "Um-hmm." And "Oh, sure." And even, "Huh." "Okay," he finally said in a normal speaking voice. "Look here." He ran his finger along the outer shell of the layout overview. "There's a buffer all around the sides of the boat. Space in-between the inner walls and the shell."

Casey followed his finger. "They were hiding things between them?"

"Ingenious, really. That way no police could find things just by going through the boat. The cupboards, storage spaces, closets—they'd all be filled with legal belongings. There would have to be an opening somewhere...I don't see it yet."

He took his time looking over the schematics, going back and forth between sheets. "There. This paneling. It would look like solid wood paneling, but see here? He's drawn in sliding sections. He would have had it constructed so no one would even think it was anything but a normal seam. You can see them all over—in the closets, behind the kitchen cabinets, even the breaker box. Behind each storage space is a hidden compartment. Fairly small."

"But plenty of space for drugs or gems or cash."

"Absolutely."

Casey and Eric looked at each other.

"What does this mean?" Betsy asked.

"It means your uncle really was a criminal," Casey said. "Or was at least working for some. And that opens up all sorts of possibilities as to who would want him dead."

Chapter Forty

"So where exactly are we going?" Eric pulled onto the road heading southeast.

"Cyrus' old workplace." Casey wished she could have access to all of the files Death had scanned, but it seemed those were out of her reach now that she'd apparently become more okay with the idea of living. She was sure there would be information about Cyrus' old workplace that she could use.

"I thought they went out of business, and that's why Cyrus lost his job."

"No, Wayne said he was laid off, but I don't think it was because they closed down. Maybe they just couldn't afford his services anymore. His expertise made him expensive."

"So why wouldn't he just lower his rates?"

"I don't know. Made him feel taken advantage of?"

"This from a guy who wouldn't accept charity? You'd think he'd be glad to have a job at all."

"These were the nineties, remember. Not today, when folks will take anything they can get. But maybe it was something else. Supposedly, like people have told us, he just wanted to be his own boss and had trouble working for someone else. He wouldn't be the first person fired for not playing well with others."

Signs for Galveston Bay began decorating the side of the road, and Eric followed them across the flat, marshy land toward the coast. The GPS on Eric's iPad took them south of the bay, as far as a marina, before saying they were at their destination.

"This is it?"

Casey understood Eric's confusion. The Gulf sparkled under the sun, and extended as far as she could see, into the horizon. Beautiful. Amazing. But the marina itself, tucked into a marshy inlet, was not the hub of busyness they had expected. A floating dock bobbed on the water alongside several old fishing boats and a pontoon. One old houseboat was moored to a different, permanent dock, and looked like it had seen better days. Many of them. Casey didn't see anyone out and about, except on the other side of the inlet, too far in the distance to recognize faces, or even genders.

A low but large building with two over-sized garage doors, made for accommodating boats, sat far enough off the water it wouldn't get hit by incoming tides. Weeds had grown up around it, and all three of the visible windows were broken, with tell-tale holes in the panes where someone had thrown a rock or a heavy seashell. A sign hung crookedly on a post, one of its chains broken and trailing as the sign swung with the breeze. The sign said, "Harbor Houseboats," although the paint was so faded it was hard to tell. No vehicles sat in the parking lot, which would have been a surprise at that point if there had been any. Casey ignored the sinking feeling in her stomach and got out of the car.

"Where are you going?" Eric came after her.

She picked her way across the weedy bank up onto the parking lot and peered through one of the busted windows. "I guess they're out of business *now*. Let's see if we can get in."

The side door was easy to open, since the building had apparently been broken into long before they'd gotten there. Casey stepped into the muggy space, which had been the front office. An old metal desk sat in the middle of the room, along with an office chair that had been home to more than a receptionist in the past few years. The walls held faded photos of houseboats in spotted wooden frames, and a curling, yellowed calendar from 2007 hung to the left of the desk.

Eric worked at the top desk drawer to get it open. "Old envelopes, all empty, some letterhead, bunch of paperclips…" He went through the rest of the drawers, but found nothing more interesting than outdated phone books and a broken model of a houseboat.

Behind the desk was a doorway, and Casey stepped through it into a large workspace. She ducked as something flew down from the rafters, wings beating a hasty retreat.

"What was that?" Eric came in behind her.

"Bird of some kind. There's nests all around." Other things, too, by the look of it. Including people, although all that was left was the trash they left behind. Beer cans, food wrappers, probably syringes and who knew what else. Casey didn't want to get any closer to find out.

The large room was fronted by the first of the two huge rolling doors. Hoists were attached to the ceiling, and workbenches, littered with refuse, lined the walls. The shell of a houseboat lay lopsided on the cement floor, as if someone had taken one of its legs out from under it. It was the flat style, so the windows to the house were at eye level. Casey walked around it, looking in the windows, hoping she wouldn't find anything disgusting inside. There were newspapers and a couple of old blankets and cardboard boxes, but nothing that looked too hopeful. Or gross.

"I'm assuming this wouldn't be Cyrus' boat," Eric said.

"Too small. Plus, we don't know that it ever got built." She walked quickly to the next room, which was another garage with the second huge door. Nothing was in there except trash and bird poop. Casey continued on to the final door. This one led to a small hallway with offices and a bathroom. The offices had been stripped of all furniture, and the utilities had obviously been turned off long ago. That didn't stop people from using the restroom. Casey tried not to vomit, and beat a hasty retreat outside, where she stopped and stared out toward the ocean.

Eric followed. "What now?"

"We find someone who knows what happened to this place."

That someone was Mr. Howard Thornville of the Whitley Chamber of Commerce, a jovial stick of a man nearing retirement age. His office fronted Main Street in Whitley, the closest town to the defunct shipyard. Main Street wasn't as busy as you'd expect from being the central street, but then, the town itself was smaller than Casey had expected this close to the shore. Thornville was more excited about relating the story of Harbor Houseboats than Casey thought natural, but perhaps it was good that someone wanted his job.

"They went out of business in 2007," he said, which Casey had already guessed from the aging calendar on the wall of the warehouse. "It was a sad thing, but people were losing their regular homes, and could hardly afford a second, vacation one."

"But I thought people lived in the boats."

"Sure, some did. Some still do. But the bulk of the houseboat business—at least this particular one—was made up of wealthy people who wanted a unique place for the winter. Harbor Houseboats prided themselves on their workmanship and their leaning toward luxury."

"Do you know anything about the people who owned it?"

He indicated his computer screen, on which he had brought up their file. "Brothers. Three of them. Their last name was Pinkerton—"

"Like the detective agency?" Eric said.

Thornville smiled. "Just like that. Don't know if they're any relation. I heard a rumor that—"

"Anyway…" Casey said. "There were *three* brothers?" Her head began to buzz. *The Three.*

"Yes, of course, sorry. Their father had started the business long ago, in the seventies, and the brothers took it over when he retired. This was the oldest, Zeke. He was the boss once the dad left."

Casey looked at image on the screen, but Zeke was no one she'd seen before. Her buzz began to fade. "And the others?"

Thornville clicked back to the home page. "The second brother, Dan, he was the most hands-on. Knew his stuff as far as boats." He brought up a photo of him. Again, someone Casey didn't recognize. So much for that theory.

"Zeke took care of most of the business end. The numbers, schmoozing the rich folks, all that. Dan pretty much ran the workshop. They employed eighteen people at one point, including themselves, but that number began dropping as early as 1995." He brought up a photo of a group of people, mostly men, and enlarged it. "This was their staff before the lay-offs began."

"There he is," Eric said.

"Who?" Thornville asked.

"Cyrus Mann. He was a woodworker from Marshland."

"Of course. He was one of the first lay-offs, I'm afraid. And," he cleared his throat, "I hear he met his end not long after that."

"That's actually why we're here."

Thornville sat back. "Really? Has new information come to light about his murder?"

"Well, it's his daughter," Eric said.

"The poor girl who disappeared? Did they find her?"

Casey tuned them out and looked at the men on the photo. She picked out the older brother, Zeke, in the back row, wearing a suit. Dan, the garage foreman, stood on the end of the middle row in blue coveralls. There were a few women, most wearing office-type clothes, one in coveralls. Casey looked carefully across each row, studying the faces, until she stopped, her heart in her throat. "One of them's here, Eric."

Eric stopped talking and looked where she was pointing. "I see him."

"Who?" Thornville angled the screen so he could see, too.

"This man. We have him on another photo. Do you know who he is? Is he still around?"

"Well, of course he is," Thornville said, laughing. "He's the youngest Pinkerton brother. He works right down the street at the police station."

Chapter Forty-one

"He's a *cop*?" Casey couldn't believe it.

"No, no." Thornville waved his hands, like he needed to stop her. "He's the motor pool manager. Oversees the fleet. Keeps their vehicles ship-shape. His name's Randy."

"So what was he, a mechanic for the boat company?"

"Yes. Wasn't always happy working for his brothers, but he was the baby, by several years, and not always the most reliable member of the staff. Between you and me, I think they would have rather laid him off than some of the others, but how are you going to do that to your own brother? Although eventually, they sort of did. He didn't work with them during the last, oh, ten years of the business."

Casey stood up so fast her chair tipped. Eric caught the chair, and her wrist. "Casey."

"We need to go see him."

"In a minute. We need to ask a few more things first."

Casey took a deep breath and sank back into the chair.

"You have the picture?" Eric said. "Of the men?"

Casey pulled out the shot of Cyrus talking to Randy and the other guy. "You know this person?"

Thornville held the photo at arm's length. "Well, that's Randy, of course, back when he was young, and Cyrus."

"But what about the other guy?"

Thornville pinched his lips. "I recognize him. Les Danvers. Small-time crook, but a child of the town, so we put up with him. He's been in and out of the police station different times. Nothing ever stuck except for a shoplifting charge, and he got off with a slap on the wrist. Should have been a slap on the behind, you ask me." Thornville's sunny demeanor had darkened. "He was not a good influence on Randy. I know Mr. Pinkterton wished he wouldn't hang around him. Tried to get him to stop, but there's only so much you can do."

"So did Randy get in trouble, too?"

Thornville dropped the photo onto the desk and sat back. "What are you really here for?"

"These guys," Casey said. "We wanted to find out who they were."

"But *why?*"

Casey glanced at Eric, and he nodded. "Because we think they might have had something to do with Cyrus Mann's death. And now his daughter's."

Thornville's face was blank for a moment before his expression changed. "His daughter? She's alive?"

"No. She *was*. Until last week."

"Wait a minute. She disappeared all those years ago. The papers always thought she was dead." He paused. "Or that she had killed her father and run."

"She didn't kill him. But she did run." Casey hoped it was true, but she had to go on the assumption that Elizabeth was innocent.

"And you think these guys—" he tapped the photo "—killed her father? And now her?"

"That's what we're trying to figure out."

"Oh, geez." He rubbed his face with both hands. "Oh, geez. That's just…just awful."

"Did Randy ever get in trouble?" Casey asked again.

Thornville wouldn't look at her. "I'm not comfortable with this. I don't think I should talk to you anymore. Randy is part of our community, but I don't know you. If you have any more to ask, you should probably just go ask him."

"Fine." Casey stood. "But one more question. Was there a third guy they hung out with? We have information that there was."

Thornville's expression remained stubborn, but Casey could see him thinking. "Do you know any more details about this man that could help trigger my memory?"

"No. Just that there were three of them. And he was sort of creepy."

Thornville picked up a pen and turned his computer toward him, like he was ready to resume work.

"Mr. Thornville?"

He closed his eyes, and let the point of his pen rest on the desk. "Yes, there was a third one. His name was Marcus." He shook his head. "Marcus Flatt."

"What was he like? What do you know about him?"

He shook his head again, like if he did that enough he wouldn't have to answer. "He was trouble, too. But in an entirely different way." He looked up at her, his eyes bleak. "God help Cyrus' daughter if Marcus Flatt was the one who found her."

Chapter Forty-two

Casey stormed out of the office and headed toward the police station to grab Randy Pinkerton by the throat. Eric jumped in front of her.

"Get out of my way, Eric."

"No."

She tried to dodge past him, but he stepped in her way again. "Casey, look. He works for the *police department*. Charging in there and accusing him of murder isn't going to fly. We have to think about this."

"He's right, you know." Death stood behind Eric, also in-between Casey and the police station.

Surprised, Casey looked over Eric's shoulder. "What are *you* doing here?"

Eric glanced backward, and frowned. "Casey. Are you all right? You know I've been with you all along."

"You're obviously back to old form," Death said, sighing. "Ready to die."

"I'm not ready to die."

"That's good," Eric said uncertainly. "I guess that means we'll take this slowly?"

"Listen to the man," Death said. "Running in there like an unprepared avenging angel isn't going to solve anything. You've got to be smooth. Like me. In and out, nobody knows you were even there. Well, except that someone's dead."

She looked at the sky, then back down. "What do you suggest?"

"Ask around," Eric said. "Find out if he's been gone lately. See if we can locate the other two."

"And you might want to do it before the Chamber of Commerce guy decides it's his civic and neighborly duty to warn them." Death indicated the window of the Chamber office, where Thornville stood watching them.

Casey glared at him. Eric plastered a smile on his face and waved, pulling Casey across the street to a coffee shop.

"I'm not thirsty," Casey said.

Eric kept dragging her. "It's not about the coffee."

"Although it should be," Death said. "From my research this place is supposed to have the best lattes around." Death held up a Nook with the banner "Best Coffee in Texas!" across the bottom of a screen that showed the shop.

Casey stopped resisting. "Fine."

Eric left her in a window booth and took out his phone. "Why don't you give Chief Kay a call, tell her we identified the men in the photo." He left her and went up to order a couple drinks, while Death fashioned a steaming mug of something that said, "Nothing like a little *Elixir of Life* to start the day!" with a yellow smiley face. Death took a sip and considered it. "A bit bitter, but some sweetness to it. Perhaps a taste of honey. Or is it ambrosia?"

Chief Kay wasn't in, so Casey left the information with the officer who answered, which unfortunately was the same one she "assaulted" in the street. It wasn't the most pleasant conversation.

Eric stayed at the counter longer than she thought necessary, talking to the pretty young barista. He came back with a blueberry muffin large enough to feed all of southeast Texas. Eric cut it in pieces and took a bite. "Mmm, good." He spewed crumbs, and grinned. "Whoops."

"Ricky is in jail," Casey said.

Eric took another bite. "I know. That's why I was chatting up the girl at the counter."

"Is that the only reason?"

Eric grinned some more. "Jealous?"

Casey looked out the window.

"You're pathetic," Death said, and took another sip.

Casey gripped her cup. "So what did the girl say?"

"She knows Randy and the other guy, Les Danvers. They come in here on most Wednesdays. Apparently, Les works over at Galveston Bay, loading and unloading ships, and that's his day off. When he comes to town they try to be the civilized business types and hang out at the coffee shop, but they don't quite pull it off."

"According to the girl."

"Britney."

"*Britney*. Of course that's her name."

Death laughed, and raised a toast. "To Britney."

"She says Randy tries to keep it cool, but Les usually gets too loud, or complains about the coffee, or offends another customer somehow. Also, it seems Randy has been trying to get her to go out with him since she started working here two years ago."

"Not exactly a surprise," Death said.

Casey took a sip of her coffee, but refused to admit she enjoyed it. "What about the third guy? Marcus Flatt?"

"She's not sure. She says there was another guy who stopped by once, but he didn't get a drink, and he didn't stay long. She was glad, because just looking at him gave her the creeps. She said his eyes were like a shark's."

"Bingo," Death said loudly, and raised another toast, making Casey wonder exactly what was in the mug.

"I don't suppose she has any idea if Randy and his buddies have been out of town?"

"Actually, she said he and Les missed their usual Wednesday last week. She hadn't really thought anything of it, except that she hasn't had to refuse Randy's advances for a nice, two-week stretch."

"The timing would fit."

"Sure would."

Casey took another drink and gazed out the window. Thornville no longer stood watching. She hoped he had just gone back to work, and wasn't tattling to the police. "When was it she saw Flatt?"

"A while ago, I guess. She didn't really remember."

"So now what? Can we go talk to Randy?"

"Or is it time to call the cops?"

"Um, Eric?" Britney was calling him.

"She knows your *name*?" Casey said.

Britney was still talking. "The guy you were asking about? Randy?"

"Yeah?"

"He's right over there." She pointed toward the street.

Randy Pinkerton was driving away in a red Camaro.

Casey stood up so fast her coffee spilled. Eric caught the cup, so his hands weren't free to stop Casey this time.

"Come on, Eric!"

She ran out to their car and waited impatiently for Eric to catch up.

Thornville peeked out at her from his window. Obviously, he had called and warned Randy Pinkerton they were coming.

"Do you want this?" Eric ran up holding out her half-full drink.

"Eric, get in the car!"

He tossed the drink in a trash can and beeped open the car. They jumped in and sped after Randy Pinkerton.

Eric squeezed past a yellow light. "Where do you think he's going? Home? To warn Les Danver?"

"Which direction are we headed?" Casey grabbed Eric's iPad and pulled up the GPS. "We're not going toward Galveston Bay, where Les works."

"Where's Pinkerton's house? See if he comes up in the white pages."

She struggled to figure out how to find that information, but eventually came up with an address. "Nope. Not going toward that, either."

"Brothers? Girlfriend?"

"How do I know who his girlfriend is?" But she knew his brothers' names. "I guess it could be the older brother. Zeke. He lives sort of out this way. Do we think he's involved?"

Eric groaned as a bakery truck pulled out in front of him, blocking their view of the escaping Pinkerton brother. He rode the truck's bumper, waiting for a break in the solid yellow line.

Casey flipped through several hits on the iPad. "From what I'm seeing here Zeke is Mr. Upright Citizen. So is Dan. Can't really find much about Randy. The most recent photos that involve the business just show the older two brothers, but that fits with what Thornville said."

"Dang it," Eric said, "where did he go? Do you see him?"

Casey looked up. "We lost him?"

"No. There he is." They could see the little red car darting around a corner. The bakery truck lumbered straight, so Eric was free to turn after Pinkerton.

"He's turning again," Casey said.

"I see him. Why does this look familiar? Did we drive past here before?" Eric realized he was too close, and slowed to put more distance between the cars. "He's on his phone."

"Talking to Thornville, maybe?"

"Who knows. Maybe he's calling his brothers. Or Les Danver. Or even the other guy."

The Other Guy. Marcus Flatt, the one who creeped out Britney just by stepping into the coffee shop, and who made Thornville shudder, and Elizabeth leave if she saw him coming. A man with shark's eyes.

"I think I know where we're going," Casey announced suddenly.

"You do? Where?"

She held up the GPS and pointed out their route. "We did drive past here before. We're going back to Harbor Houseboats."

Chapter Forty-three

Eric let the car drift farther back. "Why would we be going there?"

"A couple of reasons. He's either going to hide or get something he doesn't want us to find. He's meeting the other guys to tell them about us. Or he's leading us into a trap."

"Lovely."

Eric drove even slower.

"If they're going to hide incriminating evidence we have to get there first."

"Impossible. He knows where he's going. We don't. And they've had almost twenty years to get rid of whatever you're imagining."

Casey plugged the address of the boat garage into the GPS. The first route it offered seemed to be the one they were already taking. She asked for an alternate way. The one that came up would be less mileage, but was supposed to take seven minutes longer.

"We don't have a choice," she said. "You'll just have to speed."

Following Casey's directions, Eric turned at the next intersection, then flew along the town's streets, slowing at crosswalks and roads, but ignoring posted speed limits. They managed to get close to the boathouse without crashing or getting a ticket, and parked a couple of blocks away. Casey didn't see Randy's car, or anyone at all, except for an older couple walking slowly down the sidewalk in the opposite direction, arm in arm, so she got out of the car and began walking toward the boat garage, angling through people's yards and hoping they didn't have those big guns Chief Kay had been talking about.

They snuck up on the boathouse the back way, going as quickly as they could without calling attention to themselves. But when they got there, there was no sign of Randy Pinkerton's car.

"Did we beat him by that much?" Eric asked. "Doesn't seem possible."

"Or we were just wrong about where he was going."

"Crap."

They watched the building for a half hour, but there was no activity, so they made their way back to their car.

"Didn't you say we could have been going to his brother's house?"

"Yes, the older one. Zeke."

"Should we check it out?"

"I guess. Not sure what else to do. He's obviously not going back to work today, where we could find him."

They drove to Zeke Pinkerton's house, but there was no sign of Randy or his car. Not knowing what else to do they looked up Randy's house, but there was no action there, either.

"What about Les Danver's place?" Eric said.

Casey felt as weary as Eric's voice sounded. "I'll look him up."

But he wasn't listed anywhere, not even in the database they'd paid to belong to.

"Thornville would know," she said. "The little prick."

Eric laughed. "I think it's time for some food."

"I don't want another blueberry muffin."

They found a quick Italian place between the Gulf and Whitley, and were almost done when Eric's phone buzzed.

"Britney?" Casey said. "I suppose you managed to exchange phone numbers while you were at it."

He ignored her and read the text. "You're going to love this. Hometown Interiors? They've been around for ages."

"You're wrong. I don't love that."

"No, listen. They've been around, but they haven't done anything. Just sat in the corporation listings. The last thing they did? Bought out a small business and took it over seventeen years ago. Since then they've done nothing but exist until last week, when they apparently did a few small jobs before the work on your brother's house."

Casey let that sink in. "How is he supposed to have found this business if they haven't been active for that long?"

"Doesn't matter, because we know he really didn't. If the police would have dug a little farther they would have seen all this. Instead, they believed the voice on the other end of the phone, as well as the fake emails and phone calls they planted."

"You can do that?"

"I can't. Other people can, without breaking a sweat. Or, actually, without even waking up much, knowing those folks. But that's not the part you're going to love."

"So tell me already."

He smiled. "That little business they bought out? It just so happened to be owned by someone here in Texas, by the name of Cyrus Mann."

Chapter Forty-four

"I don't understand." Thornville was wringing his hands, like an old woman in one of those books where old women do that sort of thing. "How did you find me?"

"*That's* what you don't understand?" Casey stepped into Thornville's front door—the door at his house. "Or you don't understand about Hometown Interiors?"

"Either one."

"May we come in?" Eric said.

Thornville hesitated, so Casey pushed past him, into a little foyer.

Eric followed. "Thank you. We appreciate your time."

"But…"

"I assume you have computer access to your files here at home?" Eric said.

"It's not really something I like to do—" He hustled after Casey, who was making a self-guided tour around the first floor.

He lived alone, that much was obvious. The living room and kitchen were exceptionally neat and tidy, as was the bathroom, and the small office at the back of the house. Casey stepped in and turned on the light. An extremely fat cat sat on the leather office chair. It took one look at her, rolled off its perch, and waddled out, tail held high.

"Here's the deal," Casey said, going around to the other side of the desk. "We know Cyrus Mann was bought out seventeen years ago. His relatives didn't understand it. They'd thought he was doing great. But all of a sudden, he was out of a business and working for someone else. The Pinkertons. Can you explain that?"

Thornville stood in the doorway, blinking rapidly, like his brain was trying to compute. "I don't know, I didn't know anything about—"

"And who do you think bought out his company? I'm betting I know, and I'll give you one guess."

Thornville swallowed. "Um, the Pinkertons?"

"Ding, ding. But not all of them. Just one."

His face pinched, like someone was stepping on his toe. "Randy."

"You're getting good at this. Now, you want to tell me why Randy, who is apparently a little pet of yours, seeing how you warned him about us today, would travel up to Marshland just to buy out some business that's owned and run by one guy?"

Thornville swayed on his feet. Eric grabbed him and led him to the chair behind the desk.

Casey pointed at the computer. "See what you can find out for us."

"Please," Eric added.

Thornville blinked some more. "But I don't know—"

Casey leaned over him. "It's called research."

"Why are you being so mean to me?" Thornville whined.

"Because you sold us out today."

"But I don't know you, and I do know Randy."

"Yes, you know that he's a conniving little crook, and hangs out with even worse ones. You're the one who said his brothers don't even like him."

"I never said—"

"Type!" Casey said.

He began typing.

"Now I see what you mean when you say you're going to be nicer," Eric said to Casey.

She smiled.

"What do you want to know?" Thornville said.

"I want to see it for myself. Who officially owns Hometown Interiors?"

He was able to find the business, way down in some deep recesses of businesses whose sole activity was paying enough fees and taxes they remained legal.

"Well?"

Thornville cleared his throat. "It's owned by a corporation called Private Boats, Inc."

Casey couldn't breathe. "And who owns that business?"

Thornville typed some more. After a while, he swallowed loudly. "Randy Pinkterton. And Les Danvers. And…Marcus Flatt."

"Well, what do you know? Isn't that interesting? What about work history of our lovely home repair business?"

Thornville went back to Hometown Interiors, and found that the hibernating business had somehow managed to rack up several work payments in the past month, after years of remaining stagnant.

"Amazing, isn't it?" Casey said. "How they decided to get back into the workforce so suddenly?"

"What details can you get us?" Eric asked.

"None. It's private business activity."

"You can't see who their customers were?"

"Not without getting into their files, and before you ask, I don't know how to do that." He flinched, as if afraid of Casey's reaction.

"That's no problem," Casey said. "There's an easier way. Eric, may I borrow your phone?"

"Of course." He handed it to her, their politeness seeming to make Thornville even more nervous.

Casey dialed the business number on the screen and smiled at Thornville as she waited for it to connect. After several rings a man answered. "Yeah?"

She continued smiling at Thornville. "Hello, I'm calling to talk with someone about some work I need done."

"Sorry," the man said. "We're scheduled through the winter. It will have to wait."

"Oh, that's too bad. No chance you could squeeze me in before then?"

"No can do."

"Well, okay. How about—Is there any chance I could see some of your work to see if I want to wait for you? Could you put me in touch with one of your customers?"

"Look, lady, we can't give out private information. We do good work. No complaints. Ask the Chamber of Commerce."

"Good idea. Thank you. I'll do just that."

She hung up, still smiling. "How about that? They don't have room for any new customers right now. They suggested I ask you for a reference. Why would they say that, do you think?"

Thornville shrank in his chair. "I really have no idea."

"Nobody else has come calling, asking about them?"

He shook his head.

"Not even, say, the police in Colorado?"

His eyes filled, and tears shone in his eyes. "I didn't know. I didn't know what they were asking. They asked if it was a legitimate business, and I said yes. That's all. Because it is. And look, you can see for yourself that my database reports recent activity." He angled the computer screen toward Casey, and he was right, she could see the work orders.

"I suppose this is what we were talking about earlier?" she said to Eric.

"I suppose it is. Easy as sweet potato pie to fake, as I believe they might say down here."

Thornville dropped his head into his hands. "I didn't know. *I didn't know.*"

"No," Casey said. "I don't suppose you did know *exactly* what they were asking. But now you do." She handed him Eric's phone. "And now you are going to tell the cops *exactly* what you've found out."

"I'm not sure—"

Casey snatched the phone from his hands and gave it to Eric. "How 'bout you make the call? Once you have the right person, Thornville here can start talking." She dropped her hand onto Thornville's shoulder, and he about leapt from the chair. She kept him in it.

Eric wasn't able to connect with Detective Watts, but got someone on the line who would listen. He said they had the director of the Whitley, Texas, Chamber of Commerce on the line with information pertinent to the Alicia McManus case, and handed the phone to Thornville.

"Talk," Casey said.

Thornville cleared his throat. "Um, hello?"

Casey squeezed his shoulder, just a tad, and he squeaked. And began talking. When he'd given them all the information about who owned the company and how much work had actually been done in the past seventeen years, he looked up at Casey. She was still smiling. He cringed.

Eric took back the phone. "Got all that? Great. We'll be in touch." He hung up. "So, are we done here?"

Casey took her hand from Thornville's shoulder. "I believe we are. Unless you have something else to ask?"

"Nope."

Casey considered leaving Thornville with a physical reminder of their visit, but decided she wasn't quite that angry. Instead, she smiled at him again, and walked to the door. As she was leaving, she heard Thornville say, "Doesn't she scare you?"

Eric replied, "Every single day. But then, we're friends, so I don't have to worry. At least, not too much."

Casey smiled to herself. That was exactly the way she liked it.

Chapter Forty-five

"You're awfully quiet," Eric said as they drove back toward Marshland. They had decided they didn't actually need to track down Randy Pinkerton or his buddies. The cops had the new information, and the connections would hopefully be enough to at least bring the men in for questioning, as well as make it possible to check gun registrations, although alibis for a date several years ago would be impossible to come by. A week ago though, that was more hopeful. It wasn't like Casey and Eric knew where Randy was, anyway, since he apparently was avoiding all his usual haunts.

Casey shifted in her seat so she could look at Eric. "I'm thinking about timing. Cyrus' business is supposedly going fine, then all of a sudden he sells out. A few months later he is working for the exact people who bought his company. Soon after that he's laid off and making the blueprints for the smuggling boat. What exactly happened?"

"Wayne said he was an expert, that people were lucky to get him to make something. I guess Harbor Houseboats wanted the best."

"So they buy out his company? He goes from being his own boss to just another grunt? It doesn't make sense. And meanwhile, his wife is ill and dying of cancer."

"He needed money for her treatment?"

"Insurance would cover that."

"Assuming he had it. He wasn't getting benefits from some large company. He would have had to supply it himself."

"One way to find out." Eric dug his phone out of his pocket. "Call Betsy."

Betsy answered almost immediately. "You found something?"

"Did Cyrus have medical insurance?"

She hesitated. "They were living in a *car*."

"No, I mean before Vivian died. Were they okay?"

"Oh. I guess so. From what I remember, she was getting the best care, always in a different hospital, trying this or that new treatment. None of it worked, of course. I mean it was pancreatic cancer. Not much you can do for that—especially that far back."

"Did he ever talk about why he sold his business?"

"All I ever heard was that he ran out of money and had to get a different job."

"Do you know how he got the one with the houseboats?"

"They came looking for him. It was like Wayne told you— Uncle Cyrus was really, really good when he was thinking straight."

"But then he got laid off not too long after."

"I don't know, Casey. I guess so. Dad always said he must have still been out of his mind a little bit because of Aunt Viv. I don't think he ever really recovered. He went a little nuts trying to keep her alive with all that medicine, and when it didn't work…"

"I understand. Thanks, Betsy. We'll be in touch."

"Uh-oh," Eric said when she hung up. "You're burning brain cells."

"It doesn't make any sense. Cyrus' wife gets sick, but he's got medical insurance, so he should be okay. He owns his own business, so he can make his own schedule—five months isn't long enough for a business to go completely down the drain, is it? But halfway through her illness he sells his company and goes to work for somebody else, farther away, who would dictate his schedule, which would probably mean spending less time with his wife during her final months. From what we're hearing about how her illness affected him and how much he loved her, I just can't see that."

"Well, maybe a few months is long enough to drain a business, especially if it was on the rocks before."

She shook her head. "It's got to mean something else."

Eric's phone rang in her hand. "It's Chief Kay. Hello?"

"We got positive IDs from your Colorado people, the cook and the neighbor."

"It was Randy Pinkerton?"

"That's the guy. We're going out to talk with him."

"Good luck finding him."

Kay was quiet for a few seconds. "I take it that means you've been to see him?"

"Tried. The stupid Chamber guy gave him the heads-up and he took off. Now he's somewhere in the wind."

"Leave him up to us now. You've done your job—we're looking at someone other than your brother—not that *I* was looking at him, mind you."

"All I ever wanted." Well, not all. But it would have to be enough.

"We'll keep you posted as much as we can." Which would mean once everything was over.

Casey hung up and told Eric what was happening.

"So we can go home?"

"I guess. I'm not sure what else we could do." She watched the passing scenery, not really seeing the blue sky and the orange leaves. "But I'm not real happy about it."

"Yeah, I know what you mean."

By the time they arrived back in Marshland it was late, but Casey was too antsy to sleep, or even to go into her room. "Want to go for a walk?"

Eric looked surprised, but agreed, and they started down the street. It was dusk, and the lights were just beginning to glow, casting a yellowish light over the sidewalk and the buildings they passed. The air had cooled to a manageable temperature, but still they went at a leisurely pace.

Without discussing their destination, they headed toward the park. When they got to Elizabeth and Cyrus' old parking lot, they sat on top of the table and looked out over the grassy area. There were a few folks using the very last of the light on the playground, and maybe the same group of boys running in circles and arguing over a football game.

"It's almost like they're still here," Casey said. "But alive, not dead. It's hard to believe this is where it all went down."

Eric didn't say anything for a while, then replied, "We did our best for them."

"Yeah, I know."

The football boys disbanded, heading out in all directions, like an explosion of testosterone. The parents and children went home. The sun set all the way.

"I'm not afraid of Death," Casey said.

Eric didn't reply.

"Ever since Reuben and Omar died, it's like I'm not really here. Not a part of what's actually going on with other people. I'm sort of half alive, half not, and I don't really want the half that is. Does that make sense?"

"I guess." He hesitated. "You wish you were dead, too?"

"I don't *want* to die—" Was that true? "—but I feel like I'm half dead already, why not go the rest of the way? What's the point of being here at all?"

"That does sound sort of like a death wish."

"Yeah, I suppose it does."

They sat in silence for a while. The last of the summer's cicadas sang weakly in the trees, but other than that they heard only the breeze through the dried leaves.

"I hear things," Casey blurted out. "And I see things."

"Okay."

"I'm not crazy."

"Didn't say you were."

She climbed off the bench and swung around to look at him. "It's Death. It won't leave me alone. Everywhere I turn, it's there. It talks to me, it follows me, I can't…I can't escape it."

Eric watched her.

"Death tells me things. Things no one else knows."

"Like Alicia McManus' real name. Or what she said when she was dying."

"*Yes.*" She inhaled a sob. "Yes."

He watched her some more, and then he nodded. "Okay."

She hugged herself, trying to stop shaking, trying to stop whatever was happening. Whatever was taking her farther away from Reuben and Omar. Farther away from the life they had shared. Farther away from everything that surrounded her.

"Hey." Eric came over and bent his knees to look into her eyes. "Hey, it's all right. It's all right." He held out his hands, like he was approaching a jumpy colt. "I'm here. I'm real. All right? Okay?"

She felt his hands on her arms, then on her back as he pulled her close, holding her, tipping her face down against his shoulder. She wanted to protest. She wanted to hold him. She took a shuddering breath, then another, until she was hyperventilating.

"*Shhh,*" he whispered. "It's okay. *Shhh.* It's all right." He held her tighter, resting his head against hers, rubbing her back.

She held her arms tight against her stomach, curling into him, burrowing into his warmth, his smell, his body. "*I don't want...I don't want...*" She shuddered, and he held her even tighter.

They stood there forever. For a second. For as long as it took for her breathing to slow. For her fear to ease. Gradually she relaxed against him until it was no longer her legs holding her up, but his arms, his strength.

When she felt able, she released her hold on herself, and slid her arms around his waist until once again she stood on her own two feet. Because she chose to. Because that was what she wanted. She dropped her arms, and he let go, keeping his arms out, in case she wasn't ready.

She let out one long, cleansing breath. "Can we go now?"

"Of course."

Halfway back to the motel, Eric took her hand.

She didn't pull away.

Chapter Forty-six

"What if his insurance wasn't good enough?" Casey said. Their motel had just come into view. Her fingers were interlaced with Eric's, and they walked slowly, their arms against each other, shoulders touching.

"You mean a high deductible?"

"Or they'd reached the limit, maybe."

"Could be. But why would that make him sell his business?"

"I don't *know*. It just feels like there's something there. What would you do? Your wife is dying. Your insurance won't cover it, you can't afford to keep—"

"Wait." He pulled her to a stop. "Say that again."

"You can't afford to keep paying—"

"No. You said what if your insurance *won't cover it*."

"Yeah?"

"What if it's not because of your deductible. Or even that it's expensive. What if it's because the treatment you want isn't covered by *any* insurance. What if it's—"

"—off the boards entirely." Her heart raced. "Your wife has untreatable pancreatic cancer. You're freaking out. You'll do anything. Including sell your so-far profitable business."

"But *why*?"

It was beginning to click. "Because the people buying your business are going to pay you more than you could ever get by doing legitimate work. They're going to hire you on to make it *look* like you're doing legitimate work, but they're really going to pay you to make them something that not just anybody could make. Something illegal."

"You think Zeke and Dan Pinkerton knew?"

"No. I think Randy found this master woodworker, and they were impressed their little brother was finally doing something right, so they hired Cyrus. Randy just used him for his own purposes."

"But then Cyrus' wife died. He didn't want to make a smuggling boat anymore. He didn't want to be a criminal. He had a daughter. He was a good guy. They kept hounding him, but he was stalling, so they began threatening. *That's* why he wouldn't live with his brother and his family, and why he tried to get Elizabeth to live with them, even if he wouldn't. Not because of pride. Because he wanted them to be safe. Then finally, when they realized he wasn't going to build it, they came looking for the blueprints, and he wouldn't give them up. So they killed him."

"No." Casey wasn't convinced. "They wouldn't kill him if they didn't have the blueprints. They would get those first."

"Unless they assumed they were in the car. Where else would he keep them? He didn't have a house. And if they weren't there they would look in his *brother's* house. They could manage that with no one knowing. Betsy didn't have the blueprints until a few months later, after the school remembered Elizabeth's gym locker, and what grown man is going to think to look there?"

"Okay. But why kill him then? Unless something else happened. Something they weren't expecting."

"Like?"

"His daughter showed up. She would have thrown off the whole thing. His priority would completely shift. Who cared about the blueprints or the stupid houseboat when his daughter was suddenly in danger?"

"But she lived."

"She *ran*."

"She would leave him?"

"If he told her to. Maybe. She was only fourteen. Might still listen to her dad."

Eric began walking again, holding Casey's hand more loosely now, swinging their arms as they talked. "But why would they let her go in the first place?"

Casey considered, and one more thing fell into place. "Because they hadn't killed Cyrus yet. All they wanted was the blueprints. They probably didn't even have the gun out yet. Another reason Elizabeth might have obeyed her dad. She didn't think he was in any real danger. And she might have been mad that he was dealing with the creepy guys in the first place. But then it got out of hand. She heard the gunshot, and she went back."

"But *why*? Why kill him? It doesn't make any sense. They would want the blueprints, and we know they didn't have them."

"Who's that?" Casey stopped Eric, then shook her hand free. Someone was waiting for them in the dim light of the parking lot, leaning against their rental car. "Stay here."

Eric gave a little laugh. "I don't think so."

Casey shook her head. "Fine. He hasn't seen us yet. I'll go around the other way."

"He's not hiding. I don't think it's anyone to be afraid of. He's waiting for us right out in the open."

Okay. So he was probably right. But she was going to be ready, anyway.

They walked closer, Casey darting her eyes back and forth, waiting for more shadowy figures to emerge. But no one did, and they arrived at the man unmolested.

"Wayne?" she said.

He looked at her with eyes of darkness. "Yes, it's me. And I think it's time I told you what really happened that night."

Chapter Forty-seven

"I went to the park to see Liz."

They were sitting in Eric's room. He'd started some coffee in the little two-cupper, and sat on the bed. Wayne perched on the edge of the office chair, and Casey stood by the door. She wanted plenty of space in case she'd need it, plus she wasn't exactly comfortable being close to both the bed and Eric.

"We often met there at night. We'd sit at the picnic table at look at the stars, talk about school, talk about her dad. But that night I could see other people there, and I could hear them talking. Men. They sounded mad, and I was worried for Liz, so I snuck up as close as I could. It was too dark to really see, and their backs were to me, but I could hear in Cyrus' voice that he was scared. Somebody was in the car, I could see him in the dome light, and I saw his face. It was that awful guy Liz couldn't stand. Knowing it was him, I could recognize the other two, the ones I'd seen before, the ones in that picture you have. I didn't know what to do, whether I should call the cops or what, but I didn't want to get Cyrus in trouble. I tried to get closer so I could see better, but I stepped on a stick, and it snapped. They all spun around, but they couldn't see me because I was behind a tree, in the dark.

"Cyrus yelled—" His breath hitched. "He yelled for me to get out of there, to run, but he thought I was Liz. One of the men started toward me, so I took off. I ran as hard as I could and hid—growing up here you know where to hide—and he hadn't found me, but he was close. Cyrus was still yelling, and then…and then the gun went off, and I heard the man after me swear and take off back to the rest of them. A car came flying by me, and I stayed there until I was sure it was gone, and then I…" He let out a sob. "I ran away. God help me, I ran. I knew if they found me, if they knew I'd seen them…" He shook his head. Tears flowed freely down his cheeks, and he dropped his face into his hands and wept.

Eric's voice was gentle. Gentler than Casey could ever be. "You didn't tell the police what happened?"

"How could I? If I told, the men would know I was there. They would come after me, too."

"But Liz *disappeared*."

"I know. I know she did. But I also knew she wasn't there when it happened. I knew she was alive." He wiped his nose. "I waited for her to come back. I thought she would at least call. Or write. Or *something*."

Casey looked at the man. He was broken. But she didn't care.

"She was there, Wayne."

"What?"

"She *was* there, probably hiding because her dad told her to. She saw him get shot. She held him as he died.'

"But—"

"You let your best friend run for her life. You knew the men heard you and thought she was there. You knew she was the one they would go after. And you didn't do *anything*."

His head shot up. "You think I don't realize that? You think I don't regret that night every minute of my life? If I could go back and change it, I would. I would do the right thing. I would save her. I would save Cyrus. I would change it *all*." He wiped his face with both hands. "But I can't. I can't save Cyrus, and God knows now I can't save Liz, either. I wanted to." He deflated, his voice dropping to a whisper. "I wanted to."

Casey took a step toward him, but Eric got in-between them. "We got the story, Case. We got it now. He'll tell the cops. With what we've learned it will help, right? They'll get them."

She hated his soothing voice. She hated that he was standing between her and a good beat down.

She hated that he was right.

She spun and opened the door, then looked back to see Eric bending over Wayne, his hand on his back.

"You'll make sure he goes to the cops?"

"I'll take him right now."

"No," a voice said. "I don't think you will."

Chapter Forty-eight

Randy Pinkerton stood several feet outside the door. Casey swung the door shut, but a booted foot stopped it. The door pushed open, knocking her backward, but she righted herself and waited for the man to come forward.

Les Danvers, the second man in that long-ago photo, stepped into the door. He was middle-aged now, mostly gray, and paunchy. His eyes were wide-set and bloodshot, and his nose had those tiny little spider veins all over it. He hadn't aged well.

"How cute," he said. "If it isn't the little lady who was looking for us in Whitley. Just stay calm, sweetheart, and nobody gets hurt."

Casey threw a front kick into the guy's crotch, and he froze for a moment of pained surprise before slowly crumpling to the floor. Before he hit, Casey followed up with a side kick to the chin, and his upper body shot backward, blocking the door.

"Hey!" Randy Pinkerton leapt over Danvers, fists up. He looked better than Danvers, still in shape, his hair thinning but still with some color, and his eyes clear.

"Get back," Casey ordered Eric.

"But—"

"*Get the hell back!*"

She heard the office chair spin and hoped that meant he had grabbed Wayne and gotten him out of the way, too. She glanced quickly to the side and saw the empty chair. She shoved it back as Pinkerton approached, shuffling forward in baby steps. There was nothing for her to use as a weapon. The only things close to hand were the TV remote, bed linens, and the chair, which would be more of a hindrance than anything. It would have to be hands and feet.

"Come on," Pinkerton said, "let's talk this out."

"You killed an innocent woman."

"I don't know what you mean."

"I think you do."

He smirked. "Technically, *I* didn't kill anybody. *He* did."

Marcus Flatt stepped over the still-moaning Les Danvers and stood behind Randy Pinkerton. His entrance brought a chill to the room, and Wayne let out a moan as anguished as Danvers'. Flatt's expression was like his name, as flat as a night lake, and the look in his eyes just as dark. His arms hung loose at his sides, and he stood with his legs shoulder-width apart. A quick study of his clothes gave Casey no indication that he was carrying a gun, but she couldn't be absolutely sure.

She held up her hands, as if in surrender. "We can be civilized here, can't we? We all have things to trade."

Pinkerton smiled. "I'm not surprised to hear you say that. Marcus often brings out the cooperation in people. Shall we talk, then?"

Casey took a step forward and held out her hand. "Truce. For now."

Flatt's eyes widened in the split second it took Pinkerton to take Casey's hand. Casey yanked Pinkerton forward and spun him around, twisting his arm behind his back so he wouldn't even think of moving. He gasped, and his head arched back over Casey's shoulder, his pelvis thrust forward as he tried to escape the pain. It wasn't working.

"Get out, Marcus," Casey said.

Flatt smiled, but it didn't reach his eyes. Casey was reminded of the man called Bone, whom she had killed only weeks before. This deadly killer type was cropping up way too often, and she was growing weary of it.

"I think I'll stick around," Flatt said.

His voice sent shivers up Casey's spine.

"Marc," Pinkerton gasped.

"Quiet, now. I'm negotiating."

Pinkerton wiggled, and Casey yanked his arm up higher. He let out a shriek.

Marcus shook his head. "What happened to negotiating?"

"Somehow, I don't think that's why you're really here."

His smile grew. "I guess you know more than I thought."

"And we know about the night you shot Cyrus Mann. And how you killed Elizabeth."

"Oh, I don't think you know all about any of that."

Danvers was up on all fours now, breathing hard. He struggled to his feet and pointed at Casey. "You...I'm going to get you."

Flatt held his arm up, bent at the elbow, like he was indicating a right turn. "You stay put, Les."

"But—"

"*Stay.*"

Danvers sulked, his lips pushing out like a little boy's. His eyes narrowed, and the nostrils on his bulbous nose flared.

"You stay, too." Flatt pointed behind Casey. "Push one button on that phone, the woman dies. Give it to me. Now." He waggled his fingers, and Eric's phone went arcing past Casey. Flatt stuck it in his pocket.

Pinkerton squirmed again, and Casey reached up to find some pressure points in his throat. He stilled.

"Where are the blueprints?" Flatt said.

"Not here."

"I figured that. That's why we'll leave one of you alive."

"Why do you even need them anymore? It's been forever since Cyrus came up with those, and it's not like blueprints alone could put you in prison."

He didn't reply, and the last thing clicked into place.

Casey tried not to show her surprise. "You actually made one of the boats."

Flatt' eyelids twitched just the slightest bit.

"You made a boat, but it got seized."

Pinkerton made a sudden try for escape, but the way he jerked and the way Casey gripped his arm brought his shoulder right out of its socket. The pop was audible in the small room, and he screamed.

"My God, Pink," Flatt said. "You need to shut up."

Pinkerton slumped, but Casey grabbed him under the chin and squeezed her arm around his throat.

"Tell me," she said. "You were making a run and the boat got captured? But that can't matter anymore, either. The stuff would be long gone—drugs?"

Flatt shrugged as if saying, "what else?"

"So there has to be something else. What?"

Flatt' eyelids lowered even further. "Why don't you keep guessing. It's more fun that way."

"You crossed another drug smuggler who's out for revenge, and you think the blueprints will give you some leverage."

His only response was the slight lift of his eyebrows.

"You want to build another one."

No.

Eric's voice came from behind her. "Someone died, didn't they? When the boat was captured, there was an attack, and someone got killed."

Flatt went still.

"But that's not all," Eric continued. "It wasn't just another guy. Another drug smuggler. It was *law enforcement.*"

Casey remembered the conversation she and Eric had had when they'd first discovered the importance of the blueprints. The early nineties. The smuggling. The violence. It made sense.

"Those blueprints could be the end of you guys," Casey said. "They could tie you to the boat and to the deaths of those cops."

Flatt held his hands out. "So now you see. There's no way we're leaving without the blueprints. Wouldn't it be easier if you just told us where they were?"

"Easier for you, maybe, because then you could just leave us for dead, like you did with Cyrus Mann."

"It would have been easier for Elizabeth if she would have told us. But then, maybe she really *didn't* know what we were talking about. That would be a shame. All that pain, and nothing to show for it." He shook his head. "But at least we had a little fun first." He smiled. "Like I'm going to have with you."

Eric made a sound, and Casey held up a hand, sort of like Flatt had done to Danvers. The last thing she needed was Eric trying to be a hero.

Danvers' face had grown stormier and stormier as they talked, and Casey could see he was about done with waiting. His hands were clenching and unclenching, and his feet shifted.

"Eric?" she said.

"All right."

Danvers launched himself past Flatt, hands outstretched, going for Casey's eyes. Casey swiveled, throwing Pinkerton back into Eric, then swung forward, sweeping Danvers' hands up with her left arm and serving him a roundhouse with her right. He spun backward into Flatt, who grabbed him and tossed him toward the door like a ragdoll. Danvers crashed headfirst into the doorjamb and fell, out cold.

Casey took a deep breath and let it out, allowing her body to relax. It all came back to her, just like it had at the *dojang* the other day. Her. Flatt. Her heartbeat. That was all there was.

And then he pulled out a knife.

Sweat sprouted instantly on Casey scalp and her breath hitched.

"Not a knife fighter?" Flatt said. He turned it in his fingers and held it upright, like they do on choreographed movie knife fights. Not like a real fighter. Not like the thug in Louisville had been. That was something, anyway.

"I haven't got a knife," she said.

"Oh. That's too bad."

Flatt took a quick stride forward and jabbed toward her stomach. She sucked in her middle and rolled across the bed to the other side, but that trapped her between the mattress and the wall, and left Eric over on the other side with Flatt. Casey grabbed the pillows from the bed and flung them at Flatt. He batted them away, but she used those seconds to somersault across the bed so that she was on his far side. He lunged toward her, knife swinging sideways. Casey crouched and exploded upward, banging his arm with her left and following through with a jab to his face. She connected, and he stumbled back.

He recovered and moved toward Eric. Eric shoved Pinkerton between them. Pinkerton howled with anguish.

"Flatt!" Casey threw the TV remote at his face.

He ducked, then came back at her, knife raised. He swung the blade at her head. She blocked his arm with hers and threw herself into his stomach, shoving him back and to the side. He had a lot more heft than she did, so he didn't go far, but it was enough to place him on the side toward the door, away from Eric. He fell to his knees, but was up instantly, rushing at her.

Casey grabbed the desk chair and swung it, cracking his knees and sending him face first onto the bed. Casey leapt on his back and grabbed the wrist of his knife hand. She drilled her knee into his back as he writhed, trying to turn over. He was so much bigger, so much stronger.

"Casey!"

She turned just in time to see that Danvers had awakened and was lurching toward her. Eric dumped Pinkerton on Wayne and ran forward, leaping over the chair. Flatt used the distraction to flip onto his back and yank his wrist from her hand. He raised the knife and thrust it down. Casey spun from his grip just as Danvers and Eric each lunged for her, and Flatt's knife found its mark.

"No!" Casey screamed.

Everything froze, Casey staring at Flatt's hand, that still held the hilt of the knife. Eric's eyes were wide and staring, and Flatt gaped at what he had just done. Danvers' mouth flapped open and shut, and then he fell face forward on top of Flatt.

Casey pulled Eric away, feeling frantically for a wound, but Danvers was the one the knife had found. Flatt yanked the knife from Danvers' chest and came up off the bed, swinging for Eric's back. With a roar, Casey hit Flatt's hand with a roundhouse kick and knocked the knife from his fist, splattering Danvers' blood over the bed and carpet. She followed up with a side kick, smashing Flatt's nose, then a front heel, bashing his chin and tossing him back onto the floor. She was winding up for another when arms gripped her from behind, lifting her off the floor. She fought to get free, but it was Eric's voice in her ear, saying, "Stop, Casey. You got him. He's done. Stop."

She batted at his hands, and he let her go. She rushed to stand over Flatt, but her last kick had knocked him out. Danvers lay on his back, gasping for breath, red bubbles foaming out of his mouth. Pinkerton lay on the floor by Wayne, holding his arm and crying.

Eric was right. They were done.

When Casey had regained her breath, she reached into Flatt's pocket and pulled out Eric's phone. He used it to call the cops. Within minutes they heard sirens.

Chapter Forty-nine

The door clanged open, and Ricky stood in the sunlight, blinking. Casey ran to him, taking him in her arms and squeezing him until she realized he wasn't squeezing back. In fact, his arms lay at his sides. She stepped back, not letting go of his shoulders, and looked into his face.

"What now?" he said.

"Now you start over."

He nodded once, and Casey led him to the car. She put him in the back and turned to Don, who had come to finalize the paperwork and see the whole thing through. "Thank you."

He shook his head. "It was your doing."

"But you believed in him. As you have in me."

He frowned, and looked away. "I guess that's my job, isn't it?"

She held out her hand. "Don. Please."

His nostrils flared, and he waited several seconds before looking her in the eye. "You're welcome. For this."

"And for all those other times?"

Something close to a smile crossed his lips. "And for those, too." He finally took her hand, and she gripped his hard.

He nodded again, at her, at Ricky, at Eric. And then he climbed into his car and drove away.

Ricky sat hunched in the back seat of Eric's car, looking like a little lost boy.

"Come on, hon," Casey said. "Let's get you home."

Eric drove, and Casey sat in the back with Ricky, holding his hand, trying not to lapse into a waking coma. It had been a long few days since the motel. Long hours talking with the police, long hours convincing them to indict the Three. Long hours waiting for Danvers to die. She and Eric had flown home together, but in their own worlds, shrouded by their warring emotions and exhaustion. Casey felt like they had drifted a million miles from where they had been at the park just the other night.

She looked at him now, driving, for the second time an integral part of her life where it had met violence and death. A part she never wanted to share again. Especially not with him.

Texas also felt like another world, along with the people they'd left there. Betsy and Scott would be okay, as would Billy. They had each other, and Billy was young, with family support. Wayne was a different story. A guilt-wracked conscience, a wife who wouldn't talk about it, and a son who had basically told the killers where to find Elizabeth. A longer road for the Greers. Could they be redeemed? Casey hoped so.

Instead of driving to Ricky's own empty house, Eric took them to their mom's. When they arrived, Ricky didn't move, or even seem to notice where they'd stopped. Eric met Casey's eyes in the rearview mirror, then went around to the other side of the car to help Ricky out.

Their mother didn't respond to the bell, so Casey used the key and opened the door. "Mom?"

She sat in the same chair, looking as lost as she had when Casey had seen her earlier that week.

"Mom, look who I brought."

She swiveled her head toward the doorway. When she saw Casey something in her eyes sparked, but when her eyes landed on Ricky, it was as if a fire had truly been ignited. She jumped to her feet and held out her hands. Ricky didn't move, so Casey gently pushed him forward. Once he took the first step, his momentum carried him, and he threw his arms around his mother. They stood there for a long time, hugging and crying, until their mother raised her head and looked over Ricky's shoulder at Casey. She took one hand from around his waist and held it out. This time Eric had to nudge Casey before she grabbed her mother's hand and was pulled into the familial embrace.

Finally, her mother pulled away, face glistening with tears, and put one hand on each of her children's faces. "All together. At last." She smiled, and Casey felt something in her chest break loose and crumble.

"But," her mother said, "there's something missing."

Casey closed her eyes. It wasn't like she needed the reminder of why it had been so long. Of why she had stayed away from home. Of those finals moments of fire and smoke. Of the fact that her father was gone, as well.

But her mother looked over her shoulder. "This young man is standing all by himself over there. Aren't you going to introduce us?"

Eric looked as surprised as Casey felt, but he recovered faster, and stepped forward, looking as pleased and nervous as a teenager meeting his date's parents for the first time. "I'm Eric, Mrs. Kaufmann. I'm pleased to meet you."

She beamed. "And polite, too!" She elbowed Casey. "Why haven't we met him before?"

No one filled the awkward pause until Casey reached out her hand to take Eric's. She smiled slowly, and shyly, but with conviction. "Because this is a new thing, Mom. There hasn't been a chance before."

Eric looked at her, disbelief in his eyes, until that turned to warmth, and a full-out smile. He squeezed her hand, and she smiled back, this time without hesitation.

Her mother broke the moment with a loud clap. "Now let's do something to celebrate all these good things. Order out. What do you want, Ricky? You choose."

He blinked, looking as he had outside the jail, just as confused, and just as lost.

Casey wasn't even sure she was hungry, what with... everything.

"How about some good pizza?" Eric finally said. "I'm sure Ricky hasn't had that for a while."

"Wonderful idea!" their mother exclaimed, and bustled off to make the call.

Forty-five minutes later a kid delivered two large pizzas, breadsticks, wings, and several two-liter bottles of pop, as well as a gigantic take-out salad. Casey figured her mom would have enough leftovers to last until the next year.

As the evening wore on, Ricky became more animated, not revealing his whole self, but showing glimpses of who he had been before Alicia. Casey was relieved to see already that he wasn't completely broken, and allowed herself to relax enough to laugh and play a game of canasta and eat more than she should have. She and Eric shared many glances throughout the time, and hardly was there a time when they weren't touching in some manner.

It was close to midnight by the time Ricky almost fell asleep in the easy chair, and Casey and Eric said their farewells. She gave Ricky an extra-long hug. "It will be hard, bro. You know it will. But you'll make it through." When she let go, both their eyes were wet, and she could see his weariness.

"I'll be all right, eventually. Right?" He looked to her left, where Casey saw only air.

Something cold traveled up her spine. "Ricky?"

He looked back at her. "Your friend is pretty wise, Casey. And I have to tell you, it's nice not to be alone."

Casey looked frantically around, but couldn't see anything. She didn't understand. What was going on? Had she really become fearful of Death so suddenly? Did she want to live that badly?

"Hey," Ricky said. "You all right?"

She wasn't sure, but she said, "I'm fine. Goodnight, bro. Be careful."

"Of what? Sleeping in my old bed?"

She put her hand on his cheek, not sure what else to say.

"Casey, honey." Her mother was reaching for her.

She gave her mom a hug. "Thanks, Mom. Ricky will be best staying here for a while."

Her mother squeezed her back. "I wouldn't want him any other place."

Eric shook hands with Ricky and endured a hug from Casey's mom, and they left. Casey still didn't see an extra houseguest.

She and Eric didn't speak for the entire ride back, and didn't hold hands or even look at each other. When they arrived at Casey's house she unlocked the door and they went in. She took extra long making sure the door was locked before turning toward Eric.

"Casey," he said.

They crashed together like two long lost lovers, stumbling into the living room, falling on the couch. Eric held her face in his hands, and Casey gripped his back like he was going to disappear if she let go. He kissed her eyes, her lips, her neck, and she arched toward him, wanting his touch. Wanting him.

She yanked his shirt from his waistband and ran her hands over his skin. He shuddered and pulled her upright so she straddled him. He yanked her shirt over her head and pressed his face against her chest as she worked the buttons on his shirt and dragged it from his shoulders. Their bare stomachs touched, and fire ran through her veins. "Eric…"

He laughed softly against her, then stood, hefting her into his arms.

And he carried her upstairs.

Chapter Fifty

Casey woke up with a start. It took several seconds for her to remember where she was, and why there was another person under the covers with her. It was her house. Her bedroom. Hers and Reuben's.

But not anymore.

She looked over at Eric, who lay on his back, eyes twitching, as if he were dreaming. Casey wondered what he was dreaming about. Home? Near death? Revenge? Tortured young women? Prison? Or perhaps something more pleasant, like what had just happened in this bed? His light hair flopped over his forehead, one thatch of it close to his eye, and she fought the impulse to move it.

His coloring was the opposite of what she used to see there, Reuben's dark, Mexican heritage having been burned into her soul, into these sheets, these pillows. But he breathed evenly, like her husband, his face relaxed, except for the moving eyelids. One arm was flung above his head, the other reaching out, as if to touch her.

Casey closed her own eyes and tried to go back to sleep, hopefully the dreamless kind. She didn't need any more images crowding into her mind. She thought of Ricky, in his old bed at their mother's house, free at last from his undeserved jail cell. Of Betsy and Wayne, finally freed from their waiting, only to have to deal with the knowledge of what they could have had, but had lost. Of Zeke and Dan Pinkerton, forced to face the deeds of their brother. How long would it take any of them to move on? To live life as they had? But perhaps that wasn't the point. Perhaps the point was that they had to take what had happened and learn to live their life in its light.

Oh, for heaven's sake, it was no use. There was no way she was going back to sleep. Moving slowly, with the same focus she had used in Texas, only this time for gentleness, she slid from the bed, pulled on shorts and a T-shirt—Reuben's old one that she kept in her bag, which still lay almost entirely packed—and made her way downstairs.

The moon was nearly full and cast shadows on the back steps, where she chose to sit. The yard looked foreign in that eerie light, as if Casey had landed in some other time, at some other place. She gripped the cement of the stairs, so solid underneath her. So unchanged in the past years.

She closed her eyes and breathed in the night. The air smelled the same, tasted the same. Its composition had not changed since she had last experienced it. But at the same time…

She got up and walked across the yard. When she reached the end, she turned to look up at the house. Reuben. Omar. Eric. A building that once held a family, that now saw what could be referred to as a beginning. Or was it an ending?

A train whistle floated over the breeze, and Casey's nerves tingled. Where was the train coming from? Where was it going? Casey tried to tamp down a nagging feeling that something wasn't as it should be. That her priorities had shifted too far. Reuben. Omar. They'd shared a life there, in that house. They were supposed to still be there, with her. That had been the plan. They weren't supposed to die in a flaming wreck, only for her to replace them with other things, with other people.

God, what was happening? What was her problem? What was she *thinking*?

Something rustled in the pine trees, but Casey didn't have to look to see what had caused it. She stood silently in the moonlight. Waiting.

For Death.

To receive a free catalog of Poisoned Pen Press titles, please contact us in one of the following ways:

Phone: 1-800-421-3976
Facsimile: 1-480-949-1707
Email: info@poisonedpenpress.com
Website: www.poisonedpenpress.com

Poisoned Pen Press
6962 E. First Ave. Ste 103
Scottsdale, AZ 85251